THE
LAKE
HOUSE

BOOKS BY LAURA WOLFE

Two Widows
She Lies Alone

LAURA WOLFE

THE LAKE HOUSE

bookouture

Published by Bookouture in 2021

An imprint of Storyfire Ltd.
Carmelite House
50 Victoria Embankment
London EC4Y 0DZ

www.bookouture.com

ISBN: 978-1-80019-009-2
eBook ISBN: 978-1-80019-008-5

This book is a work of fiction. Names, characters, businesses,
organizations, places and events other than those clearly in the
public domain, are either the product of the author's imagination
or are used fictitiously. Any resemblance to actual persons, living or
dead, events or locales is entirely coincidental.

For my truest friends

PROLOGUE

We could have avoided the whole thing. That was the worst part. Only a minor change here or there would have done the trick—a few minutes more spent researching before booking the trip or a different decision made last week or twenty years ago. Instead, every choice had led to this terrifying place. A breath heaved from my lungs. My soaking shoes tumbled over each other as I scurried across the uneven ground, searching for a hiding place. The night was silent and black around me, the air so filled with terror that even the stars hid behind the clouds. *Never ignore your instincts.* That's what I always told my clients, but I hadn't followed my own advice. I'd been pushing away the tightness in my chest and pangs in my gut for days. Now my body's animalistic instincts consumed me, muscles contracting, and fear exploding through every cell. I could barely see where my next footstep would land, but my legs stretched forward, again and again. Sturdy tree trunks materialized from the shadows like strangers waiting to capture me. I kept running.

A twig snapped through the darkness, and my feet stopped, my throat constricting. The faces of the dead flashed in my mind. Even the release of breath might give me away.

My thoughts spun toward alternate realities as I darted into the cover of the trees. Why hadn't I made up an excuse to stay home with my family? It would have been easy enough to lie. Or I could have insisted on hosting the get-together at my house in the safety of suburbia. Or, twenty-two years earlier, the people at campus housing could have placed the incoming freshmen in different dorms and different hallways than the ones they'd chosen for us. Then I would have made another group of friends, friends who would have insisted on meeting at a less remote location and who steered clear of reckless decisions. They might have been friends who, when we hugged, could have detected the sour odor of festering secrets.

CHAPTER ONE

Five years had passed since we'd seen each other. My insides hummed along with my car as I eased my foot against the brake. The drive from my house in Brookfield to Charlotte's address in Hartland was less than thirty minutes—a straight shot west on the highway through Milwaukee, Wisconsin. The quick trip made it difficult to ignore our recent lack of effort to get together. My arms felt heavy as I approached the driveway. I let my car idle in front of the modest ranch-style house where Charlotte lived with her second husband, Reed, and her teenage son, Oliver. An open garage door revealed a blue-and-white cooler, two large suitcases, and several reusable grocery bags waiting behind Charlotte's red minivan. A silver hatchback filled the other half of the garage.

I took a breath, turning up the driveway and parking under a rusty basketball hoop and next to a gleaming blue Tesla. Kaitlyn had beaten me here, even though her drive was twice as far. We would stop at the airport later to pick up Sam and Jenna. Nerves held me in place as I leaned my weight into the upholstered seat. People always said old friends could pick up where they left off, but I wasn't sure that was true. Five years was a long time.

A door slammed. Kaitlyn emerged from the garage, the sun catching her blue-green eyes. She flashed her Hollywood smile, wavy tendrils of auburn hair reaching past her shoulders. She was still breathtaking with her lithe frame and carved features. A fashionable linen pantsuit skimmed her curves, and she wore lipstick the shade of ripe berries. It had always been a struggle not to feel frumpy in Kaitlyn's presence.

Charlotte followed a step behind, her head barely reaching Kaitlyn's shoulders. Her billowy sundress fluttered in the wind, and she pulled her jean jacket closed. I did a double take. Charlotte's cheeks were the same rosy pink I remembered, but her face was rounder and her hips wider. She'd grown her dark hair to just below her shoulders, and her brown eyes held their familiar girl-next-door charm. She waved and bounded into the air.

I abandoned my nerves and jumped from my car, hugging Kaitlyn first, then Charlotte.

"Yay, Megan! You're here." Charlotte pulled away and smiled at me.

I wondered what changes they noticed in me. I'd made an effort to cover the gray hairs poking up from my light brown roots, but my hand instinctively moved to cover the paunch in my gut that had formed after Wyatt had been born, becoming even more pronounced when I'd stopped training for marathons two years ago.

"Can you believe we're forty?" I lowered my hand.

Charlotte closed her eyes and tipped her face toward the sky. "No. How the hell did that happen?"

"In my head, I'm still twenty-five," Kaitlyn said.

Charlotte fluttered her eyelashes at Kaitlyn. "How have you not aged? You probably still get carded."

"Bitch," I said.

We laughed. I'd been silly to feel nervous. Despite the long absence, we'd slipped back into our friendship easily, like rediscovering a favorite pair of shoes in the corner of the closet.

My group of college friends and I turned forty this year, and we deserved a weekend away to celebrate. At least that's what Jenna had claimed in the barrage of texts that began three months ago: *Happy Birthday to us! Girls' weekend. No excuses! No husbands or kids allowed!* Jenna, a New York City attorney and always the organizer, was the one who sent the initial message urging us to plan an exotic getaway.

Charlotte and Kaitlyn had immediately responded with sentiments like *Count me in!* and *Yes! I'll be there!* Even Sam, who lived in Denver and ran a multimillion-dollar corporation, quickly joined the fun. I didn't share their unbridled excitement. The talk of planning a trip stressed me out, my jaw tightening and my finger flicking across the emails the same way I'd bat away a pesky fly. I'd hoped the planning would fizzle out like it had when Jenna had made a similar push two years ago. But my friends were two steps ahead of me; an Excel spreadsheet soon followed with each of our names above the top row and three months of weekend dates across the side. I couldn't write *no* for all of the dates; that would be too obvious. I was trapped. Anxiety had gripped my chest at the mention of faraway destinations—a luxury spa in Tucson or an all-inclusive eco-resort in Costa Rica. I worried about my kids, eight-year-old Marnie and five-year-old Wyatt. Four nights was a long time to be away. My husband, Andrew, was perfectly capable of caring for them, of course, but he'd have to waste two vacation days for my trip to work. Either that or I'd have to get my mother-in-law involved. They were both options I preferred to avoid.

How about something closer to home? I'd suggested, hoping Kaitlyn would offer to host again, but she hadn't.

Now I hovered in Kaitlyn's shadow on Charlotte's driveway, thinking back to how our unlikely crew had become friends in the first place. By accident or fate, the five of us had met freshman year at Marquette University in Milwaukee. I'd chosen the private Jesuit school over several others, even though I wasn't Catholic. Marquette was only forty minutes from my parents' house, had an excellent academic reputation, and was about the right size—not as big as a state school, but large enough to keep my anonymity if I desired. Out of nearly 2,500 incoming first-year students in 1997, Campus Housing had placed me, Sam, Charlotte, Kaitlyn, and Jenna in the same corridor in the utilitarian 1950s dormitory. That was twenty-two years ago. Even though we didn't see each other often anymore, we had forged our loyalties. We'd shared too much to abandon each other, no matter how much time had passed.

Kaitlyn smoothed back a lock of her windblown hair. "So much planning, but we made it work!"

"I can't believe it," I said, and I really couldn't. The weeks of back-and-forth texts from my friends scrolled through my mind as I opened the trunk of my car to unload my suitcase.

Megan, you coming? It won't be the same without you.

Of course she's coming! Look at the spreadsheet. The weekend of 17 Sept works for everyone! Jenna had responded. I'd shaken my head when I read it. Twenty years later, Jenna was still talking over me.

The messages had continued to pop on my phone, poking and prodding. My friends laid the guilt on thick. Despite my hesitation to commit, the plans rolled forward. I'd cut back my hours as a therapist at the family clinic. Turning forty *was* kind of a big deal, and I'd been feeling lost both at home and work lately—a possible midlife crisis. When I'd mentioned the plans to Andrew and asked if I should join in on the four-day girls' weekend, he'd only shrugged and said, "Sure. Why not?"

That was when I realized a weekend away with old friends was exactly what I needed to excavate a forgotten piece of myself, to remember my identity before marriage and kids. Taking a few nights for myself wasn't such a sacrifice, so I officially committed. Now, the weekend had finally arrived.

Charlotte and Kaitlyn helped me load my things into the back of the minivan, including a case of wine I'd picked up at the liquor store a few days before.

Charlotte widened her eyes at the box and chuckled. "Jeez, Megan! Do you think you packed enough wine?"

"There was a discount if you bought twelve bottles."

"You did the right thing," Kaitlyn said, crinkling her button nose. "Now, we don't have to worry about running out, even with Jenna around."

We laughed at Kaitlyn's dig at Jenna, who was the partier of the group. I locked my car.

Reed stepped into the shadowy garage wearing gray athletic shorts and a black Nike T-shirt. He smiled at us, his biceps straining against his shirt. "Hey guys. It's been a while."

I stood taller, noticing how he and Charlotte didn't quite match each other. "Hi Reed. Nice to see you."

"Likewise." The stubble on his face became visible as he lowered his chin.

Charlotte gave her husband a playful shove. "He's counting the seconds until I leave so he can go for a run, watch TV all day, and make whatever he wants for dinner."

"I'm debating between pancakes and greasy carry-out."

Kaitlyn chuckled in Reed's direction. "You and Derek would get along well."

"We eat pancakes and greasy carry-out at our house almost every day," I said.

Reed smiled and leaned against the minivan. "How's the fam, Megan?"

"Everyone's good. Thanks."

"Are you still living in Brookfield?"

"Yep. I work there too. The clinic is still in the same building. It's a short commute."

Charlotte nodded. "Reed works over in that direction now."

"We're about ten minutes down the road, just past Elm Grove."

"Really?" I motioned toward him and Charlotte. "The three of us should meet for lunch sometime."

"That would be fun," Charlotte said.

"We all need to make more of an effort," Kaitlyn said. "I mean, it only took me an hour to get here, and you guys are all so close."

Charlotte did a little hop. "Yes. We need to set a regular date, like the third Saturday of every month we'll meet at someone's house for dinner. Or we can find a restaurant that's halfway."

"Let's include husbands and kids too," Kaitlyn said. "Wouldn't it be fun if our kids were friends?"

"Oliver is a little too old," Reed said.

"He can babysit," I said, only half-joking.

Kaitlyn smiled. "Perfect!"

We agreed on striving for more regular meetups and exchanged a few niceties as Reed tightened the laces on his running shoes. He wished us safe travels and promised Charlotte he'd hold down the home front. "Love you," he said, wrapping his sturdy arms around his wife and kissing her. A pang shot through me. I thought of my departure from Andrew less than an hour earlier. He had only glanced up from his phone call, pointed at my handwritten list of instructions, and mouthed, "Have fun." I'd nodded and given him a thumbs up, not making any effort to kiss him goodbye either—something I'd later regret.

CHAPTER TWO

We buckled ourselves into the minivan with Kaitlyn riding shotgun and me in the back.

"I can't believe this is finally happening!" Charlotte said as she started the ignition.

Kaitlyn looked over her shoulder. "We did it. Yay!"

It had taken weeks for everyone to complete the spreadsheet, work out a date, and agree on a location. We decided to stay in Wisconsin. That way, only Sam and Jenna had to book flights. I remembered the vacation rental listing of the quaint cottage on a private lake that had caught everyone's eyes: *Secluded Cabin on Crooked Lake Sleeps Six.* The cabin we'd rented for the weekend was almost a five-hour drive from Milwaukee, but it wasn't too far from a small airport. Charlotte had plenty of room in her minivan and had offered to drive us. We would make one pit stop to pick up Jenna and Sam, who had coordinated their flights from New York and Denver into the remote airfield.

The drive was long in miles, but with all our talking, it passed quickly. The suburban houses transformed into endless farmland and, eventually, dense forest. We stopped once for gas and two more times for bathroom and snack breaks as we took turns updating each other on our lives—husbands, kids, careers, and in Kaitlyn's case, charity work. We reminisced about Jenna's failed attempt to get the group together two years ago. The plan had evaporated as soon as a couple of us had conflicts with the proposed dates.

Our last girls' weekend had been a little more than five years earlier. Kaitlyn had hosted at her posh house in the upscale Madison suburb of Shorewood Hills. I'd gasped when I'd first laid eyes on her sprawling brick colonial, which looked like someone had plucked it from the pages of *House Beautiful* magazine. Not that my spacious home in Brookfield was anything to complain about, but Kaitlyn and Derek's house surpassed another level of luxury with an infinity-edge swimming pool, golf course view, wine cellar, and movie theatre. Derek's finance career had skyrocketed faster than Kaitlyn's, and she'd decided to stay home after their second daughter was born. Derek had taken their girls to stay with his parents that weekend. Still, traces of their daughters appeared everywhere—stuffed animals neatly stacked against a wall, tiny chairs sitting beside the regular chairs, and Tupperware containers filled with cookies. I remembered feeling guilty about displacing them.

Kaitlyn had given us a tour of the property, pointing out all the renovations she and Derek had done. The rest of us had smiled and nodded and said all the right things as we admired the many upgrades, but there'd been an undercurrent of tension as we paraded around the patio, the afternoon sun searing our skin. My sandals had clicked against the natural stone slabs surrounding the pristine swimming pool as Kaitlyn led us around the edge. I glimpsed defeat (or was it jealousy?) flickering behind the eyes of my friends, their jaw muscles twitching, almost as if they wouldn't mind if Kaitlyn slipped and fell into the water. Or maybe I'd only been projecting my feelings onto the others. Kaitlyn had one-upped us all, not that she would ever say that. She was too kind. I'd dropped my gaze, letting it drift across the chlorinated water; it stopped near my toes, where stray leaves and a handful of dead bugs floated in the corner.

There had been more uncomfortable moments as daylight dwindled. I'd been pregnant with Wyatt then, so I hadn't been able to drink alcohol like everyone else as we gathered around a massive table positioned beneath a wisteria-covered pergola. Jenna sat with arms crossed, throwing back glass after glass of wine as she gazed out at the fairway and described the grueling hours she worked at the law firm. She'd been going through a difficult period. Her dad had recently passed away, only weeks before her latest boyfriend had dumped her. Jenna's face contorted as she critiqued the form of the occasional golfers passing at dusk. The rest of us gabbed about our babies and toddlers, told birthing stories, and complained about our husbands. Jokes were made, many of them by Jenna and most in bad taste. That was Jenna in a nutshell—loud, dramatic, intense, funny. Memories were dug up. Past tensions surfaced, leading to gaping silences, tightened jaws, and sideways glances. Because of my training as a therapist—and without the haze of alcohol—I'd probably noticed the defensive body language and backhanded compliments more than the others. My eyes kept traveling back to Kaitlyn's shimmery pool, landing on the pile of debris floating in the corner.

That other weekend had only been for two nights. This time we were meeting for four. At least now I could drink. I exhaled, envisioning the twelve bottles of wine clinking in the back.

As Charlotte sped along the highway, we lamented the two times we'd planned to meet for dinner but had to cancel at the last minute, once because of an emergency illness with Marnie and the second time because of an unexpected conflict with one of Kaitlyn's daughters. Just like our weekends away, life had gotten in the way, and we'd stopped trying.

My legs ached by the time we reached the tiny airport, which was located amid dozens of empty fields carved into the forest. I perched in the back seat, staring out the window. A single prop plane accelerated down a runway beyond the underwhelming brick building that housed only four gates.

My phone beeped with a text message from Sam: *Got our luggage. Out in a sec!*

"They're coming out." My hands sweat as I waited for my first glimpse of Jenna and Sam.

Kaitlyn turned from the front passenger seat and clapped her hands excitedly. "It's happening!"

Charlotte's fingers gripped the steering wheel. "I'll pull into the pickup lane." I caught a glimpse of her eager smile and reddened cheeks in the rearview mirror. She must have been tired after so many hours of driving, but Sam and Jenna's arrival had energized all of us.

"There they are." Kaitlyn lowered her window. "Hey guys!" She waved and smiled as her designer sunglasses reflected in the late-afternoon sun. "Oh my gosh. Look at what Jenna's wearing!"

I craned my neck to see Sam and Jenna ambling toward us, pulling wheeled suitcases behind them. A sparkly, silver headband with the number "40" stuck up from two antennas on top of Jenna's head. I couldn't help but smile. Jenna had always loved being the center of attention. But the lilt in her step caused me to lean forward and hold my breath. Even after all these years, she hadn't fully recovered from the accident.

"Too funny." Charlotte unlocked the doors and jumped out.

I watched my friends hop up and down and load their suitcases in the back. I moved back to the third row as nerves bubbled in my stomach. The doors swung open.

"Megan!"

"Hi! So good to see you." I extended my arms as they ducked inside, taking turns hugging Kaitlyn and me while we commented on Jenna's headband. The flowery scent of Sam's perfume, coupled with the low-pitched intonation of Jenna's laugh, immediately soothed me, like the time I'd returned to my childhood home and found the rusty swing set standing in the same corner of the backyard. My friends had changed but were recognizable in all the important ways—Sam's vibrant white smile set off against her dark skin and black hair, the sparkle in Jenna's sea-blue eyes as she slid the glittery headband over her blonde crop cut. Only minor differences had emerged—a few more crow's feet around the eyes, deeper lines around the mouth, a stray silver hair peeking through from Sam's ebony tresses. It was both comforting and disconcerting to know that time didn't stop for anyone. Well, maybe except for Kaitlyn.

"I'm so happy you found flights that landed at the same time." Charlotte peeked over her shoulder as she pulled away from the curb.

"There was only one flight from LaGuardia every day," Jenna said.

Sam shook her head. "I know. Same from Denver. It's crazy how it worked out."

As Charlotte exited onto a two-lane highway and drove toward our destination, Jenna updated us about her life in New York City and a case she was working on representing an environmental group fighting to keep pesticides out of the city. She motioned with her arms as she talked, sitting a few inches taller than me and looking over her shoulder every minute or two. She'd been a soccer player in college and hadn't lost her athletic build.

I slipped my phone out of my purse and texted Andrew: *Just picked up everyone from the airport. On our way to the cabin. Not sure if I'll have time to talk later. Kiss Wyatt and Marnie for me. xx.*

A minute later, he texted back: *Have fun! Love you.*

Despite the flippant goodbye this morning, Andrew was good to me. Sometimes I didn't think I deserved him. I tried to remember the last time he'd taken a weekend for himself, away from the kids, but couldn't. I swallowed back the guilt rising in my throat and focused on Sam's voice as she filled us in on her family in Denver. Her sons, Leo and Brett, were eight and six now and obsessed with Legos.

"How's your MedTech company?" I asked, remembering all the hard work Sam had put in over the last fifteen years. She'd left her research position at a major hospital to pursue an idea to make affordable prescription drugs available online for everyone.

"It's going great. We had our biggest profit margin ever this year. I can tell you more about it later." Sam's brown eyes found mine as she tucked her thick hair behind her ear. She had plucked her eyebrows into perfect arches and her maroon lipstick accentuated her dark complexion. Her hair wasn't frizzy anymore, like it had been in college. She was even more beautiful, more confident.

"Wow. Look at you, overachievers." Kaitlyn flashed her movie-star smile from the front seat.

Sam threw her head back. "Look who's talking! How many charities are you running this year, PTO President?"

"I dropped out of the PTO. Some of the parents were too much." Kaitlyn waved her manicured hand in the air. "I'm focusing my time on a new initiative to get books into the hands of inner-city and rural kids. And I'm still helping new immigrants get settled."

"Kaitlyn saves the world. Again," Charlotte said, a smile pulling at her lips. Jenna and I chuckled.

Sam nodded her approval. "Good for you, Kaitlyn."

"I love that." I nodded toward Kaitlyn and noted the familiar sinking feeling she had always sent through me, like I should be doing more with my life. Kaitlyn had never stopped using her privileged position to help others. I imagined she didn't quite fit in with the country club set where she lived.

The trees flitted past outside the car windows as we caught each other up on our day's travels. I looked around at the women who sat near me inside the minivan. They were my closest friends in so many ways, but the passing of time had also made them strangers. Besides an occasional photo one of us posted on social media, I knew close to nothing about their day-to-day lives. I studied their faces as they talked, wondering which of us would still be friends if we met each other today, rather than twenty-two years earlier. My eyes traveled from Sam to Jenna in the second row to Kaitlyn and Charlotte in the front seat. I pinned my elbows close to my body and didn't let myself think too long about the answers.

CHAPTER THREE

The tires hit another pothole and I pressed my palms into the seat to steady myself. The forest swallowed the minivan, blocking out the sunlight. Eventually, Charlotte turned down another road identical to the one we'd just been on, but with even fewer cars. It was the second weekend in September and the summer travelers had already returned south for school and work.

Jenna narrowed her eyes out the window. "Where is this place we rented?"

Kaitlyn squinted at the GPS directions on her phone. "I don't know. I knew it was kind of far out there, but this is crazy."

"I'm looking for a sign for Crooked Lake," Sam said, craning her neck toward the far side of the car.

"We're in the middle of nowhere." Charlotte kept her eyes focused on the bumpy road. "But don't worry. I have a cooler of food, Kaitlyn brought four bags of groceries, and Megan brought every bottle of wine in her house."

"True story," I yelled from the back, picturing the bags of groceries and twelve bottles of wine rattling behind me.

"What more could we need?" Kaitlyn motioned toward the window. "This is what we wanted, right? Seclusion, nature, no distractions. Just four days of catching up."

Jenna stared at the passing landscape. "I've never seen so many trees before. It's such a nice break from the city."

We sat in silence for a minute, watching the trees flit by, the same scene repeating over and over, like the backgrounds of old cartoons.

"I'm hungry. What time do the food trucks come by?" Jenna asked, making the rest of us laugh.

"We're having pizza tonight. I hope that's okay. No meat." Kaitlyn winked at Jenna and then looked back at me. Jenna and I were vegetarians—Jenna, since college, and me more recently, after watching a horrific documentary about factory farms.

"Thanks," I said. It was just like Kaitlyn to be so accommodating. Outside of party planning and fundraising, empathy was one of her top strengths.

"I brought a salad too and some appetizers."

"Wow. Thanks," Sam said.

Jenna shifted. "Yeah. That's great."

"I can't wait to get there." From my spot in the back, I strained against my seat belt, fighting the onset of nausea. All the lurching and bumping gave me the feeling of being trapped in a cave during an earthquake.

"Hey, Charlotte. Slow down." Kaitlyn leaned forward. "I think our turn is coming up."

The minivan slowed as we passed a few run-down storefronts attempting to pass for a town. A gas station featured pumps reminiscent of the 1950s; only a discolored pickup truck lingered in the corner of its crumbling parking lot. A beauty salon doubled as a real estate office: *The Hair Cuttery. $12 cuts!* And below it: *Wooded lots for sale!* Next door, a grocery store displayed a black-and-white sign through a murky front window: *Night crawlers * Live Bait.*

Sam squealed. "Oh my God! We're staying in a place that sells worms in the grocery store."

I cringed at the sign as belly-aching laughter filled the van.

"There's a lake near the cabin, so it kind of makes sense," Kaitlyn said.

More jokes about scheduling haircuts with the town realtor followed as the fleeting glimpse of civilization faded, and our vehicle was submerged back into the forest. A mile or so later, we approached an unmarked dirt road.

Charlotte slid her hands lower on the steering wheel. "Is this it?"

Kaitlyn scrolled through the GPS. "It looks like this is the turn. We still have twelve miles to go down this road. Then we take a right for half a mile. Then a left, and we're there."

"Twelve miles! Seriously!" Jenna leaned toward the front seat. "Where is this place?"

A motor rumbled behind us and Charlotte sped up. I caught her nervous glance in the rearview mirror. "Look at this guy. Why is he following so close?"

I turned toward the back window where a black pickup truck hovered only a foot or two behind the minivan. The truck sat on oversized tires and had an extra exhaust pipe affixed to the hood. A reflection on the windshield obscured the driver's face.

"I can't go any faster. I'll fly off the road," Charlotte said.

Kaitlyn rubbed her arm. "Just ignore him. We're the only cars here. He can pass you if he wants."

Jenna leaned past me toward the other driver, throwing her arm in the air. "Go around us, jerk."

The minivan hit a pothole and I clutched the door handle to keep myself steady. "Slow down, Charlotte."

An engine revved from behind as the truck swerved to the side and sped past us. A tattered sticker of a skull and crossbones was affixed to the truck's back window. A cloud of black smoke trailed behind the mammoth vehicle, polluting the otherwise pristine air.

Jenna scowled. "Looks like someone's not concerned about his carbon footprint."

"I'm guessing he's a local," I said.

"What makes you say that?" Jenna asked with a straight face, and I couldn't help but chuckle.

With the truck out of sight, Charlotte's shoulders had relaxed, but her eyes remained glued to the road as we continued traveling at a slightly slower speed.

"Where are you guys taking me?" Sam asked.

Kaitlyn glanced back. "Isn't there a land trust that owns over a thousand acres of forest out here? I remember something about it in the rental listing."

"I didn't realize it was so remote." Charlotte shook her head. "The cabin looked charming online."

"We got a good deal," I said. "I can't wait to get there."

I thought of the cabin we'd agreed to rent for our long weekend. After running into a few dead ends on the mainstream vacation rental sites, Jenna recommended a mom-and-pop site specializing in off-the-grid properties. Charlotte had quickly bookmarked the cabin based on its location and price. The heading read: *Secluded Cabin on Crooked Lake Sleeps Six.* The online pictures portrayed a rustic country cabin with baskets of red geraniums hanging along a front deck. A steep wooded incline led to a private lake. The property sat on over thirty wooded acres, surrounded by a thousand acres of forest owned by a land trust on one side and a two-hundred-acre summer sleepaway camp on the other. Beyond the camp sat state-owned forest land. Although the cabin's description presented it as "a no-frills escape to rustic living," it cost less than half the price of everything else we'd seen and was relatively close to the small airport. Charlotte claimed their money was tight. She and Reed were saving up to take Oliver to Europe the following spring. Jenna had her heart set on going "off the grid" for a few days.

It's kind of like glamping, Jenna had written in one of our group texts, which had made the description sound more appealing. None of us cared about going out to restaurants or bars, so the decision had been easy.

I envisioned the photo of the glassy lake in the early morning light with a sailboat gliding past. "I can't believe it has a private lake. It sounds so peaceful."

"What the heck." Kaitlyn smacked her phone against her hand a few times and pushed the power button. "The GPS is frozen. It says we're still back on the County Road."

The minivan continued bumping along the dirt road, nailing a pothole every few seconds despite Charlotte's attempts to swerve around them.

Jenna's eyebrows furrowed as she studied her phone. "My phone's not loading either. Don't tell me there are no cell-phone towers out here."

I leaned toward her, noticing my phone had lost its bars too. "The rental listing said something about spotty phone reception. It was in the fine print below the description. I told Andrew he might not hear from me until Monday."

"Yeah. I told Derek we might have to drive into town for me to call him."

Jenna looked back at me. "Yeah. I saw that too, but I thought it said reception was 'spotty,' not non-existent!"

"I warned Reed that I might be off the grid for a few days." Charlotte adjusted her hands on the steering wheel. "Hopefully it will get better once we get to the cabin."

Sam held up her phone and frowned. "Mine's out too. At least I texted Thomas from the airport. He knows we're headed out to the boonies."

"How far do you think we've gone?" I asked. "You said twelve miles on this road and then a right, followed by a left."

"Yeah." Charlotte glanced over her shoulder. "I'll keep going for another five or six miles and then we'll look for a turn."

The sun sank lower in the sky as we rambled down the road. Kaitlyn sat motionless in the front passenger seat; her euphoria had evaporated. A crease of worry formed across her forehead every time she turned back to look at us. Meanwhile, Jenna relayed every detail about a new series she'd been watching on Netflix and then told a long story about an attractive man who owned her favorite vegan food truck in Brooklyn. Jenna was the only one in the group who wasn't married and didn't have kids, and it was exciting to live vicariously through her. But there was one thing about Jenna that had always been aggravating; she made it difficult to get a word in.

A wooden sign flew past my window, blending into the trees.

"Wait," I yelled, interrupting Jenna's story. "There was a sign."

Charlotte slammed on the brakes. We lurched forward against our seat belts.

I pointed behind us. "You just passed it."

The minivan reversed for five seconds until the sign materialized in the trees. The placard was homemade, constructed of plywood, with messy white lettering painted across it.

Sam read it out loud, "Camp Eventide. Next Right."

My eyes traveled over the uneven words. "That sign is so creepy. It looks like a serial killer painted it. Who would send their kids there?"

"Next right to your death, kiddos. Hahaha!" Jenna said in a bad imitation of a villain's voice.

Sam covered her face with her fingers. "You guys are horrible."

"I can't believe I forgot to tell you this." Kaitlyn studied the sign then flipped back toward the rest of us. "I saw that camp on the map yesterday when I was looking for the nearest grocery store. I wondered what Camp Eventide was, so I looked it up."

"What is it?" Charlotte asked, her wide eyes reflecting in the rearview mirror.

Light filtered through the window and cast wavering shadows across Kaitlyn's face. "It was a summer retreat for at-risk youths. The place shut down earlier this summer after someone on the staff died."

"Who was it? A counselor?" Charlotte asked.

Kaitlyn pinched her berry-stained lips together. "I don't know. Probably. The person who died was a woman, but the article was vague. It was written right after it happened, so the police hadn't even notified the victim's family yet."

"How did she die?" I asked.

Kaitlyn shrugged. "I don't know. It only mentioned 'suspicious circumstances.' Maybe it was an accident. I meant to find out more about it, but Julia had an emergency with some cookies she was making. I'm talking smoke billowing out of the oven. She's really into baking right now. I forgot to go back and look up more information."

"I wonder what the suspicious circumstances were," I said.

Jenna touched her fabric headband and sighed. "Oh man. So that whole camp is sitting empty? Her family probably sued the owners."

"Spoken like a lawyer," Kaitlyn said as the rest of us chuckled.

Sam straightened up in her seat. "Wait. There's a deserted camp sitting across from our cabin out in the middle of nowhere? And someone just died there under suspicious circumstances?"

Charlotte glanced toward her. "That's what it sounds like."

Sam adjusted her sunglasses atop her head. "This is terrifying. Why didn't I know about this?"

"You should never leave the planning to us," Jenna said with a playful wink.

Sam couldn't help but smile, although I noticed a sheen of sweat across her upper lip. "You're right. I should have known better. Can we talk about something else?"

Kaitlyn pointed ahead, attempting to get everyone back on track. "Okay. So when we get to the next road, we'll take a left instead of a right. The cabin is across the lake from the camp."

Charlotte nodded. "Sounds good. See? Who needs GPS when we have Kaitlyn?"

A few minutes later, guided by Kaitlyn's directions, we turned down a long, winding dirt driveway. My stomach churned with a mixture of nausea and hunger. Jenna lowered her window and breathed in the mossy air, a smile stretching across her face. "Is this what fresh air smells like?"

Just as I was enjoying the sing-song melody of chirping birds and the refreshing breeze, a shot cracked through the serenity of the woods. A second one followed. My muscles jerked, and Charlotte hit the brakes.

"What was that?"

"It sounded like gunshots." Charlotte looked back at us.

Jenna's fingers gripped her seat belt. "Holy crap!"

"Maybe someone is hunting." Dread tunneled through me. "Wonderful."

This cabin in the woods was already giving me a bad vibe. I was trapped in the back of the minivan, hours away from my family. The air thickened around me, my muscles cramping. I wanted to go home. I kicked myself for not offering to host. Andrew could have taken the kids to his mom's house for the weekend. My friends and I could be sitting on our back patio with music and laughter floating through my fenced-in backyard instead of gunshots.

Charlotte crouched behind the steering wheel, guiding the minivan up the long driveway.

"I thought there wasn't going to be anyone else around," I said.

Kaitlyn shook her head. "The website said the owner lives down the street, but his house is over a half-mile away. I emailed him a few questions last week before Charlotte sent the payment. He only responded that he'd leave the front door unlocked."

Charlotte nodded. "Yeah. He emailed me a copy of the house rules—all pretty straightforward. Don't worry. We don't have to see him at all unless there's a problem."

The minivan rolled up to the cabin, and all talking ceased. I gasped at the sight of the dilapidated structure. Even chatty Jenna failed to produce words. The wooden cabin bore only a vague resemblance to the building in the photos, like a long-lost sibling who'd fallen on hard times and lived a much more difficult life. The cabin wasn't rustic and quaint; it was a dump. Cobwebs covered the corners of the windows. A broken piece of wood siding dangled down from the outer wall. The place was falling apart. A thick layer of moss grew across the shingled roof, and cracked steps led to the front door. The deck was suffering from wood rot. The pots of red geraniums that had popped vibrantly from the photos on the website were nowhere in sight.

Charlotte turned off the ignition, staring straight ahead. "Tell me this isn't the right place."

Sam blinked her thick black eyelashes. "This doesn't look anything like the photos."

"Maybe the inside is better," Kaitlyn said, but the high pitch of her voice was hollow.

Jenna exited the minivan. I slipped out after her, sucking in a breath and appreciating the solid ground beneath my feet. I stretched out my cramped legs and stumbled across the gravel driveway in my strappy sandals. My eyes were drawn forward, past a steep, wooded drop-off leading to a lake. Crooked Lake spread out below us, glittering and beautiful. I blinked at the sight, so spectacular in contrast to the drab cabin. At least the information about the private lake had been accurate. Nothing but trees rimmed the shoreline. The surface of the cobalt water rippled in the wind, stealing my breath. Maybe this view would make up for the disappointing accommodations. As I stepped forward, my toes bumped against something soft and warm.

I jumped and screamed. A dead squirrel stared up at me, its tiny hands stretched upward, its eyes vacant. A circle of blood seeped into its fur. I stumbled to the side, trying to erase the sensation of the warm body against my bare skin. Someone had shot it.

CHAPTER FOUR

"What kind of person shoots a squirrel?" Jenna stood next to me with her eyebrows furrowed. "This little guy wasn't hurting anything."

I looked away from the murdered animal. "This is so messed up."

Sam and Kaitlyn wavered next to us.

"Just leave it, you guys. It might have rabies." Charlotte eyed a dirt path that led over the wooded hill. "The owner was probably here."

"Is this his idea of housekeeping?" I followed Charlotte's gaze toward the trees. No one else was around.

Charlotte bit her lower lip as her eyes flickered across us. "Sorry. I didn't know this place was going to be like this. Hopefully whoever did this will stay away from the cabin now that we're here."

I nodded, not wanting to make Charlotte feel bad. The property's condition wasn't her fault, even though we'd chosen the cabin because she wanted to save money. The photos of the vacation property had been stunning, and no one had argued with the price. We'd all reviewed the same listing for the rental, and we'd all agreed on renting the secluded cabin.

Kaitlyn stretched her arms as she surveyed the cabin. "Yeah. Let's unload our stuff. We'll have to make the best of it."

"Do you hate me right now?" Charlotte asked Kaitlyn, whose mouth had turned down.

Kaitlyn's head snapped up as if she'd woken from a trance. "What? No. Of course not! I could never be mad at the person who introduced me to my husband."

"I'm good for something." Charlotte offered a sheepish grin and Kaitlyn squeezed her. Charlotte had invited Derek to one of our house parties during our junior year. Every time we got together Kaitlyn made a big deal of thanking Charlotte for her matchmaking skills.

We grabbed our suitcases and headed through the front door. Jenna walked in front of me, favoring her left leg. Sweat gathered in my armpits as I tried not to think of the accident back in college.

I tore my gaze away from her uneven stride, finding myself standing in a dim living room. A hint of lemon cut through the musty air. Someone had attempted to clean the rustic space. A red plaid couch and matching love seat surrounded a worn coffee table. A wicker rocking chair sat in the corner, displaying a cross-stitched cushion with a blocky red heart above the words *HOME IS WHERE THE HEART IS*. A fireplace with a stone mantel covered most of the far wall. There was no TV, not even the old, boxy kind with an antenna. A deer head stared down at me from the opposite side of the room.

I turned away, missing the warmth of my own living room and wishing I hadn't agreed to four nights away. I'd crossed paths with two dead animals in under five minutes. "This place gives me the creeps."

Jenna pulled her suitcase close to her legs, gawking at the surroundings. "Where are we? We should have read the reviews more carefully."

"I did read them carefully," I said. "I assumed the bad ones were from miserable people. Most of the reviews were positive. They raved about the lake, mostly. No one mentioned that the roof is rotting away or that dead squirrels fall from trees as you arrive."

Jenna chuckled.

"At least it's clean." Kaitlyn was in the kitchen, peering into a white refrigerator. "It could be worse."

Charlotte lowered her chin as her eyes darted around the living room. "Sorry about this. I had no idea. Maybe we can get our money back if we complain."

Jenna waved her away. "Nah. We'll make it work. It'll be an adventure."

"Yeah. It's not like there's anyplace else to stay around here," I said.

Jenna kicked the floor and smiled. "Something tells me this is one weekend we'll never forget."

"That's for sure," Sam added, hugging her arms in front of herself. "We'll have good stories to tell when we get home."

I observed my friends who hunched together, silent. Despite the reassuring words coming out of their mouths, their faces twitched, and their gazes avoided one another. Panic rose inside me. My lungs constricted, making it difficult to breathe. I recognized the sensations as the onset of a panic attack. It was the same feeling I'd had in the back of the minivan, but now that my nausea had faded, the terror was even more pronounced. The cabin walls were closing in on me. My body told me to run, but I couldn't move. The therapist in me could have diagnosed the condition in someone else immediately, but it took a few seconds longer to see it in myself. I needed to focus on something I could control and to get some fresh air.

"I'll go get the wine." I turned away and forced my heavy legs through the kitchen door and onto the rotting deck. Once I reached the minivan, I averted my eyes from the lifeless squirrel and sucked in the woodsy breeze. The sound of lapping waves pulled me off course. My eyes traveled toward the lake and across the bobbing waves, landing on an empty rectangle of beach on the far shore. The early evening sky cast a gray light over the sand. Besides the sandy area, only trees were visible beyond the water. The beach must have been part of the abandoned summer camp. Happy memories of my own childhood experiences at a different sleepaway camp fluttered through me.

My shoulders straightened, and I found my breath again. I turned away from the shimmering water and opened the back of Charlotte's van, pulling out the box of wine and lugging it toward the cabin. The glass bottles clinked together with each step. My stomach rumbled, and I wondered if Andrew had fed Marnie and Wyatt yet. It must be getting late. I'd forgotten to tell him about the leftover mac and cheese in the fridge. I set down the load and dug my phone out of my pocket, finding no reception. I wrote a text to Andrew anyway and pressed send. A second later, a notification popped up; the message was undeliverable. I sighed, shoving the phone back in my pocket and closing the back of the minivan.

As I bent to lift the box, a shadow shifted in my peripheral vision. I paused, leaning forward and squinting. *Was it the person who'd shot the squirrel? The owner of the cabin? Or someone else?* I watched and waited as my heart hammered in my chest, searching for someone with a rifle hiding in the trees. Only a black crow flapped its wings and cawed, flying away from a nearby branch. I exhaled, my arms dropping to my sides—*stupid crow.* I'd freaked myself out and I was imagining things that weren't there.

I shook away my paranoia and continued carrying the box into the kitchen, where I stashed a few bottles of white in the refrigerator. Thumping footsteps and loud conversation sounded from upstairs. I moved toward the commotion.

Charlotte met me at the top of the stairs, holding my suitcase. A mischievous look flashed across her face, an expression I'd seen her make so many times in college whenever she couldn't wait to tell me something. "Looks like you and I are roommates. Jenna's got the bed across the hall, and Sam and Kaitlyn are in the master bedroom." Charlotte made quotes with her fingers as she said the word "master."

"Sounds good." I climbed the narrow wooden staircase and followed Charlotte into a small bedroom on the left with two twin beds covered in yellow-flowered quilts. I pulled back the covers on the bed closest to me, relieved to find crisp, white linens. I peered further into the sheets, searching for signs of spiders or bed bugs, but didn't see anything. When I looked up, Charlotte was standing with her hands on her hips, watching me.

"Are you okay?" she asked. "You look a little pale."

"Oh. Yeah. I'm fine. I think I just got some motion sickness on the way up."

She stepped closer. "I'm sorry this cabin isn't the greatest, but hopefully we can make it work. It's only for a few nights."

I heard the note of guilt in Charlotte's voice and loosened my shoulders. "It looked so different online. It's not your fault."

I meant what I said, even though Charlotte had been the one who pushed for something affordable. She and Reed both had professional careers, but she was excited about their upcoming trip to Europe. It wasn't my place to question her financial decisions. Besides, Jenna had wanted to escape city life for a few days and this place fit her requirements too. We'd all thought it was a good choice. I didn't want Charlotte to think any of us blamed the accommodations squarely on her. She'd been nice enough to drive both Kaitlyn and me up here and pick the others up from the airport. It wasn't a five-star hotel, but we had high standards because we were spoiled. I thought of the last trip Andrew and I had taken together almost a year ago. We'd gone to San Francisco and stayed at The Ritz. I could deal with a run-down cabin for four nights.

"Yeah. We'll make it work. We're all together. That's the important thing."

Charlotte's face softened.

"And if we drink enough wine, none of us will notice, anyway." I shoved my bag toward the wall with my foot. "I'm starving. Should we make some food?"

"Good idea."

*

Thirty minutes later, we sat in a semicircle on the sturdiest part of the deck, drinking wine from glasses we'd found in the cupboard, and eating cheese and crackers while we waited for the frozen pizza to cook. Jenna had located a broom and swept the debris and cobwebs away. The sun sank lower on the horizon, an orange ball against a pink sky glowing through the trees.

"It's pretty out here, isn't it?" Jenna gazed out toward the lake. "I almost had a heart attack when we first pulled up."

We nodded in agreement. Now that we'd gotten settled, the rustic cabin wasn't so bad. The moss and spiderwebs had all but disappeared in the dwindling light.

Our moment of silence was followed up by a solid hour of non-stop talking and laughing, just like old times. We only paused to refill wineglasses, remove the pizza from the oven, and dole out a pre-made salad onto some paper plates. Kaitlyn pulled out her phone and showed off photos of her three girls, Julia, Peyton, and Maddie, who looked like mini versions of their mom, all tall and thin with ivory skin and silky auburn hair. The photos started a chain reaction, with everyone locating pictures on their phones. When Sam handed me her phone, I studied her sons, who shared her brilliant white smile and tufts of black hair against tawny complexions as they proudly held up their Lego creations. Another photo showed Sam's husband, Thomas, hiking up the side of a mountain. Sam had met Thomas when she was in medical school. None of us knew him well, but he was soft-spoken and had kind eyes. Sam always spoke highly of him, as if she'd won the husband lottery. Charlotte shared a photo of Oliver gripping the steering wheel of the minivan during his first driving lesson. I wished Charlotte luck, finding it impossible to imagine my young ones in the same position in a few years. When it was Jenna's turn, she flashed photos of her dog, a black lab mix named Rufus, who she'd rescued from the shelter, as well as a posh new condo she'd purchased in Brooklyn. I showed off my kids, too, catching everyone up on Marnie and Wyatt's swim lessons and art projects.

"How is Andrew, anyway?" Kaitlyn asked.

"He's good. He's coaching Wyatt's soccer team this fall. And he likes his job." I slumped forward and cleared my throat. Not able to tell the rest. We'd hit a rough patch recently, and my voice dried up whenever the conversation turned to Andrew.

Charlotte set her paper plate on the rickety table in front of us. "And everything's good between the two of you?"

"Yeah. I mean, we have our ups and downs, but who doesn't?" I forced a smile, pressing my back into the metal chair. There was so much more to say, but my insides compressed, trapping the truth like a clenched fist. I wasn't ready to loosen the grip, even among friends. Otherwise, I would have to tell them how the resentment had grown between Andrew and me after Wyatt had been born. I'd been quick to criticize him, and he'd been slow to help. Andrew rarely kissed me or complimented me. There were no surprises, no dinners out, no flowers. To avoid confrontation, I'd retreated into my work while he'd chosen his phone. We ate dinner side-by-side, watching TV. I didn't feel appreciated or loved. Sometimes I stayed at work extra-late just to avoid him, even though it meant less time with my children. I was a failure at marriage and commitment. I was a family therapist who didn't know how to communicate with her husband in any productive way.

"Yeah. Who doesn't have marital problems?" Charlotte chuckled, but there was an edge to her laugh. I remained quietly confused, remembering the way Reed had kissed her.

The rest of us had stayed unmarried and focused on graduate school and careers after college, but Charlotte, who'd always been flirtatious and boy crazy, had been married and pregnant by the age of twenty-four. She and her first husband divorced four years later. Then she dated a long string of men before landing on Reed eight years ago. Charlotte was the only one of us with a teenager.

She'd stayed home with Oliver when he was young but had gone back to school when Oliver was in elementary school. Around the time of our last get-together five years ago, Charlotte had earned her certification as a physical therapist. Now she described how her long hours at the medical center had become her life. She placed a hand on her stomach. "I don't have time to exercise anymore. And my diet's obviously not working."

Sam shook her head. "You look great, Charlotte."

"We're our own worst enemies," Jenna said as the rest of us nodded.

Kaitlyn played with the ends of her hair. "You guys should give your husbands a not-so-subtle hint to cherish you. Derek surprised me in March with an all-inclusive vacation to the Dominican Republic. He even arranged for his mom to stay with the girls. All I had to do was pack my suitcase." She lowered her long eyelashes and smiled. "It was heaven."

Sam leaned in. "That's awesome. I can't complain about Thomas. He's always doing nice things for me. He collected all the press clippings about MedTech and made a photo book out of them. The title was, 'My Brilliant CEO Wife,' which was quite an exaggeration, but I'll take it." Sam shook her head. "He's so involved with the boys, too. I don't know what I'd do without him."

"Aw. That's so sweet," I said.

Jenna raised her chin. "Looks like everyone's life has turned out rosy and perfect, except for mine." Her voice sliced through our laughter and chatter.

I pressed my back into my chair as my thoughts plummeted. I wondered if Jenna was thinking about the accident that had altered the course of her life, and I braced myself for the drama that was sure to follow.

CHAPTER FIVE

Jenna's angry words hung in the air as the rest of us sat in stunned silence. Kaitlyn widened her eyes. Charlotte's mouth opened. Sam shifted in her chair.

I sat up. "What? Don't be crazy, Jenna. No one has a perfect life. And your life is amazing, anyway. Don't you know we're all jealous of your freedom?"

Charlotte nodded. "Yeah. How many people can claim to be a successful attorney in New York City?"

A shadow passed over Sam's face as she raised her gaze toward Jenna. "I didn't mean to say my life is perfect. Of course it's not."

Jenna tugged at the ends of her chin-length hair and flattened her mouth.

"Look at your trendy condo." Kaitlyn motioned toward Jenna's phone. "You have the most exciting life of any of us. We're all at home in the suburbs trying to come up with new ways to make grilled cheese sandwiches while you're out drinking martinis and dancing to live music."

A smile cracked Jenna's lips.

Sam tapped the table with her manicured nails. "Seriously. I'm sorry. I thought we were having braggy time."

I chuckled at the phrase. "Braggy time?"

Jenna touched her chin. "I don't mean to rain on anyone's braggy time. I'm just feeling old and bitter, I guess."

"Join the club," I said, offering a look of exasperation.

Sam slapped her hand down. "Okay. We're all still young in the grand scheme of things, and braggy time is over."

"Hey guys. I found an old photo album in my basement." Kaitlyn slid back her chair and reached into a reusable grocery bag sitting nearby. She removed a thick book with a sea-blue cover and placed it on the table, flipping it open. "There are some real gems in here. This was our junior year, remember?"

We hunched over it. Shrieks and squeals filled the air as we studied the images of our former selves.

Charlotte tossed back her head. "Oh my God! Why didn't anyone stop me from wearing that ugly shirt?"

"Look at my hair," I said. "Could my ponytail be any higher?"

Jenna pointed at another photo. "I remember when I used to have long hair." She narrowed her eyes. "Who's that guy with Sam?"

Sam stood behind them, peering toward the book. "That's Johnny Franklin. We dated for a few months."

A flood of lost memories returned to me. "Oh, yeah. The guy from Vermont, right?"

"Uh-huh." Sam scratched her nose, and I noticed she wore the same wood-beaded bracelets she used to wear in college. "Thank God I didn't end up with him."

"He was a big pothead, wasn't he?" Jenna asked.

Sam nodded. "Yeah. Here's the crazy thing. I'm connected to him on LinkedIn. He owns a marijuana growing facility in California. I guess he's super successful."

"Way to follow your passion, Johnny," Jenna said as I laughed.

A group photo at the bottom of the page caught my eye. It was the five of us, plus one. "Oh my gosh. Is that Frida? I almost forgot about her."

Charlotte leaned closer. "Yeah. That's her. Frida King. My freshman-year roommate."

"Look at her scowl," Kaitlyn said, chuckling. "She was always the life of the party."

I leaned forward, taking in the image. Frida stood at the edge of the frame a foot away from the rest of us, as if she wasn't sure whether she should be in the photo. Her dark hair framed her face, and her small eyes peered uncomfortably toward me like she'd flipped over a rock and was cataloging everything she found underneath. Frida had never been at the center of our group but always seemed to be lurking nearby, watching. I shook my head. "I never understood what you saw in her, Charlotte."

Sam's smile flattened. "She always made me feel weird."

"She didn't wash her hands. Remember, you had to teach her about soap?" Kaitlyn said as she wrinkled her nose.

"That was because her parents were off the deep end. Frida was nice enough." Charlotte shrugged. "Just a little socially awkward. I know what it's like to grow up in a small town out in the middle of nowhere."

I studied my friends, breathing in the damp night air, as my thoughts drifted back over the years.

*

"I hope you don't mind. I took the top bunk. You can choose whichever desk you want." My new roommate, Sam, tugged at the hem of her navy-blue-and-gold Marquette T-shirt. The whites of her eyes showed as she glanced toward the bunk beds. She looked as nervous as I felt.

"It's fine. I wanted the bottom bunk, anyway," I said. "I'll take the desk by the window if it's all the same to you."

"Sure thing."

My parents had left five minutes earlier after helping me unload my things into the dorm room and make up the bottom bunk with sheets and blankets. Sam had already claimed the top bed. Now it was just the two of us, along with a steady stream of incoming freshmen and their parents passing by our doorway.

"It's a pretty small room for two people, huh?" I lifted a box of school supplies onto the desk by the window. My new dorm room was

approximately half the size of my bedroom at home. Still, we had a decent view of a leafy treetop shading a courtyard where parents carried boxes and suitcases toward the door.

"Yeah, but it's ours." She flashed an eager smile.

My shoulders loosened, and I smiled back.

I'd roomed blind and immediately realized how lucky I was to have been paired with Sam. She was stunning, with dark skin and long black hair. The first thing she told me was that she was from Phoenix, which I already knew from the letter I'd received from student housing three weeks earlier. I told her I grew up in a boring suburb forty minutes away, which didn't sound nearly as cool but made Sam laugh. She'd chosen Marquette because her parents had lived in Milwaukee before she was born, and she wanted to go somewhere no one else in her high school was going. Also, because of the school's strong pre-med program. Sam shared details about her life in the desert, including a cactus and a pool in her backyard. The warm climate sounded so exotic to my eighteen-year-old self that she might as well have been from Zimbabwe or Acapulco. I'd never traveled out of the Midwest other than to go to Florida to visit my grandparents.

Sam had a bohemian style, with wooden beads and a bandana made of patchwork fabric. Her jeans hung loosely at the ankles. She was so much more relaxed than me.

"Hopefully you brought some warm clothes, too? The winters are brutal here."

Sam stopped playing the beads around her wrist and looked toward the window. "I have a down coat, but I didn't pack it."

"Don't worry. We have a few months. Plus, I have tons of extra hats and mittens. Consider them yours."

Bellowing laughter echoed from the hallway. A second later, knuckles rapped against our open door and two tall women popped their heads inside our dorm room. One had a muscular body and looked like an all-American athlete with blue eyes and a blonde ponytail. The other one was drop-dead gorgeous with silky reddish hair and a face like a doll. She had a kind smile, which was the only thing keeping me from hating her.

"Hi neighbors! We live next door."

Sam and I stood from our seated positions on the lower bunk.

"I'm Jenna," said the one with the blonde ponytail. "I'm from Chicago."

The redhead waved. "I'm Kaitlyn. I'm from Michigan."

Sam and I introduced ourselves. Jenna told us she was attending the university on a soccer scholarship. She was supposed to have lived in a different hall with the other athletes, but someone in the housing department had messed up and put her in the room next door.

Jenna shrugged. "I'm going to stay here, though. It seems cool."

"Don't leave me." Kaitlyn elbowed Jenna before telling us she planned to major in economics. We chatted about our dorm's location and shared rumors we'd heard on whether our dorm's cafeteria lived up to the food in the other cafeterias. Then we made dinner plans because the food service didn't begin until the next day.

Movement in the hallway caught my eye, and the others turned to see where I was looking. Someone's parents exited the room across the hall. They looked much older than my mom and dad, and I wondered if they were grandparents instead of parents. The man wore shapeless beige pants and a button-down shirt that was a size too small. His jowls sagged around his frown, and his stern eyes avoided contact with everyone around him. A woman walked two paces behind him. Short, tight curls covered her head, the same way my grandma wore her hair. But I could see now that this woman was younger than I thought—closer to my mom's age. Her wide and desolate face held two stony eyes. A flowered pink dress resembling a nightgown hung over her stout frame. She stepped awkwardly because of the chunky sandals on her feet. The unusual couple hurried down the hall, clearly out of their element and eager to leave.

Jenna raised her eyebrows at us. We chuckled nervously as the man and woman disappeared into the stairwell. Curiosity pulled me forward, toward the room across the way. Jenna barged past me and knocked on the closed door. A petite woman with thick brown hair, pale skin, and full cheeks stepped into the doorway.

"Hi. I'm Jenna." Jenna waved toward the rest of us. "This is Kaitlyn, Megan, and Sam. We live in the two rooms across the hall from you."

"Hi. I'm Charlotte."

"Where are you from, Charlotte?" It was Sam who stepped forward now, offering Charlotte the same easy smile she'd shown me earlier.

"Northeast Wisconsin. A small town you've never heard of."

I smiled at Charlotte's joke, immediately drawn to her shy grin and down-to-earth vibe. We took turns telling Charlotte about ourselves.

"Were those your parents?" Jenna asked.

Charlotte blinked down the hallway. "Oh. No. My mom left a while ago. I have a roommate. Frida. That was her mom and dad." Charlotte made a face. "Frida's from an even smaller town than mine."

As if on cue, a broad-shouldered woman sulked down the hall. She had the same plain face and intense eyes as the curly-haired woman who'd hobbled away a few minutes earlier. The young woman stopped several steps short of us with a bag of garlic bagels dangling from her hand. The hair near her part was greasy and dotted with dandruff. I looked away.

"Hi Frida," Charlotte said, speaking louder than she needed to. "These guys live in the two rooms across the hall."

Frida raised her chin toward us but didn't smile. "Hey," she said, then ducked past us into the room.

Charlotte shrugged. We stared at each other for a minute before Kaitlyn suggested we hang out in her and Jenna's room. They kept the door open and played music, encouraging others in our hall to stop by and introduce themselves. Two guys from around the corner joined us, one of them telling Kaitlyn she reminded them of Nicole Kidman. She only fluttered her eyelashes and directed the conversation away from herself, which made me like her even more. A couple of hours later, the visitors had left. The five of us headed out for dinner.

I paced down the hall, excited to be going out to eat with my new friends, Sam, Kaitlyn, Jenna, and Charlotte. But halfway to the stairs, the weight of watching eyes pressed into my back. I flipped around, finding Frida peering through a narrow gap in the door. Her unflinching stare sent a chill through my bones. I hesitated, debating whether I should yell down the hall and invite her to come with us. Before I could decide, Frida dropped her gaze to the floor and stepped backward, disappearing behind the door like a child banished to the attic in a creepy Stephen King novel. I turned away from the empty hallway and trotted to catch up with the others as a shiver skittered across my skin.

CHAPTER SIX

An owl hooted from somewhere beyond the lake. I scooted my chair forward, looking closer at the photo in the album. "Frida was a strange duck."

Kaitlyn pursed her lips. "She became more normal, didn't she? After she got away from her parents?"

"And after she started using soap," Jenna added.

"She was smart to get away from them," Sam said. "Weren't her parents involved in some extreme fundamentalist religious sect?"

I nodded, remembering bits of information I hadn't thought about since we'd gotten together five years ago. "Frida's parents homeschooled her through high school. Didn't they?"

"Something like that," Kaitlyn said. "I remember Frida would come to Mass with us sometimes, right, Charlotte?" Kaitlyn twirled a strand of wavy hair around her finger.

"Yeah. She did."

"It was so strange," Kaitlyn continued. "Frida didn't know the real words to any of the prayers because her parents had taught her some twisted version of them."

Charlotte crossed her arms and leaned back. "That's right. I totally forgot about that. Frida's parents thought the Catholic church was too liberal."

"Oh, for the love of Mother Universe." Jenna chuckled. "In fairness, most of us here didn't know how to say the prayers."

Sam, Jenna, and I smiled at each other. We had a long-standing private joke about how a Catholic university had managed to bring the three of us together—two fallen Protestants and a non-practicing-Jew. The university's efforts to diversify their student body had succeeded.

"Frida studied social work, right?" Sam looked at Charlotte.

Charlotte nodded. "Uh-huh."

"Do you ever hear anything from her?" I asked, vaguely recalling a similar conversation we'd had about Frida the last time we'd gotten together.

Charlotte shook her head. "Not really. We met for dinner a few times after graduation. But after Oliver was born, it was hard to find the time."

I released my breath, relieved we'd all lost touch with Frida, even if she had turned her life around.

Charlotte gripped her glass. "We're still Facebook friends, but she doesn't post much anymore."

Kaitlyn's face brightened. "I saw your post yesterday, Charlotte. About the five of us finally getting together on Crooked Lake to celebrate turning forty. We should take a group photo tomorrow and add it to your post."

"Okay. Good idea."

Jenna raised her finger. "Let's be sure not to include the cabin in the background. We don't want people to think we've failed at life."

I lowered my head and giggled. Jenna's sense of humor still killed me.

"I can't stand Facebook," Sam said. "I canceled my account last year. We should definitely take a group photo, though."

Jenna slid back a pink fabric headband that had replaced the show-stopping one she'd been wearing earlier. "How'd you get off Facebook, Sam? I'm jealous."

"No, kidding," Kaitlyn said with a frown. "I hate social media. I have to use it for my charity stuff, though."

"I have to use it to find bad dates," Jenna said, and everyone laughed again.

Kaitlyn flipped to the next page in the album, where we continued ridiculing our former fashion choices.

Jenna pointed at a photo, smiling. "Remember Charlotte's morbid phase?"

"Oh, yeah!" I studied photos of Charlotte, wearing all-black and chunky combat boots. Kohl eyeliner rimmed her eyes. In one photo, she even wore black lipstick and a black knit cap.

Charlotte shrugged. "I thought I was cool. Anyway, don't be so quick to judge. I remember your hippie phase, Sam."

Sam shook her head. "I don't."

Jenna threw her chin in the air. "Yeah. Too much weed from Johnny Franklin."

We howled with laughter, my insides aching from not being able to catch my breath.

Sam scooched forward and smirked. "Charlotte, tell me the truth. Did you have a thing for Johnny? Remember how you were always so flirty with him?"

"Wasn't Charlotte flirty with everyone's boyfriends?" Jenna raised an eyebrow.

A giggle slipped from my mouth, but my hands balled into fists under the table as I remembered how Charlotte used to flutter around any new boy who showed the slightest interest, especially those in relationships. She'd been so desperate for male attention, always scanning her surroundings for anyone who would talk to her, wearing spandex shirts and too much makeup to class. I didn't judge her for those things anymore. We'd all done stupid things back then. The sight of Frida in the photo had reminded me of that.

Charlotte's cheeks reddened as she forced a smile. "What can I say? I was insecure."

"I'm only messing with you," Jenna said.

Sam set down her glass and picked up her phone, a perplexed look stretching across her face.

"Still no reception?" I asked.

Kaitlyn pulled her wavy hair back and twisted it into a bun. "I'm thinking there's not going to be any reception, no matter how many times we check."

"We need a Wi-Fi password," Sam said. "I thought I saw an available network earlier."

Jenna looked at her phone. "I don't see any network on mine."

Someone coughed in the distance. It sounded like a man. Footsteps crunched from further up the path, and I strained to see through the dwindling daylight.

A tremor slid down my back. I tilted my head toward the path and stopped breathing. "Someone's there."

Sam perched forward in her chair.

A shadowy figure materialized from the trees. "Evening, ladies." A wiry guy with a shaved head marched toward us, only pausing to spit at the ground. He wore greasy jeans and a stained T-shirt. A tattoo of a knife marked the side of his pale neck. His eyes sank into purplish hollows and a rifle hung from a strap on his shoulder.

My mouth went dry.

"Is this your cabin, sir?" Kaitlyn asked, her voice artificially loud and overly friendly.

He gave a nod. "I'm Travis. I forgot to leave a key. I know how city folks like to lock up." His icy eyes traveled over us. His body twitched every few seconds. It wasn't clear if he suffered from a nervous tick or if he was on drugs. The muscle in his sinewy forearm flexed as he reached across his chest to touch the gun strap. He strode closer and slapped a single key down in front of me.

"Thanks." I resisted the urge to hide under the table.

Travis leered at me, then Kaitlyn. "You're a good-looking group of ladies, aren't you?" A sickening smile curved onto his lips.

I felt as if a thousand spiders were skittering across my skin. Jenna cleared her throat, Kaitlyn and Charlotte stared at the ground, and Sam crossed her arms.

Travis's demeanor—and his rifle—made me nervous. I pictured the lifeless squirrel and clenched my teeth. Nothing about this place felt safe, especially now that we'd met the creepy owner.

"Okay. Thanks for the key. Good night." Charlotte spoke quickly and I could tell she also wanted Travis to leave.

The man twitched again but didn't move. His reptilian stare stuck on Sam for a beat longer than the rest of us, as he seemed to notice her for the first time. His bloodshot eyeballs protruded from his face, a flash of hate in his pupils. My pulse accelerated, and I wished I could trade places with her. I wondered if Travis had ever seen a person with dark skin before.

An incident from college played in my mind. I'd been shopping with Sam freshman year. We'd taken the bus to a mall on the outskirts of town. As we strolled toward Macy's to check out the coat sale, a man with white hair and a tattered jacket had stepped in front of us, blocking our path into a department store. He motioned at Sam. "Where you from?"

Sam had stared the man directly in his face. "Phoenix."

"No. Where you *really* from?"

"I was born in Phoenix."

The man grimaced, narrowing his eyes. "No. I'm trying to figure out what country you're from."

I'd wanted to run, but Sam stood her ground. Sam's mom was of Indian descent and had grown up in southern California. Her dad was African American and had been born and raised in Milwaukee. Sam's beautifully unique look often caught people's eyes as if they'd spotted a rare bird or a polished seashell. I'd never witnessed an ugly confrontation like this.

Sam squared her shoulders at the older man. "I'm American. Just like you."

The man shook his head and grunted. Finally, he stomped away. I'd turned toward my roommate, so proud of her for holding her own, for not playing the man's divisive game.

"I can't believe that guy," I'd whispered to her, my heart pounding.

She looked at me like I was from another planet. "It happens all the time."

"Really?"

"ALL the time." Sam turned on her heel and continued into the department store. The pungent scent of perfume stung my nostrils from the nearby cosmetic counter. I hung my head, feeling naïve and useless.

A clink of a wineglass brought me back to the present. Sam cleared her throat and lifted her chin, locking eyes with the jittery cabin owner. "Do you have a Wi-Fi password?"

Travis narrowed his too-small eyes at her. "Huh?"

My fingers tightened around the edge of my chair. I could see Sam was using the same technique she'd used with the man at the mall all those years ago. She showed no weakness. She didn't back down.

Sam jutted out her chin and hardened her voice. "Is there an internet password we can use, *sir*? We're not getting any cell-phone reception out here."

Travis adjusted the gun on his shoulder and pulled his stare away from Sam. "Ain't many cell towers in the area. And I ain't got no internet for guests. It's all part of the experience." The man's thin lips pulled back, exposing yellowed teeth.

I pressed my palms into the top of my legs, feeling the overwhelming urge to run.

Travis jerked his hand toward the path. "I got a landline at my house in case of emergency. Same deal as the last time you stayed here."

"We've never stayed here before," Jenna said.

He spat at the ground and leered at each of us. "Sure you have."

Jenna shook her head. "No. We haven't."

We flashed confused looks at each other, not sure whether to argue. Dread pooled in my stomach. Jenna coughed. I clenched my teeth, hoping she wouldn't make any condescending comments about the accommodations.

"You must have us confused with another group," Kaitlyn said.

The man grunted. "Huh. Maybe." The same sick smile pulled on the corners of his lips. He threw his hand in the air and turned to leave.

My breath finally left my lungs.

"You always carry a gun around with you?" It was Jenna who spoke. I cringed, familiar with her psyche. She hated this man's effort to intimidate us as much as I did. But, unlike me, she couldn't keep her mouth shut.

He turned back, glaring. "Sure do. There's coyotes in these parts. Seen bears too."

Jenna leaned forward with a defiant gleam in her eyes. "That's funny. I just watched a documentary about coyotes. Their diet consists mainly of rodents. Bears eat fish and berries. They only attack humans if they're starving, so there's nothing for a big tough guy like you to worry about."

Travis shook his head as another twitch jerked his shoulders. "Sounds like you're from the city."

"Have a good night." I blurted out the words before Jenna could antagonize the man any further. Anything to get him away from us.

Travis grunted, raised a hand toward us, and strolled back up the hill, disappearing into the woods.

Jenna tilted her head back and lowered her voice to a loud whisper. "Holy shit! Was that guy for real?"

"Could he be any creepier? Was he on drugs?" I asked.

Kaitlyn covered her mouth with her hands. "I don't know. Were you trying to start a fight with him, Jenna?"

Jenna rubbed her eyes, not responding. She hadn't lost her flair for drama.

I shook my head. "I guess we know who shot the squirrel."

Sam hugged her arms in front of her. "Thanks for renting a cabin from an armed redneck, guys. This is lovely. Next time, I'll choose the location."

"You know what they say—the bigger the gun, the smaller the penis." Jenna raised her eyebrows.

"Yeah," I said. "If Travis shows up driving a Lamborghini tomorrow, we'll know the truth, for sure."

Our nervous laughter filtered through the air, but I couldn't shake the unease dripping through me.

Kaitlyn shook her head. "All of the misspelled words in his email are suddenly making a *lot* more sense."

Jenna stared into the distance. "Do you think he's a flat-earther?"

Charlotte looked confused. "A what?"

"A flat-earther. One of those crazy science deniers who believes the earth is flat despite overwhelming scientific proof to the contrary?"

"I don't know, but he's probably a strong candidate."

"He seems more like a child molester to me."

A cough sounded from somewhere beyond the trees. We froze.

My hand flew to my mouth. I leaned forward and lowered my voice to a whisper. "Oh my God! He's still here. Do you think he heard us?"

Fear stretched across my friends' faces. We waited in silence, listening. I pressed my back against the metal chair, hearing nothing other than chirping crickets and lapping waves.

At last, Jenna exhaled. "I think he's gone now."

Sam shook her head. "This is bad, guys."

Charlotte studied her empty glass. "I can't believe the reviews didn't mention him. Or that there's no internet connection."

"There were a few bad reviews," I said, "but like I mentioned before, they were down at the bottom. I assumed they were from difficult people."

"Most people come here to get off the grid," Kaitlyn said. "That's probably all they care about, especially if they didn't meet Travis in person."

"Well, we've already met him." Jenna made a face. "We can't unring that bell."

I tucked my feet under my chair. "I say we drive back toward the airport and find another place to stay if Travis comes anywhere near us tomorrow. Something is really off with him."

Charlotte grinned. "Is that your professional opinion, Megan?"

"Yes. He's off."

My friends glanced at each other. Then their eyes darted from the cabin to the woods to the lake and back to me.

Kaitlyn bit her lip. "We drove all the way up here. Let's give the little cabin a chance. I bet that lake is awesome in the daytime."

"We can give it a chance. I'm only saying, if that guy does anything else to make us feel unsafe, we should leave."

"Deal," Kaitlyn said as the others mumbled in agreement.

Sam squinted at her phone. "I'm sure I saw a network fading in and out when we arrived. It's not there now."

"It's probably Travis's home network," Kaitlyn said. "He claimed there isn't one for the guests."

Charlotte made a face. "Why can't he just let us use his network?"

I cracked my knuckles and looked out at the blackened lake. "I don't know."

The only thing I knew for sure was that we were out in the middle of nowhere, down the road from a scary guy with a gun, and if he tried to do anything to us, we had no way to call for help.

CHAPTER SEVEN

It was after midnight by the time I washed my face and brushed my teeth in a pedestal sink, turning away from the rust stain circling the drain. After changing into a T-shirt and cotton shorts, I joined Charlotte in our shared room, crawling under the sheets and checking again for bugs and spiders. Charlotte rested her head on the pillow on the twin bed across from mine.

Jenna's heavy footsteps—signaled by her uneven gait—clomped down the hall. I held my breath and tried not to listen.

Jenna popped her head into the bedroom. "Good night again, ladies. I double locked all the doors. All the downstairs windows are locked, too."

"Thanks," I said, although I wondered about the purpose of locking the doors when the owner surely had a key. I hoped Travis hadn't overheard us making fun of him.

Jenna blew us kisses and left. Her comment from earlier in the night replayed in my ears—"*Looks like everyone's life turned out rosy and perfect, except for mine.*" If only I'd been able to tell her how imperfect my life was. I shifted my legs against the scratchy sheets, feeling unsettled. My unease stemmed from multiple sources—Jenna's angry words, my lack of forthrightness with my friends, the creepy cabin's remote location, and Travis's gun.

I pulled the edge of the sheet up to my chin. "Do you think we're safe in here?"

Charlotte reached for the lamp and turned off the light. "Travis is a little scary, but this rental is probably his only way of making money. I'm sure he doesn't want us to leave a bad review—or five bad reviews, for that matter. He's given us the key now. I bet we won't see him again."

I rolled onto my side, hoping she was right. The pillow smelled musty and I wished I'd brought my own. It was strange to be in this room with Charlotte, skipping my bedtime routine with the kids. Normally, I read them each two books and sang a song before saying I love you back and forth five times. They loved their routines. I guess I did, too. Andrew was taking care of it, though. I wondered again if he'd spotted the mac and cheese on the shelf in the fridge. My mundane concern suddenly felt utterly important. Homesickness needled through me. I wished I'd been there to pick Marnie and Wyatt up from school, collect their art projects, and hear about their day.

"I was thinking about what you said earlier. About marriages having their ups and downs."

Charlotte's voice made my eyes pop open, despite my heavy lids.

"Yeah," I said.

"Mine is down."

"Oh. I'm sorry, Charlotte."

My head weighed a thousand pounds. It had been a long and draining day, and I'd had one too many glasses of wine. Listening to Charlotte's marital problems was the last thing I felt like doing. But having people confess their troubles to me was a hazard of my profession. And Charlotte was a friend. I opened my eyes wider, searching for the outline of her shadow through the darkened room. "Do you want to talk about it?"

Her sheets rustled. "Reed has become so distant."

"Yeah?"

"Sometimes, I think if I stood naked next to the TV, he wouldn't even see me."

"Really? It didn't seem like that this morning." I pulled my quilt over my shoulders and inhaled. The vision of Reed kissing

Charlotte on the lips before we'd left her house played in my mind. Andrew had only pecked me on the cheek. After Wyatt was born, our carefree lifestyle had transformed into a never-ending to-do list. We'd replaced our family outings with a "divide and conquer" attitude. Every weekend, each of us took one child to their activities and split the list of errands. It was exhausting keeping up with the house, the yard work, the kids, and our careers. When a task didn't get accomplished, we were quick to blame the other person. Somewhere along the line, we'd gone from planning romantic candlelit meals together to microwaving frozen dinners and eating in front of the TV. We'd lost the spark that had brought us together. I'd hoped to find something better in its place—the unbreakable bond or comfortable friendship that older couples often hinted at—but something between indifference and resentment hung between Andrew and me instead. It was time to set aside my personal issues, though, and turn on my therapist mode.

Charlotte sighed. "Reed was only putting on a show for you and Kaitlyn, so you would see what a great husband he is."

"Have you talked to him about your feelings?"

"I've tried. I'm afraid of pushing too hard. I'm afraid of the answer I might get."

I lifted my head. "You're afraid Reed might leave you?"

"I don't want to get divorced. Oliver needs a strong man in his life." Charlotte's voice cracked as she said the words, and my heart shattered.

I remembered Charlotte's frequent visits to my room back in college and how she'd fed me tidbits of her upbringing on her family's eighty-acre dairy farm in northeast Wisconsin. Amid the tales of back-breaking chores, fall harvest festivals, and boring Saturday nights, her stories often circled back to the unreasonable demands of her strict parents. They had charged their daughter with looking after her two younger brothers. The boys, who were three and five years younger than Charlotte, were wild and rebellious and often got into trouble. Charlotte's parents blamed their sons' shortcomings on her; she should have done a better job watching them. Charlotte was the one her father berated and whipped with a leather belt, leaving welts across her skin. Charlotte's mother hadn't been strong enough to stand up to her short-fused husband. It made sense now, so many years later, that Charlotte would want someone calm and kind like Reed—someone the opposite of her own dad—to be the father figure for her son.

I propped myself up on one elbow. "You and Reed don't have to split up. It doesn't have to come to that. It's not too late. You can talk to a counselor. Take a romantic trip together like the one Kaitlyn mentioned. You have that trip to Europe coming up, right?"

"Yeah."

"I work with a lot of couples in my practice. There are so many things that can help. You need to find a way to communicate with each other." I thought of the months of strained conversations between Andrew and me and felt like a hypocrite. I was thankful Charlotte couldn't see my face through the darkness.

"Okay. Thanks, Megan."

"Sure."

"You know, just between you and me, Andrew and I have had our struggles lately too. We started neglecting each other after Wyatt was born. Now he's five. We're working on not doing that anymore. Things are getting better." That was a lie. Things weren't getting better. Still, I wanted to offer Charlotte some hope.

"I'm glad you're working things out. Children can strain a relationship. I know that from experience." Charlotte's breath heaved in and out, and I wondered if she was thinking about her first marriage. "I know it's late. Let's go to sleep."

"Okay. We can talk more tomorrow."

"Good night."

"Good night." I turned to the other side, facing the wall and cradling the bunched-up blanket in the crook of my arm. If only

Marnie or Wyatt were lying next to me instead of a pile of sheets. I wanted to press my face against their silky hair and smell the fruity scent left from their watermelon shampoo. I wanted to tell them a funny joke and feel their laughter cascading through me. I wanted to sing whatever song Andrew had sung with them tonight.

My eyelids lowered and I shifted my arm, trying to imagine Andrew lying next to me, telling me to relax and have fun, and reminding me that he'll see me soon.

"You're so beautiful."

I hung on to each remembered word, the raspy voice sweet in my ear. But remorse tunneled through me because it wasn't Andrew's voice whispering to me. This was the massive, horrible secret I was hiding from my friends, and from my husband. The flattering words were from the other man in my life. The one I'd secretly been seeing for the past eight months. The one with the boyish grin and interesting eyes who showered me with compliments and surprised me with flowers. The man who rearranged his schedule to make dinner reservations and book hotel rooms. I'd never meant for it to happen. I never thought I was one of those women who self-medicate, using the fleeting attention of a charming man to make themselves feel better. And I certainly wouldn't reveal what I'd done to anyone. I was a family therapist for God's sake. I had to protect my professional integrity. People couldn't know that my life was a disaster.

I'd thought about my actions frequently, and about why I'd done what I'd done. I concluded I'd cheated on Andrew because he didn't appreciate me anymore. It was a cliché, but it was the truth. At the very least, Andrew didn't know how to express his love. He treated me like another item on our to-do list.

Take out the garbage. Check. Pay the bills. Check. Tell Megan to have a good day. Check.

That must have been why I'd strayed, why I'd jumped into the arms of the first man who showed me an ounce of passion.

"*Can I buy you a coffee?*"

That's how the affair had started. He'd spoken that single question in a deep, gravelly voice. I'd seen him at the cafe across from my clinic three days in a row, noticing his tailored suit and strong jawline. On the second day, his gaze hung on to me too. We'd chatted while waiting in line, talking about bland subjects like road construction, the weather, and our kids' favorite non-caffeinated drinks. It was nothing more than a coffee with a man I barely knew, but a stronger person would have said no. During that brief twenty-minute date, a magnetism had pulled us closer, an easy familiarity warming me to him. It felt like we'd already confessed our secrets and shared our stories, as if I could see my entire future in his gold-brown irises. He'd lowered his left hand beneath the table when he caught me glancing toward his wedding band. Without realizing it, I'd mirrored his actions, hiding my ring too. The mutual seduction had been quick and inevitable. His allure had rushed through me as beautiful and dangerous as a tropical waterfall spilling off the side of a cliff. It was the kind of fresh excitement that accompanied intense physical attraction. *Lust at first sight.* So different from anything I'd felt with Andrew in months, if not years.

Now guilt consumed me, panic attacks hitting me at unexpected moments. Oddly, it was the affair that finally made me realize Andrew was enough. The problem had been with me, not him. Instead of talking to him about my feelings and telling him what I needed, I had shut down. I was the one who hadn't been smart enough to appreciate my spouse. I still wasn't smart enough to end it. I'd lost my confidence over the years. I hoped this weekend with old friends would help me reclaim a piece of my former self, to glimpse the determined, happy young woman who used to occupy my body. I'd held my goals and dreams close back then, like shiny coins in my pocket. Somewhere along the line, the stitching had come undone. Now my pocket was empty. I needed to find myself again. Maybe then I'd have the courage to come clean with Andrew and put in the work to repair our marriage.

My eyelids closed, my body aching for sleep, but my mind reeled as I pictured my current location so far away from my unsuspecting husband and my precious children. Instead, I was lying in this room listening to Charlotte's heavy breathing, a stone's throw away from the creepy owner of the cabin. Nothing but acres and acres of woods surrounded us. I would sleep with one eye open. Morning couldn't come soon enough.

CHAPTER EIGHT

The sun filtered through the kitchen window as coffee dripped into a cloudy pot with a cracked handle. I wondered if the coffee maker was celebrating its fortieth birthday right along with the rest of us. Still, I was grateful that it functioned. After a restless night, I was desperate for caffeine. My phone had no reception but showed the time—8:15 a.m. Charlotte and Sam sat at a square kitchen table, waiting for their caffeine fix, too. Kaitlyn and Jenna had wandered out to the porch.

Charlotte tilted her head toward Sam, who wore a gray MedTech hoodie over her pajamas. "So, who are MedTech's biggest clients right now?"

Charlotte had already asked Sam six or seven questions about her online prescription company, ignoring the fact that Sam was bleary-eyed and hadn't had her coffee yet. Sam handled the interrogation better than I would have.

"We're finding a new segment of sales through online advertising, but most of our clients are physicians in private practice. They refer their patients to us, especially the ones who've fallen through the cracks of traditional insurance."

"What's their cut?" Charlotte asked without missing a beat.

"It depends on the product and the volume."

Sam and Charlotte had been pre-med during school. After graduation, Sam had gone on to complete medical school, specializing in cardiology. Then she'd shifted gears and taken a research position at a hospital, while simultaneously building her online prescription company from her basement. Just like when we were in school, the conversation between them often slipped to medical talk.

Sam fidgeted with her phone and let out a sigh.

"Still no reception." I winked as I delivered full mugs of black coffee to them. I wished I'd thought to pack sugar or milk.

Charlotte gazed toward the window. "Maybe a signal could come through down by the lake or on a ridge somewhere. I'd love to check in on Oliver."

I paused for a second, noticing she hadn't mentioned anything about Reed. "We could drive back toward civilization later. See if we can pick up a signal." I took a sip of the coffee, my teeth clicking at the bitter liquid, which tasted more like airplane fuel.

"Wow. That's bad coffee." Charlotte wrinkled her nose and set down her mug.

I opened the fridge and pulled out the box of muffins from one of Kaitlyn's bags of groceries. There were strawberries too, but I didn't have the energy to wash and trim them. Charlotte asked Sam another question about her company, and I felt like a third wheel. I wandered out to the porch where Kaitlyn and Jenna sat hunched over the table, whispering. I thought I heard my name. The photo album lay open between them. Jenna flipped around at the sound of the door.

"You guys telling secrets again?" I asked.

"Come sit down with us," Jenna said a little too quickly, and without answering the question.

I scraped back a chair and set down my coffee, finding relief in the brisk morning air whipping off the lake. The door opened again, and Charlotte and Sam wandered toward us.

"Morning," Kaitlyn said.

Charlotte raised her chin toward the lake and sniffed the fresh air. "It's so nice out here."

They filled in the two remaining chairs.

"Look at this." Jenna stabbed her finger at the album, pointing to a picture on the very first page. We all leaned forward to get a better view. It was a photo we'd only skimmed over last night, eager to flip through the rest of the images. In the picture, Jenna, Sam, and Kaitlyn rested against a Formica kitchen counter with cardboard boxes around them and plain white cabinets stretching behind their heads. They wore grungy T-shirts and tight denim shorts, and had their hair pulled back in ponytails. A portion of my shoulder and elbow poked into the frame. The photo had been taken the day the five of us had moved into our rental house on 14th Street our junior year. I remembered that day so well—the excitement, the laughter, the stress.

"That was move-in day on 14th Street," Charlotte said.

"Yeah. But look on the counter." Jenna tapped the photo again. "There's my mom's mug. The one that somehow mysteriously disappeared a couple of weeks later."

I leaned closer. Near the edge of the frame, a white mug sat next to Jenna on the counter. The front of the mug read *#1 Mom* in dark-blue lettering.

Heat prickled across my cheeks. "Oh my gosh. You're right."

Kaitlyn raised her eyes. "Isn't that crazy?"

"So, what do you guys think happened to my mug, to the last remaining and most meaningful artifact connecting me to my deceased mom? How did it vanish into thin air? Do you think her ghost came back and took it?"

Sam sat straight up in her chair, her eyes darting from the album to me to the trees. I closed my eyes as the memories poured through me, as dark and bitter as the coffee.

*

The five of us stood in a circle in the living room with cardboard boxes and the chemical odor of fresh paint surrounding us. It was late August and a week before classes started. We hadn't worked out the bedroom assignments yet.

Jenna clapped her hands. "Here we go, ladies. It's time to draw for bedrooms." She pulled out a baseball cap with five pieces of folded paper inside. We'd been through the same routine last year, but at a different house on the other side of campus. "There's a number on each paper that determines the order we get to choose. Everyone good with that?"

Charlotte stuck out her lip, a look of concern clouding her eyes. "It's not really fair that one of the bedrooms is so much bigger than all the others."

Kaitlyn nodded. "Yeah. And the big room has its own bathroom attached."

I thought back to the house we'd rented the year before, our sophomore year. The walls were thin, there was no dishwasher, and the hot water only worked half the time. We'd faced a different drama in the months leading up to last year's move-in—whether or not to invite Frida to live with us. Charlotte had wanted to include her in the house, explaining she was Frida's only friend. The rest of us did not want strange, lurking, staring, hygienically challenged Frida living with us. The majority ruled. This year, no one had even mentioned Frida's name.

Charlotte wiped her hands on her shorts and looked around. "We should have chosen that yellow house we looked at. All the rooms were the same."

Jenna shook her head. "That house was in a horrible location, Charlotte. This one is so much better. Besides, we signed the lease six months ago. We can't change our minds now."

I cleared my throat. "Maybe whoever gets the enormous bedroom should pay a little more toward the rent." I laced my fingers together, hoping I didn't get the room. It would only cause problems. I didn't want my housemates to resent me.

"Nobody should have to pay more," Jenna said. "That's not fair. We'll randomly draw for it."

"Why isn't it fair to pay more for a bigger room with a private bathroom?" Kaitlyn asked.

Jenna touched her forehead and sighed. "Because not everyone can afford to pay more than the amount we agreed on. We shouldn't discriminate."

"It's not discriminating. If one of us wants a bigger room, we can pay a little more." Kaitlyn turned away from Jenna and widened her eyes at me.

Sam rubbed her hands together and lifted her gaze from the floor. "If you guys don't mind, I think I should take the larger room. I'm fine paying a little extra for it. I bought a queen-size mattress yesterday. It's out in the truck right now. I don't even know if I can fit it in the smaller bedrooms."

Jenna made a face like she smelled rotten garbage. "No way, Sam. We all would have bought queen-size mattresses if we knew it would get us that room. That's not fair."

I bit the inside of my cheek. This stupid bedroom was already causing problems. It made sense to give Sam the room. The rest of us had twin or double beds. But I didn't want to get on anyone's bad side. Especially Jenna's. Her mom had passed away the previous spring, losing a long battle with breast cancer. The two of them had been especially close. It wasn't my place to make Jenna's life more difficult.

Sam rolled her eyes. "Whatever. Let's draw the numbers so we can unload our stuff."

Five hands reached into the hat. I clamped my fingers around a folded square of paper, holding my breath as I opened it.

"Oh, great," Sam said, blinking her eyes at the ceiling. "I got the last choice. I can't even fit my bed into that corner bedroom."

"I got number one," I said, my voice shaky.

Everyone stared at me.

Jenna nudged my arm. "Congrats, Megan. You get the master suite."

The number in my hand felt more like a curse than a blessing. "No. I don't want it. I'll take the room in the back. The one with the hexagon window."

Sam tilted her head. "Why?"

"It's charming," I said. But that wasn't the reason. I didn't want the burden of the enormous bedroom. Besides, I barely owned any furniture, and I'd perfected my bare-bones shower routine over the last two years of communal living. A private bathroom would be wasted on me.

Charlotte's mouth gaped. "Really? You're not taking the suite?"

I shrugged. "Nah."

"Yes!" Jenna pumped her fist in the air and jumped up and down, squealing like she'd just scored the winning goal in an overtime game. "I have number two. I'll take the big room with the bathroom. Woo-hoo!"

Sam stared blankly, her lip twitching.

"I have number three," Charlotte said. "I'll take the first-floor room."

"I'll take the tiny bedroom in the corner," Kaitlyn said, smiling at Sam. "You should be able to fit your bed into that other room upstairs."

Sam lifted her face toward Kaitlyn. "Are you sure?"

"Yeah. It's no big deal."

"Thanks."

Jenna stepped back. "Glad that's all worked out. You are all welcome to visit me in my suite at any time, especially if anyone feels the sudden need to do somersaults or cartwheels across the floor. Or if there's a shower emergency."

"Or a toilet emergency?" I asked.

Jenna cringed. "I guess."

I chuckled and shook my head, but noticed Sam stood with her arms crossed in front of her, not cracking a smile.

In the days that followed, Jenna didn't have many visitors to her spacious suite. She bounded around like the queen of the rental house, loud and oblivious to the tension surrounding her handling of the room assign-ments. In contrast, Sam, Kaitlyn, and Charlotte stopped by my room frequently. Everyone wanted to talk about their feelings, how they'd been slighted or were annoyed with Jenna, or how she should be paying more for the bigger room. Sometimes, the complaints were more general—people not cleaning up after themselves in the kitchen or why a guy who promised to call one of them never did. Even Jenna stopped in occasionally to talk about how much she missed her mom and how her dad rarely returned her calls. She worried he was suffering from depression.

I was already on the road to becoming a psychologist by then, and my friends' efforts to seek my counseling confirmed that, perhaps, I'd found my calling. I found it satisfying to peer inside a friend and dissect why she felt a certain way. I imagined a computer engineer felt the same bubble of anticipation when removing a panel from the back of a machine and following which wires connected to which circuits. By talking things through, it was possible to peel back the layers and get to the root of the problem. Counseling wasn't a burden to me; it was a thrilling and rewarding challenge.

One Saturday afternoon, I sat cross-legged on my bed, reading a chapter from a textbook when a light knock sounded on my door.

"Yeah."

The door creaked open and Sam stepped inside. Her brown eyes were glassy and her face frozen.

I looked up from my reading. "What's wrong?"

"Is Jenna home?" Sam whispered, peering over her shoulder toward the door.

"No. She's at soccer practice. Why?"

"Something happened." Sam sat on the bed next to me and covered her face with her hands.

"What?"

She lowered her hands. "It was an accident. I swear."

"*What happened?*"

"*Jenna's mom's mug. I was rearranging the glasses in the cabinet. It slipped from my hand and shattered on the floor.*"

"*Oh no.*"

Jenna drank coffee from the same mug every day. It was the mug she'd given her mom for Mother's Day fifteen years earlier. It said "#1 Mom" across the side. Her mom had sipped from it every day when she'd been alive, explaining to Jenna with a smirk how the woman next door had received the same mug from her son, so she'd have to fight her neighbor for the title. Jenna had told us the story many times, always with a sheen of nostalgia in her sky-blue eyes. The emotional significance of the mug was invaluable.

"*Shit!*" *Sam bit her lip.* "*How could I have been so careless? Why did I even touch it?*"

I raised my gaze to meet hers. "*You have to tell Jenna.*"

"*No. I can't. She'll think I did it on purpose.*"

"*Huh?*"

"*She'll think I was trying to get back at her for taking the bedroom I wanted.*"

I thought of the drama from move-in day, thankful again that I'd selected one of the smaller rooms. Sam's bed filled her room from wall to wall. She could barely open her closet door and dresser drawers. She frequently complained about her cramped living quarters.

Sam paced toward the wall, clutching her head. "*It was just a fluke. The handle slipped.*"

I closed my book. "*Of course, it was an accident. Jenna will understand.*"

"*No. She won't. Please. Don't tell her. You know how Jenna is. She's going to make my life a living hell.*"

"*Can we glue it back together?*"

Sam lowered her thick eyelashes. "*It was too far gone. I cleaned it up already and threw away the pieces.*"

"*Won't she wonder where it is?*"

"Yeah, but we'll just pretend like we don't know. Stuff goes missing all the time. I still can't find the sunglasses I set on the counter last week."

I swallowed, unsure of the appropriate response.

"Don't mention anything about it to Kaitlyn or Charlotte, either."

I nodded, blowing out a puff of air. Sam was my most loyal friend, and she had never asked much of me. There didn't need to be any new drama between Sam and Jenna. Maybe Jenna would believe she'd misplaced the mug.

"Promise?" Sam asked.

"Yeah."

The next morning Jenna opened and slammed cupboard after cupboard. "Has anyone seen my mom's mug? I swear it was in here."

"No." I turned away from her as my stomach folded.

Charlotte pinched her lips together. "It was in that cupboard yesterday, same as always."

"Is it in the dishwasher?" Sam asked, staring at her feet.

Jenna pulled open the drawer and studied the dirty dishes. "No. Maybe I took it upstairs."

"You probably lost it somewhere in that enormous bedroom of yours." Sam turned toward me, our eyes locking in a moment of betrayal. All at once, something dark and purposeful hardened in Sam's face. I had the horrible and fleeting thought that Sam had broken the mug on purpose.

*

Sam picked up her coffee and set it down without drinking. Behind her, the water of Crooked Lake lapped against the shoreline. She rubbed her eyes, then blinked at Jenna. "I have a confession to make."

Jenna cocked her head. I squeezed my fingers around the edge of the metal chair, afraid to breathe.

"It was me. I broke your mug. I was taking it out of the cabinet to move things around and it slipped. I should have just told you right then, but I didn't. I thought you'd never forgive me."

Jenna's eyes popped, but she didn't speak.

Sam shook her head. "The more time that passed, the bigger the secret became, and the harder it was to tell you the truth."

Jenna flopped back in her chair, squeezing her eyelids shut. "I knew it. I knew one of you did something and didn't want to tell me. I almost went crazy looking for that thing."

Sam pressed her lips together. "I'm really sorry. I wish I'd handled it differently."

"Did you guys know, too?" Jenna peered around the circle, my blood turning cold when her stare landed on me.

"Yeah." Kaitlyn nodded. "We didn't know what to do. We all knew how much that mug meant to you."

"We didn't handle it the right way," I said.

"I found out about it later." Charlotte puckered her lips.

Sam's eyes watered as she faced Jenna. "I didn't want to cause you anymore pain after you'd just lost your mom. I thought it would be easier on you if you'd thought you temporarily misplaced the mug. It was such a stupid thing to do. I don't know what I was thinking or why I hid it from you for so long."

Jenna rubbed her forehead and smiled at Sam. "I'm just happy to know what happened to my mom's mug. I knew it was in the cupboard. I remembered putting it in there the night before. And then it was gone. It's always bothered me. I mean, I was two days away from contacting *Unsolved Mysteries*."

Sam tugged at the sleeves of her sweatshirt, a smile twitching on her lips. "Can you forgive me?"

"It's water under the bridge." Jenna's eyes skittered across all of us again like a spotlight. When her gaze hovered on me, I averted my guilty eyes. We'd repeated a lie to her for twenty years. We'd chosen to protect Sam's secret over telling her the truth. I questioned whether Jenna was glossing over her true feelings so as not to cause issues. I wondered how much the truth could sting.

CHAPTER NINE

An hour later, we were dressed in our hiking clothes and standing on the deck. The morning sun filtered through the leaves and cast spots across our skin. We'd just taken a few group selfies, making sure to capture the sparkling lake in the background. Charlotte promised to add the photos to her Facebook post once we were back within range of a Wi-Fi signal. There'd been no sign of Travis since the night before and everyone's mood had lightened. Now we took turns holding out our arms as Jenna spritzed us with her all-natural mosquito repellant. I clutched a reusable water bottle in my hand.

Kaitlyn clapped her hands. "Ready to get some exercise?"

"How far is it to get to that camp?" Jenna asked. "We should go check it out."

I remembered the deserted beach across the lake and realized I wouldn't mind seeing it up close and letting my bare feet sink into the sand.

Sam raised an eyebrow. "Isn't that trespassing, Jenna?"

"Not if no one sees us."

"Maybe we can catch a signal over there." I waved toward the lake. "Besides, I can't imagine anyone would be hanging out at a closed-down summer camp in September."

Jenna lowered the bug spray. "Someone died there. I bet it's super creepy."

"I don't know," Charlotte said, lacing her fingers together. "Sam is right. The camp is private property. Maybe we should just explore closer to where we're staying."

"Oh, come on, Charlotte. Let's do something adventurous." Kaitlyn leaned toward Charlotte as if she was explaining something to one of her kids. "Who would ever know if we hiked through the camp? Besides, who cares if anyone sees us? We'll just say we're staying across the lake and got turned around."

Sam tightened her ponytail. "I guess it's fine to wander through a deserted camp. Who would be out there, anyway? I didn't see a single house for miles when we were driving in."

"Yeah. Me neither," Kaitlyn said. "Is that because of the land trust?"

Jenna nodded. "Yeah. Depending on the terms of the trust, it probably preserves this forest from development forever. It's kind of awesome."

"Why does Travis live here then?" I asked.

"I don't know. Someone probably left all this land to the trust. I guess they didn't include Travis's parcel for whatever reason. And the camp is probably separate too."

Sam waved us forward. "Come on. Daylight's burning."

Charlotte tucked in her shirt and stepped toward us.

"Lead the way, Megan," Jenna said.

"I don't know where I'm going."

"Neither does anybody else."

"Okay. I'll do my best."

My feet stumbled along a narrow dirt trail weaving down toward the lake. The water was a deep royal blue set off against the yellow and orange of the changing leaves. The sun popped in and out of fast-moving clouds, causing the lake's color to dim and brighten. Even though it was September, the searing heat felt more like August. The slope steepened and I lost my footing. I grabbed the narrow trunk of a sapling to keep from sliding down the hill.

"Careful!" I yelled back to my friends.

One by one, they found their footing down the cliff. We walked in a single file until we reached the shore of the lake. The decrepit cabin spied down on us from its position on the tree-lined ridge.

Jenna nudged the sand with the toe of her tennis shoe. "The natural shoreline is so pretty."

"I love the sound of the water." Sam breathed in the air and closed her eyes.

Kaitlyn nodded. "It's relaxing."

The shore was narrow and rugged, strewn with rocks and sticks. It wasn't the kind of beach where parents basked in the sun while their kids built sandcastles. Nature ruled here. A decaying log rested nearby. Charlotte made her way over to it and sat down. I edged along the rocks until the shrubs reached out so far that they forced me into the water, making it impossible to continue. Something metal glinted through the leaves. I pulled back a thorny branch, finding an overturned canoe hidden in the underbrush. It was rusty and covered in spiderwebs; it looked like no one had used it in at least a decade.

"Anyone want to take a boat ride?" I asked, pointing to my discovery.

Jenna peered over my shoulder. "Ew!"

"We can't follow the shoreline. There's no room. Should we head back to the trail?" I asked.

The others agreed, and we foraged through the trees, discovering another narrow trail that traveled alongside the water but was further inland. We followed the contours of the lake as it widened in the middle, then turned like a crooked boot just as its name suggested. By the immense size of the lake, I guessed it would be another two or three miles before we reached the camp.

We traipsed along, enjoying the scenery and listening to Kaitlyn and Sam compare notes on their recent vacations to Costa Rica. I wasn't sure if the trail would lead us to the camp, but at least it was a pretty hike. As long as we could see the lake, we wouldn't get lost. The path snaked through the woods for what seemed like miles. We followed it up a steep slope as lactic acid burned through my thigh muscles.

"We're gonna feel this tomorrow."

"Tomorrow? I feel it now." Jenna made a face and we all laughed.

At last we reached the top of an incline where the path opened into a well-marked trail. I paused and pulled out my phone to check for reception. There was no signal. Through huffing breaths, Charlotte told us about a ten-year-old boy who'd lost the use of his leg after a skateboarding accident shattered his knee. "He had multiple surgeries, but still couldn't walk. I've been working with him three times a week at the clinic, guiding him through endless physical therapy exercises. He has such a great attitude. Then, amazingly, last week, he started walking on his own."

Sam beamed. "Wow! That must be so rewarding, Charlotte."

"It is. I mean, his mom was crying because she was so happy. I couldn't help tearing up, too. It's not all sunshine and puppy dogs, though." Charlotte told us another story of her least favorite patient, an older woman with severe arthritis of the spine who refused to do the exercises and berated Charlotte every chance she got.

After five more minutes of trekking, we reached a clearing in the woods. The lake was no longer in view, and the tall trees of the forest encircled us. A climbing wall towered above us with a few wooden benches positioned around it.

Jenna gasped. "This must be part of the camp."

I stepped back and surveyed the eerie scene, feeling like I'd stumbled across the relics of a lost city. "Anyone want to give the climbing wall a try?"

Jenna bound toward the wall. "I will." She hoisted herself up, finding the lowest footholds. She got about halfway up before leaping down amid our chuckles. "It's harder than it looks."

Charlotte smiled. "Yeah. Especially for a bunch of forty-year-olds!"

We laughed at ourselves as we wandered down an adjoining path that deposited us into a field. A half-dozen archery targets formed a line along the perimeter, and a wooden hut with small windows stood across the way. I walked toward it, finding the bows and arrows were still inside. I jiggled the handle, but someone had locked the door.

"They must have shut this place down in a hurry." Sam appeared next to me, staring at the bows on the other side of the murky glass.

"Hey guys, there's zip line over here!" Jenna yelled from beyond the trees.

Sam and I jogged to catch up with the others who had already moved on. They stood in a group with their faces tipped toward the sky. A thick wire ran from a high wooden ledge about thirty feet off the ground, ending at another perch about two hundred feet away. A handlebar hung from the wire close to the first ledge, but someone had tied it down.

Jenna hopped to the side. "I want to do it!"

Sam shook her head. "No way. We don't even know if it's in working condition."

"Yeah. They tied off the handles, anyway," I said, studying the tall perch. "The camp clearly doesn't want people using it."

Jenna was already halfway up the wooden ladder. "You guys are acting like old ladies. Is that what having kids does to you?" She threw her chin in the air. "Let me have a little fun."

Kaitlyn turned and widened her eyes at me. I gave her a knowing look and shrugged. Maybe Jenna was right. Becoming a mom had made me paranoid about situations I wouldn't have thought twice about pre-motherhood.

"Careful!" Charlotte yelled, shielding her eyes from the sun. "Isn't there supposed to be a safety harness or a helmet or something?"

Jenna struggled with the rope that secured the handlebars. She untied the knot and reached forward, smiling down on us. "Don't worry. I got it!"

"At least pull on the line to make sure it's secure," I yelled.

Jenna jiggled the line, then pulled the handles toward her. She gave a thumbs up. "All good!" She took a running start and leaped into the air, hanging on to the metal bar. "Wheeeee!" she squealed as she flew past us in a blur of turquoise and pink. Pure joy radiated from her, and I was suddenly glad we hadn't stopped her.

"Jenna! Say cheese!" Charlotte held up her phone to take a photo.

Jenna turned toward us, grinning. But the mid-air rotation caused one of her hands to lose its grip. Jenna's body straightened as she struggled to catch her balance. She was only ten feet from the landing site when her legs flailed and her fingers slipped from the handlebar. Her body flopped like a rag doll toward the ground. She landed with a thud.

I screamed.

We raced toward her. Jenna lay on the ground, clutching her ankle.

"Oh my God!" Kaitlyn and Charlotte said at the same time. We crouched around Jenna.

"Are you okay?" I asked.

"My ankle." Jenna's face twisted in pain. She clutched her left ankle, not her right, and I didn't know whether to be relieved or worried. Her right leg was the one that had never recovered from the car accident. Jenna's yelp forced me back to that devastating night twenty years earlier, but I pushed the memory away.

Sam crouched over her. "Can you wiggle your toes?"

Jenna winced. She sat upright with her leg stretched in front of her, giving a slight nod.

"Do you want me to take your shoe off?" Sam asked.

Jenna waved her off. "No. Leave it."

Charlotte huddled between Sam and me, placing her fingers on Jenna's ankle. "It doesn't look broken. You probably sprained it."

"Good thing we have so many medical professionals here," Kaitlyn said.

"Should we help you up?" Creases formed across Sam's face. "Or do you want to sit here for a while?"

Jenna placed her palms on the ground. "Help me up. I don't know if I can put my weight on it, though."

I stepped forward. "Put your arm around my shoulder. I got you."

Jenna raised her eyes to me and held out a hand. I pulled her up and she looped her arm over my shoulder. I took a step and she hopped next to me.

"Sorry, guys," Jenna said. "I guess your mom instincts were right. I'm an idiot."

"That's okay. We need you to keep our lives interesting." Kaitlyn offered a sympathetic smile.

Jenna waved toward the wire. "That counselor probably died in a zip-line accident. Mystery solved."

I giggled at Jenna's joke, relieved to find her in good spirits.

Sam eyed Jenna's ankle as sweat glistened across her forehead. "This will be a long hike back to the cabin."

"I think this path might get us back faster." Kaitlyn pointed toward a trail that branched toward the lake.

Sam shook her head. "Let's go back the way we came."

"Sam's right. We don't want to get lost," Charlotte said.

We paused, looking back and forth. Jenna waved toward the trail. "No. It's fine. We've come this far. Let's try the new route so we can check out the rest of the camp."

We hiked toward the trail, finding a wooden sign painted with white lettering. Sam read it aloud: *To Cabins.*

Charlotte threw back her head. "We're going in the wrong direction."

Charlotte was probably right, but curiosity about the abandoned camp tugged me forward. I recognized the same inquisitive glint in Jenna's eyes as she hopped along next to me. The trail led us up a gradual incline to a ridge overlooking a grassy expanse. Six wooden cabins perched in a row. A massive log building sat in the distance. A sign above the door read: *Mess Hall*. Another building was marked: *Arts and Crafts*. A smaller one was labeled: *Office*. Even further beyond, another six cabins dotted the landscape. It was easy to imagine a bustling summer camp filled with happy campers and fun activities. Instead, the atmosphere was quiet and empty. I wandered past the vacant cabins, supporting Jenna's weight and feeling as if we'd stumbled into a ghost town.

"This is a little weird," I said.

A trail led down a hill toward the water. I recognized the rectangular patch of sand as the beach we'd spotted from across the lake. The decline would be too steep for Jenna's ankle.

A deer darted across the field in front of us. Two more followed before they disappeared into the woods.

"Oh my God!" Charlotte jumped in front of us, her eyebrows raised. "There's someone over there." She spoke in a whisper and flicked her eyes in the direction of the distant cabins. "We should leave."

I peered toward the cabins. I thought I'd seen a flash of movement in my peripheral vision, but there was nothing there now. An ominous presence prickled over my scalp.

"Who?" Jenna asked.

Charlotte shook her head. "I don't know, but we're trespassing. What if it's Travis?"

Jenna sighed. "Travis doesn't own this land either. He'd be trespassing too."

"Charlotte's right. We should leave," Sam said, frowning.

I flipped around, just as eager as Sam to head back to our home base.

Jenna squared her shoulders. "Wait. I think we should take a look. Maybe it's a caretaker for the camp. Maybe they have an extra ace bandage somewhere for my ankle."

I inhaled a breath of courage and turned toward the cabins again.

"I guess I can go check it out," Charlotte said.

Kaitlyn stepped forward. "I'll go, too."

"Me too," I said. "Sam, you can stay with Jenna."

"Thank God," Sam said as she plopped down on the grass next to Jenna's feet.

Charlotte, Kaitlyn, and I trudged across the uneven grass. I checked my phone out of habit, still finding zero reception.

"I don't see anyone now." Charlotte craned her neck toward the trees.

We approached the camp office. If the person Charlotte had seen was a camp worker, maybe another staff member was in here. I peered through a dusty side window, but only a dim room lay before me. Its barren walls contained nothing more than a utilitarian desk with some office supplies and a wooden chair. "No one's here." My friends nodded and continued walking. I trotted to catch up with them.

"Where did you see the person?" Kaitlyn asked Charlotte as we continued trekking past the building labeled *Arts and Crafts*.

"Over by those cabins." Charlotte wiped her palms on her shorts, tipping her head toward the cabins at the top of a distant incline. A wall of forest loomed behind the tiny wooden structures. "I'm not sure it was a person, though. It could have been another deer or a squirrel or something. I shouldn't have said anything."

Kaitlyn pushed a stray piece of hair from her face. "No. It's fine. We're already halfway there. Let's make a loop behind the cabins to make Jenna happy. Then we can head back."

"Sounds good," I said, lengthening my stride to keep up with Kaitlyn.

We hiked through the tall grass for another few minutes until the cabins lay in front of us. Their matching doors were closed; spiderwebs stretched across their darkened windows.

Kaitlyn paused, looking at Charlotte and me, then facing toward the woods. "Hello!" she yelled. "Is someone here? Our friend is injured. We need a bandage." Kaitlyn placed her hands on her hips and twisted her lips to the side.

We stood still for a minute, listening for a response, or even footsteps. There was no answer, except for the wind fluttering through the tree branches.

Kaitlyn waved us forward. "C'mon. Let's take a quick look."

I followed her along a narrow dirt path that ran behind the cabins. Charlotte stumbled along behind me.

"Is anyone there?" Kaitlyn yelled as we passed a communal bathroom with a padlock on the door. Again, there was no sound except for our own shoes hitting the ground.

"There's no one around. I must have made a mistake," Charlotte said.

"Yeah."

"No worries. Let's head back," I said, nudging Charlotte's arm.

We turned past the last cabin, following the shady trail until we stepped into the sunlight. Several minutes later, we arrived back at the far hill where Jenna and Sam lounged beneath a leafy tree.

"There wasn't anyone there," Kaitlyn told them as we approached.

Jenna tossed back her head. "Oh man. I was hoping for a golf cart ride back to our cabin."

I smiled at Jenna's joke.

"Golf cart," Charlotte said under her breath as she chuckled along with the others.

Sam and Jenna stood up, brushing dirt and leaves from their legs.

"Let's get a move on," I said. "Jenna, you can lean on me."

"Thanks." She looped her arm around my shoulder, and we walked behind the others. We passed the nearby cabins and the zip line, the archery field, and the climbing wall until we reached the narrow path that branched off from the camp trail. My shoulder ached under Jenna's weight, and when Sam saw me struggling, she offered to take my place.

"Can I rest my ankle?" Jenna said after several more minutes of hobbling along the trail.

We stopped and sat on a fallen log.

Sam looked at the rest of us. "Do you think Travis followed us?"

Charlotte tugged at her shirt, her eyes traveling over the trees. "I doubt it. No one was over there when we looked. It was probably just a deer."

"Something else must have scared them," I said.

"Why is this place so terrifying?" Jenna asked. "Next year, can we meet at a hotel in Vegas?"

"I second that," Kaitlyn said.

Charlotte raised an eyebrow. "Yeah. Because nothing bad ever happens in Vegas."

Sam furrowed her brow, watching Jenna as she rubbed her ankle. "When we get back to the cabin, let's drive into town and buy an ace bandage. Your ankle needs more support."

"What town?" I asked, and the others laughed.

"Maybe the grocery store we passed has something," Sam said.

"I'm sure they keep the ace bandages right next to the night crawlers."

We all chuckled and the humor eased the tension in my neck. When Jenna was ready, we resumed our trek. We hiked along, resting, and checking over our shoulders for the person Charlotte may or may not have seen at the camp.

"I'm so happy we're all still friends," Sam said out of nowhere as we stepped along the trail.

"Yeah. There aren't any other people I'd rather injure myself with." Jenna flashed a smile. "Do you ever wonder how your life would be different if we hadn't met freshman year?"

My cheeks burned at the question. I trained my eyes away from Jenna as my breath hitched in my throat.

Charlotte shrugged. "I don't know. It sounds weird, but I feel like we still would have found each other."

"I would hate to think about the scenario where we'd never met," Kaitlyn said. "After all, Charlotte introduced me to Derek. So maybe without her, I wouldn't even have my daughters."

We walked in silence for a few steps. I hoped Jenna wasn't thinking about how her life might have been better if she'd never met me.

"Remember all the parties we had in our house on 14th Street?" I asked, attempting to change the subject.

Memories of one particular party flickered through my mind. I'd seen the photos last night in Kaitlyn's album.

Charlotte huffed. "I think I'd rather forget."

CHAPTER TEN

"One, two, three." Sam counted as we lifted the upholstered chair and moved it toward the far wall. It was a Friday night in October of our junior year. A party was underway at our rental house. Jenna had given up looking for her mug several weeks earlier, although I sometimes caught her staring at one of us when she thought no one was looking. It was clear she suspected we were involved in its sudden disappearance.

Loud music pulsed from speakers. Drums thumped through my chest, followed by techno beats on a synthesizer. Jenna's boyfriend, Pete, nodded toward us as he hoisted one side of the keg. He was also attending school on a soccer scholarship, and he and Jenna looked like two pieces of the same puzzle— both tall, blonde, athletic, and good-looking. They'd met in the weight room a month ago and had been inseparable ever since. The pairing was sickeningly cute. Sam's boyfriend, Johnny Franklin, wore a Bob Marley T-shirt and a jester's cap. He carried a keg toward us and positioned it in the spot where the chair had been. Our supply of beer cans had run dry thirty minutes earlier, but now reinforcements had arrived.

"Perfect!" Charlotte flashed a flirtatious smile toward Pete and clapped her hands.

"Easy, girl." Annoyance flashed in Jenna's eyes. She stepped in between Charlotte and her boyfriend, holding out her cup.

Charlotte scurried away, stopping to chat with my boyfriend, Dan. The two of them stood near the kitchen door as Charlotte threw her head back in exaggerated laughter.

"*Like a moth to a flame.*" Sam tilted her head toward Charlotte. Sam pulled at the ratty ends of her black hair, the beginnings of dreadlocks. The ropy clumps hung halfway down her shirt, which pictured a giant peace sign in rainbow colors. She and Johnny had discovered a shared love for weed, and they enjoyed flaunting their lifestyle.

I raised my eyebrows just as Charlotte placed her hand on Dan's arm. He said something to her, then stepped back and looked in my direction. I gave a half-wave, and he smiled.

We'd all learned not to take Charlotte's flirtatious behavior too seriously. Other than her overly friendly demeanor around men, particularly those who were already spoken for, she'd never crossed any lines. At least, as far as we knew. Sam, Jenna, Kaitlyn, and I often discussed Charlotte's quest for male attention, and we'd agreed it was a sign of insecurity, probably stemming from her emotionally distant father. Charlotte had told me plenty of stories about her not-so-perfect home life, but the first time I'd glimpsed it myself had been parents' weekend of freshman year. Only her mother had shown up as Charlotte explained how her father had to stay with her brothers and tend to the cows. Her mother joined the rest of the parents in our group for dinner at Pizza Pete's. The woman barely spoke two words the whole night and raised a few eyebrows when she ordered her fourth whiskey sour.

Dan headed toward me, while Charlotte avoided my eyes and left to join a growing crowd of people in the kitchen. A line of muscular men strutted toward the keg and shouted to Pete, and I assumed they were Pete's soccer friends. Kaitlyn sauntered in from the kitchen, drawing the soccer players' eyes toward her fiery hair and tall frame. She wore a tight sweater that was cut low in front. I chuckled to myself. Pete's friends had gone speechless. The front door opened and someone else slipped in. Unlike the soccer players' confident posturing and Kaitlyn's attention-grabbing physique, this person pressed herself against the wall as if trying to blend in with the paint.

"Hi Frida!" Sam waved toward the woman, and I did a double take. I hadn't seen Frida since the year before when she occasionally stopped

*by the last house we'd rented to pick up Charlotte for lunch or to walk
to class. I'd never been sure how much Charlotte had told Frida about
our four-to-one vote to keep her from living with us, and the encounters
had always been cordial but awkward. Frida's hair was longer and less
greasy, and she'd lost weight. Mascara and shimmery lipstick accentuated
her features. Her clothes, while not particularly trendy, fit well. She
wore jeans and a black T-shirt with black ankle boots.*

*Frida stepped toward us with a smile twitching in the corner of
her lips. "Hi."*

*I hoped to hide the shock on my face and found my voice. "Wow.
You look great. Did you have a good summer?"*

*Frida shoved her hands into her jean pockets. "Yeah. I stayed
in Milwaukee and took a few classes. I volunteered at a shelter for
abused women."*

*"That's awesome," Sam said. "I need to do something meaningful
like that."*

"I can give you their number."

"Do you want a beer?" I asked Frida, reaching for a cup.

*"No. Maybe later." Frida's eyes darted around the room. "Charlotte
invited me."*

"Yeah. I think she's in the kitchen."

*Frida nodded. "Thanks." She lowered her head and made a beeline
away from us.*

*I raised my eyebrows at Sam. "Looks like college is agreeing with
someone."*

*"No kidding. She's really transformed. I mean, comparatively
speaking." Johnny swooped behind Sam and wrapped his bony arms
around her. "Hey, beautiful. Nice dreads."*

*She flicked one of the bells hanging from his ridiculous hat. "Nice
hat."*

"Want to go smoke a joint?"

*"I guess you can twist my arm." She turned toward me. "Want to
partake, Megan?"*

My eyes found Dan across the room. "No. I'm good."

Sam shrugged. Johnny took her by the hand and led her, giggling, up the stairs.

I made my way from the living room into the kitchen, where people gathered in packs, and the music wasn't as loud. My head was light and fuzzy with the buzz of alcohol, and the air smelled of cigarette smoke and beer. I'd lost Dan to a raucous game of beer pong in the living room. I took the opportunity to slip away to use the bathroom. Charlotte and Frida stood against the counter, beer cups in hand. A tall guy with a sandy-blonde crew cut and muscular arms hovered across from Charlotte, his shorter and squatter friend at his side. The taller guy said something, and Charlotte flung her chin toward the ceiling and laughed as if she'd just heard the funniest joke in the world. Frida shifted her feet and focused on drinking her beer. I shook my head, relieved at least that Charlotte had turned her overdone giggles away from my boyfriend. I made my way over to the group.

Charlotte's eyes brightened when she saw me. "Hi Megan. You remember Frida."

Frida's dark eyes flitted toward me, then back to the floor.

"Yeah. We chatted earlier."

Charlotte motioned toward the guys. "And this is Derek and Bryce."

The two men nodded toward me and said hi.

Charlotte flashed me a knowing smile. "Derek is in my Chemistry study group. I ran into them at the coffee shop yesterday and told them about our party."

"We never turn down free beer," Bryce said, and everyone laughed.

I smiled at them and rocked to the side because my bladder felt like it was going to burst. "Glad you could make it."

"It turns out they live in the same apartment building where I lived last year," Frida said.

I nearly jumped at the rare sound of Frida's voice. "No kidding. What are the odds?"

"*Do you like that building?*" *Charlotte asked them, lowering her eyelashes.*

From the corner of my eye, I saw Kaitlyn poke her head through the doorway. I waved toward her and she grinned.

"*Sorry, I need to run to the ladies' room,*" *I said, interrupting Derek's description of the bare-bones apartment he rented with three friends. "I'll be back in a minute.*"

They nodded toward me and resumed their conversation.

A few minutes later, I returned from the bathroom, feeling a million times more comfortable. Kaitlyn stood in the spot where I'd been, and I squeezed in between her and Charlotte. Derek's friend had drifted over to another group of people. The dynamics had transformed in the short time I'd been gone. Now it was Kaitlyn who fluttered her eyelashes, flipped her hair back, and blushed like a schoolgirl every time the handsome man across from her spoke. Kaitlyn was usually on the receiving end of male attention, and it was almost uncomfortable to watch her flirting so overtly. I raised my eyebrows at Charlotte and she shrugged, her lips flat. The connection between Kaitlyn and Derek was obvious. Even Frida seemed aware of the electricity, her unsteady gaze flitting between the lovestruck couple as if watching lightning strike two trees at once.

"*I'm going to refill my beer,*" *Charlotte said.*

"*I'll come with you.*" *I followed Charlotte and Frida into the living room, where Sam had joined the drinking game.*

Charlotte's shoulders slumped as she refilled her beer and took a few long sips.

I squeezed my friend's arm, sensing her disappointment. It was sad how Charlotte lived or died by a man's approval. We leaned against the back of the couch and cheered as Dan, Pete, Sam, and a few others lobbed ping pong balls into cups. Frida made a strange comment about the weather and left a few minutes later.

Eventually the partygoers thinned out, having headed home or to different parties. Derek and Bryce left through the front door.

When our house had quieted, and we collected empty cups and cans for recycling, Kaitlyn floated toward us, her cheeks rosy, and her eyes beaming. She positioned herself in front of Charlotte and sighed. "I can never thank you enough."

"For what?"

A dreamy smile stretched across Kaitlyn's face. "For introducing me to my future husband."

"He's an awesome guy," Charlotte said. "I'm happy for you."

I nodded. "You guys looked cute together."

Jenna edged closer, a smirk on her lips. "Make sure to watch your back, Kaitlyn. Charlotte's got a thing for men in relationships."

Charlotte glared at Jenna. "Shut up. I wouldn't do that."

"Relax, Charlotte. I'm only joking."

But the joke was thinly veiled, and no one except Jenna laughed.

CHAPTER ELEVEN

After forty-five minutes of hiking, we sat on the deck, drinking from our refilled water bottles and eating leftover pizza. Refueled and refreshed, we piled into Charlotte's minivan, determined to locate a bandage for Jenna's ankle, along with some ibuprofen for her pain.

Charlotte started the ignition, and the minivan crept forward for a half-second before lurching to a stop.

"What's going on?" Jenna said.

Charlotte's face fell. An orange service light glowed from the dashboard. "Oh no. Are you serious?"

"What is it?" I asked.

"I'm not sure, but I think I have a flat tire."

We exited the minivan and crawled around opposite sides of the vehicle, peering underneath.

"I found it." I pointed to the front passenger tire, which looked like it was melting into the ground.

"No. It's over here," Kaitlyn said.

We paced around to the front, realizing we were both correct. Two front tires were deflated.

"Are you kidding me? These tires aren't even a year old," Charlotte said, rubbing her temples. "How did this even happen?"

"You must have run over something at the airport." Kaitlyn crouched down to inspect the tread. "I don't see anything sticking out. Do you?"

I steadied myself, remembering yesterday's bumpy ride down the never-ending dirt road. "Or it could have been all those potholes you hit."

Sam tipped her head back. "This is great. Now what are we supposed to do? We don't even have phone reception."

My stomach folded as I rested my hands on my thighs. A fresh layer of sweat formed across my back. This trip was turning into a disaster. Why had I let myself be pressured into this weekend away? My gut had warned me not to go. It had practically screamed at me to make an excuse or cancel last-minute. *Always listen to your instincts.* How many times a week had I offered that piece of wisdom to my patients? But I hadn't bothered to follow my own advice. I'd convinced myself the weekend would be good for me. *Healing,* even. I hadn't wanted to be the one person who didn't show up, the one person to disappoint everyone.

I was supposed to be at work right now, drinking smooth coffee with vanilla creamer and meeting with familiar faces. Fridays were always easy at the clinic. Not many people wanted to meet with their therapist right before the weekend, especially not in the late afternoon. But I had my regulars. There was a soft-spoken woman named Bev, who showed up on Friday mornings. Her forty-nine-year-old husband had died of a sudden heart attack six months ago, and she was dealing with the loss. Then there was a couple in their fifties who had lunch together every Friday before meeting with me at 1 p.m. They were intent on keeping their lines of communication open. They referred to our sessions as "preventative therapy." I'd canceled on them this week, and I wondered if they'd keep their lunch date. I always left early on Fridays. It was one of my days to pick up the kids. And tomorrow was Saturday. Marnie had her second soccer game of the season in the morning, and I was going to miss it. I'd chosen to be here, instead, barely surviving in a remote cabin with no cell-phone reception. Now we had two flat tires, too.

A cloud moved away from the sun, sending blinding light into my face and snapping me into action. "Does anyone know how to change a tire?" I looked around at my friends, already suspecting the answer. We were educated in numerous fields—medicine, law, psychology, and finance—but auto mechanics wasn't one of them.

Four heads shook as eyes focused on the ground.

"Neither do I."

Kaitlyn shrugged. "Maybe Travis can fix it."

Jenna rested her hands on her hips and stared toward the woods. "He's probably the one who did it."

It wasn't clear if she was joking, but her words sent a chill through me.

"Jenna!" Kaitlyn said. "Why would he do that? Don't jump to conclusions."

"You're right," Jenna said. "He probably wants us to leave as soon as possible."

"Anyway, I only have one spare." Charlotte waved her key fob toward the back of the minivan. "We need to replace two tires."

Kaitlyn clasped her hands together, fidgeting. "Travis said he had a landline in case of emergency. This is an emergency, isn't it?"

Sam nodded. "Yeah. I would say so."

"Who wants to go ask him?" Charlotte asked. "Or should we all go?"

"I'll go," I said, despite the pit in my stomach. "I have a premium membership with Triple A roadside assistance. I'm sure they can send someone out with an extra tire or two."

Jenna's worried eyes flickered toward the trail. "You shouldn't go to that guy's house alone."

Sam stepped toward me. "Yeah. I'll go with you."

"I can come, too," Charlotte said. "It's my car and you might need my insurance information."

"Okay." I waved toward Charlotte. "How about you and Sam come with me, and Kaitlyn stays here with Jenna, so she can rest her ankle?"

Everyone agreed. I grabbed my purse, and Charlotte retrieved her insurance card as Kaitlyn helped Jenna hobble back to the porch.

"Good luck, guys," Kaitlyn yelled as the three of us headed up the trail in the direction we'd seen Travis appear from the night before.

We trod along the dirt road. It was afternoon now and the breeze had disappeared. Tire tracks imprinted the path, which was too narrow for more than one car. We walked for nearly ten minutes before wondering if we were heading in the wrong direction. I was about to suggest turning back when a ramshackle house appeared in the distance. Yesterday's gunshots and the dead squirrel flashed in my mind as my pulse quickened. A shed materialized through a thicket of trees, a giant padlock hanging from its door. A yellow sign read: *WARNING, KEEP OUT!*

Sam pointed to the shed. "What's that all about?"

I made a face. "I'm afraid to ask." I kept walking and focused on the mission. "All I know is that I'll feel better once a mechanic is on the way."

Charlotte tugged at my shoulder and I turned toward her. Her saucer eyes darted toward the house, then back at me. "Look, I know Jenna thinks the cabin owner might be responsible for the tires, but we shouldn't accuse him of anything. I mean, we have no reason to think he'd do something like that."

I kicked at the dirt. "Jenna is quick to jump to conclusions. You probably ran over some nails at the airport. End of story."

"And you hit about a thousand potholes yesterday," Sam said.

Charlotte's shoulders relaxed, and she tried not to smile. "I didn't do it on purpose. The roads were treacherous."

We stepped toward the house. An open window revealed a ripped screen, only blackness visible behind it. The air felt thick, and I forced my feet forward. Sam had stopped talking, and I could tell she was uneasy too. Everything about the house was unwelcoming. It wasn't much larger than a mobile home and it sat on cement blocks. The windows were small. Brown stains seeped around the edges of the white siding.

A white pickup truck was parked in the dirt driveway. A faded sticker of an American flag clung to one side of the fender. An image of a semi-naked woman holding a black machine gun was stuck next to it.

I shook my head at the truck. "Ugh. Lovely."

Sam grunted and kicked the ground.

The front door swung open. "Need somethin'?" Travis wore stained jeans and a tattered, unbuttoned shirt. The shirt hung open, revealing his bony chest, and another mark below his left clavicle. I stepped forward, realizing it was a tattoo about the size of a silver dollar. I blinked, not wanting to believe my eyes as the image came into focus. The design was a swastika. A row of small numbers formed a line beneath it.

Charlotte clutched my arm. "Oh my God."

"What the hell?" My stomach dropped and I thought I was going to be sick. Travis was a neo-Nazi. I'd seen people like him on the news, but not in person—at least as far as I knew. Recent events had emboldened their hate, and their blatant ignorance blew my mind. I'd seen strings of numbers like the ones on his chest when I'd volunteered at a local prison years earlier. The authorities assigned numbers to identify the prisoners, and I wondered if Travis was an ex-convict too, or merely pretending to be tough. Either way, I felt like the crosshairs of a rifle were aimed at my forehead. Every muscle in my body wanted to turn and run.

"I said, you need something?" Travis had now buttoned up his shirt, a strange grin cemented to his lips. A tremor twitched through his body.

"We shouldn't be here." I looked at Sam, wishing none of us had come to this place. A lock of black hair had fallen into Sam's face, obscuring her glassy eyes.

I wanted to scream at him, but only a disturbed grunt shot from my mouth. Charlotte turned away. We needed to use his phone, but there was no way any of us would enter his house.

Sam pulled her hand from mine, squaring her shoulders at Travis. Her lip snarled. "No. We took a wrong turn."

He looked Sam up and down like she was a piece of meat. I couldn't breathe, fearing he might turn violent.

"Huh?" was all he said. He hooked his thumb in the waist of his jeans and spat at the dirt.

A woman with eyes that sat too close together appeared in the doorway next to him. Her scalp held a mop of over-processed blonde hair, and her body's concave hollows matched Travis's emaciated build. An oversized T-shirt hung from her bony shoulders. I wondered if she and Travis were meth addicts or merely so poor they couldn't afford three meals a day.

"Those the renters?" she asked Travis in a gravelly voice.

My heart pounded as I pulled Sam's arm. "Let's go," I said, forcing my friend to come with me. Her bronze skin radiated heat.

I could feel the man's eyes watching us as we strode away. I was too angry to speak. Sam and Charlotte's faces pinched with disgust, mirroring my own expression. Partway down the path, our feet trod faster. We picked up speed and began to run. As we rounded the bend, I got the terrifying feeling we were running for our lives.

CHAPTER TWELVE

"We need to find another way to get out of here." My breath clogged my throat as I bounded up the porch steps. We'd sprinted the entire way back from Travis's house, but there could never be enough space between the hateful man and us.

Kaitlyn leaned forward in her chair on the deck. "Why? What's going on?"

I clenched my fists. "We rented this crappy cabin from a member of a hate group. There's a fucking swastika tattooed on his chest."

"Seriously?" Kaitlyn said under her breath. She blinked a few times and bit her lip. "Oh my God."

"He tried to cover up the symbol, but not before we saw it. He had some numbers tattooed underneath it too. He might be an ex-con," I said, struggling to catch my breath. "This guy is bad news."

"It's not like this is a big surprise. Didn't you see him last night?" Jenna forced herself up from her chair, using the table as a crutch. "He had a knife blade tattooed on his neck. He was looking at Sam like he wanted to murder her. I can only imagine what he'd do if he knew I was Jewish. Not to mention he twitches every five seconds like he's going through withdrawal. Great job finding this place." Jenna's eyes landed on Charlotte.

Charlotte shook her head. "I had no idea it was going to be like this. I told you that. You guys saw the same description and photos I did." Charlotte's eyes traveled around the group, but no one spoke. "Anyway, I found the rental website through the link that *you* sent me, Jenna. So maybe you should be blaming yourself."

Jenna sneered. "Oh, come on. This stupid cabin was available on multiple sites. You pushed it on everyone because you wanted something cheap."

Anger brewed in Charlotte's eyes. She flung her hand toward Jenna. "*You* were the one who wanted to be in the woods! Remember that text you sent about needing a break from the city? You wanted to go off-grid. *Off-grid!* And now here we are trapped in the middle of nowhere with no cell-phone reception. Congratulations!"

We looked at each other. The tension stretching between Jenna and Charlotte was enough to strangle us. I held my hands in the air, trying to diffuse the situation. "It's no one's fault. We didn't know."

From what I could remember, we'd all chosen the cabin after several rounds of emails and texts. Charlotte had requested something affordable due to her upcoming trip to Europe. Jenna suggested meeting in Wisconsin, so the three of us who live here could drive, and so she could get a break from city life. Sam was quick to offer to fly from Denver. Someone had discovered the tiny airport up north. We'd all searched online, using various vacation rental sites. Charlotte had emailed the cabin to us as one potential option, along with a few others. But the secluded cabin with the private lake was affordable and close to the airport. Our plans had quickly fallen into place. There hadn't been any mention of the neo-Nazi owner.

Charlotte's mouth puckered. "As much as we don't like Travis, he has a right to his opinion. This is America."

"Are you for real?" Jenna heaved herself forward, leaning close to Charlotte's face. "That piece of shit is a terrorist."

Charlotte squinted. She held up her hands and stepped back. "Calm down. I agree with you. I'm only saying that you haven't had much experience with people like him…"

Jenna rolled her shoulders back and stepped away, huffing.

I released a breath. Jenna and Charlotte were from such different backgrounds. Charlotte's parents had never made it past high
school and had spent their entire lives in their unpopulated farming
town in northeast Wisconsin. The furthest they ever traveled was
thirty minutes every Sunday to the nearest Catholic church. In
contrast, Jenna had grown up in the hustle and bustle of downtown
Chicago, the product of expensive schooling and top-of-the-line
athletic training. Her Jewish father and agnostic mother had been
community activists and professors at the University of Chicago.
Long before Jenna's mother had lost her battle with cancer, she'd
been a college athlete herself—a track star at the University of
Illinois. Even under the happiest of circumstances, Charlotte
and Jenna's ideologies could be like oil and water. I worried their
friendship wouldn't survive the weekend.

A long sigh drew our attention. Sam stood in the corner, her
manicured fingernails touching her face. "I'm sorry, guys, but I
don't feel safe here. I want to go back to Denver as soon as possible.
I have my family to think about." She looked around the group,
searching our faces. "Will someone hike back to the camp with
me? There might be a phone in the office. Or maybe we can find
that person Charlotte saw? Maybe we can still get the minivan
fixed today if we go now."

Unease expanded in my chest, making it difficult to breathe.
"Sam's right," I said, as Marnie and Wyatt's faces flashed before
me. "I want to leave, too."

"Wait." A sad smile tugged at the corners of Kaitlyn's mouth.
"No one has to leave. Let's not give that stupid guy the power to
ruin our weekend. We can ignore him, or we can go someplace
else. We never get to see each other."

Charlotte placed her hand on Sam's arm. "I agree with Kaitlyn.
It's getting late, and we've already hiked so far today. I don't want
to get lost out there in the dark. We can eat a good dinner and

rest up tonight. We'll figure out the tire situation in the morning. Then we can find a hotel in a nearby town."

My gut wrenched at the thought of staying in this place for another night. "We can try to drive out on the flat tires. Maybe we could make it to a gas station."

The others looked at me, considering my idea.

Jenna let out a low whistle. "Look at how deflated those tires are. I don't think we can make it to the end of this driveway, much less to the main road."

"It's worth a try, though. Isn't it?" Kaitlyn said.

Charlotte shrugged and dug out her keys. "You're right. What's the worst that can happen?" She climbed into the passenger seat, starting the ignition. Metal groaned as she slowly backed up the van. The tires were angled and rolled straight toward one of the many deep pits in the dirt driveway.

"Turn the wheel. Turn!" I yelled, but the awful groaning noise continued.

Charlotte threw her hands in the air. "The wheel won't turn. It's locked in place." The minivan lurched backward. The deflated front tire on the passenger side dropped into one of the deep potholes. The vehicle jerked to a halt. Charlotte slumped forward and turned off the car.

Jenna slid her hand across her forehead. "I guess that was the worst that can happen."

Sam kicked the dirt and closed her eyes.

Charlotte exited the minivan and turned toward Sam. "Look, we're losing daylight. How about I walk back to Travis's house on my own first thing in the morning? I can pretend I didn't see his tattoo and ask to use his phone."

Kaitlyn slid her palms down the outside of her leggings. "We still have two nights after tonight. What if we find a hotel in a bigger town for the rest of our time? Wausau isn't too far away. Like I said, we don't have to let this disgusting idiot ruin our weekend."

"What about Jenna's ankle?" I asked.

Jenna grunted. "I can deal with my ankle for one night, as long as we can find someplace a lot better to stay tomorrow. Let's hunker down and get the hell out of here in the morning." She looked at Sam. "Are you on board, Sam?"

Sam raised her eyes from the ground. "Okay. Yeah, I guess."

I inched toward her. "Are you sure?"

"It's fine. As long as we leave as soon as possible tomorrow."

Jenna peered in the direction of Travis's house. "I'm going to leave the worst vacation rental review the internet has ever seen."

Everyone nodded as bodies shifted. We moped toward the deck and found chairs. My arms weighed heavily at my sides as I wondered how our society had failed so miserably at valuing things like diversity, compassion, empathy, and education. Despair loomed over me. I closed my eyes and followed my breath inside my body, grounding myself in the moment as I often advised my patients to do when they felt overwhelmed. After a few deep inhales and exhales, a speck of hope buoyed in my chest. I identified the bright spot, latching on to it. I was lucky to have this time with my friends. There was safety in numbers, and we had each other's backs. We could salvage the second half of our four-day weekend. All we had to do was make it through the night.

A few minutes later, we were back in the kitchen, chopping vegetables for a stir-fry. Kaitlyn had packed all the ingredients, microwavable packets of rice, and a printout of a recipe she'd found on a celebrity blog. Stifled conversation passed between us. Jenna's endless chatter had dried up, her words sporadic and carefully chosen. She sat on a chair, watching the rest of us measure and chop. Sam appeared in the doorway from the living room and handed her a bottle of ibuprofen.

"I found it at the bottom of my bathroom kit."

"Oh, thank God." Jenna opened the lid and popped a pill in her mouth, not bothering with water.

Jenna wasn't the only one who wasn't acting like herself. My eyes watered as I peeled and diced an onion. The encounter with Travis had knocked me off-kilter, making me feel as if I was teetering on the edge of a sinking boat. Charlotte took long pauses in between measuring the soy sauce and the cornstarch, her eyes distant, her positive energy deflated. Sam stood in the corner with her back to the rest of us, quietly chopping a stalk of celery.

"Just think of the story we're going to have to tell when we get back," Kaitlyn said.

I blinked, narrowly missing the tip of my finger with the blade. "Yeah. Andrew will think I'm exaggerating."

Sam turned toward me with a hint of grin. "When have you ever done that?"

I chuckled, grateful for the lightened mood.

A few minutes later, Kaitlyn had filled everyone's wineglasses and ushered us all out to the porch. It was 7:45 p.m. and dusk was setting in. The wine relaxed our bodies and loosened our tongues. We ate our concoction, trying to keep our napkins from blowing away in the wind as we complimented each other on the flavors.

"Look at the beach across the lake." Jenna's eyes held a distant look. "I wonder if there's someone over there. I wonder if they can see us."

Charlotte set down her fork. "I don't think there was anyone there. Kaitlyn yelled pretty loudly and no one responded. I must have made a mistake."

My eyes drifted over the water toward the empty beach. I kept staring, hoping to catch sight of a person on the other side. Maybe there was someone who could make a phone call for us. But the light was dim and, as far as I could tell, Charlotte was right. There was no one there. We refilled our wineglasses again as daylight faded faster. I slapped a mosquito off my arm, and Charlotte lit a citronella candle. An animal skittered through the woods below us. I crouched forward with my teeth clenched.

"What if Travis killed the counselor at that camp?" Jenna's face flickered in the candlelight.

A laugh escaped my mouth. "I love a good conspiracy theory, but that's a big leap, Jenna."

Kaitlyn shook her head. "The article said she died under suspicious circumstances. It was probably a boating accident or an arrow that strayed from the archery field."

"Maybe she drowned," Sam said, staring toward the lake.

Jenna raised her finger in the air. "Or the zip line got her."

I smiled at Jenna's joke again, then peered toward the blackened water and the wall of forest that blended into the night sky. We were trapped in this remote location without a car or our phones. It was a view toward the end of the earth.

I thought of the shed near Travis's house with the *KEEP OUT!* sign and giant padlock, assuming it housed a collection of guns. And what were the odds that Charlotte's car would have *two* flat tires? I'd gotten a few flat tires over the years, but never two at the same time. The guy who owned this cabin was a threat. Our lousy luck didn't feel like a mere coincidence.

I straightened in my chair. "I don't know. Jenna might be onto something. Wasn't the camp aimed at helping at-risk youth? Maybe the counselor who died wasn't white. Or maybe she was helping kids from different ethnicities and religions. I'm sure the neighborhood hate group wasn't cool with that."

"People like Travis will use any excuse to kill. History repeats itself," Sam said in a quiet voice.

Jenna scowled toward the woods. "Don't worry, Sam. We're going to get out of this hellhole tomorrow."

"I know." Sam lifted her chin. "I'd feel so much better if I could call Thomas. Then he could contact the police and have them send someone out to us."

"We'd all feel better if that happened." Charlotte stared at her nearly empty wineglass. "But no one should wander off in the dark. It's not safe."

Kaitlyn stretched her arms over her head and yawned, causing a chain reaction of yawns around the circle. "Maybe it's time to call it a night."

Sam clutched her phone. "Yeah. The sooner we go to sleep, the sooner morning will get here."

A mattress spring creaked from across the room and my eyes popped open. It took a second to remember where I was and why the air smelled different than my bedroom at home—not of sandalwood candles and cotton linens, but of antique furniture and flea-bitten blankets. The shadowy outline of Charlotte's body rolled to the side, followed by deep breathing. My bladder strained with pressure. Once again, I'd had one too many glasses of wine. I blinked against the darkness, letting my eyes adjust to the light. Now that the thought of going to the bathroom had entered my brain, I couldn't erase it. I inhaled a breath and slid back the sheet, carefully moving my feet to the side of the bed so as not to make any noise. I pressed my toes into the wooden floor and stood up, feeling dizzy for a moment. When my head rush passed, I tiptoed across the room and gripped the door handle, turning slowly and slipping out to the hallway.

My feet skittered toward the bathroom at the end of the hall as I told myself to ignore the elongated shadows and darkened hiding places. A faint nightlight glowed from beyond the open bathroom door. I locked myself inside the tiny room. A minute later, feeling relieved, I stumbled back toward the bedroom.

As I passed the top step of the stairway, a muffled cough sounded from downstairs. Someone was awake. I froze, craning my neck toward the noise and noticing a sliver of light piercing onto the bottom step. The kitchen light was on.

I crept down the stairs, curious to see who was hanging out in the kitchen in the middle of the night. Not wanting to scare anyone, I let my feet land heavier as I approached. Jenna sat at the round table. Her head snapped up as I stepped into the doorway. Kaitlyn's old photo album lay open in front of her, along with a cloudy glass of water.

"Hey." I stepped toward her. "Can't sleep either?"

"Nope." Jenna's bloodshot eyes followed my gaze to the photos. The book was opened to a snapshot of her and Pete back when they were still a happy couple.

I pulled out a chair and sat down, ignoring the way my skin turned cold. "It seems like so long ago, doesn't it?"

Jenna flattened her lips. "In some ways, yeah. In other ways, it feels like yesterday."

"I guess that's true." While I'd completely forgotten some people's names and faces, and much of what I'd learned in my classes, I vividly remembered other things. The emotions had stayed with me. I'd never felt more excited or alive than when I'd been a twenty-year-old away at college with a future full of hope and possibilities lying ahead of me. I could recall how empathetic friends had lightened my worries. I could feel the stress of final exams tightening my chest and the thrilling euphoria of young love. And, as much as I tried to forget, I remembered every moment leading up to the car accident. The trauma that followed could still suffocate me.

Jenna looked away from the photo album and rubbed her red-rimmed eyes. I dug my fingernails into the table, deciding it was better not to relive that horrible night.

"Do you ever hear anything from Pete?" I asked.

She closed the book and frowned. "No. Pete never looked back, and neither did I."

"He was an idiot." I realized my mouth was dry. I stood and walked to the cupboard, where I found a glass and filled it with water from the sink. A gust of wind blew outside, causing a branch to scrape against the window above the sink. I sipped the lukewarm water. "This place gives me the creeps."

"Yeah. There's a reason no one's sleeping."

I looked toward the darkened living room. "Is someone else awake?"

"I don't know. Probably. Charlotte was in here eating a slice of pizza when I came down. I think I accidentally scared the crap out of her. And then Sam came down to get some water. I wouldn't be surprised if everyone slept with one eye open tonight."

I envisioned the repulsive man who lived a stone's throw away from the remote cabin, the man who'd shot a squirrel from a tree for no other reason but to watch it die. The camp across the lake sat empty because a counselor had died under "suspicious circumstances." I tightened my jaw. I didn't know if Travis was responsible for the counselor's death, but the theory wasn't outside the realm of possibility. We needed to leave this place as soon as possible.

CHAPTER THIRTEEN

The coffee tasted even worse than it did yesterday. Last night's sleep had been spotty, at best, but we'd survived the restless night and now sipped tentatively from our mugs, wrinkling our noses with each bitter gulp. Low-hanging clouds dimmed the morning light and added to the subdued atmosphere on the deck. I yawned and squeezed my eyelids closed.

"Okay, so here's the plan," Jenna said between yawns. "Charlotte can head back to Travis's house and ask to use his phone."

My fingers tightened around the mug at the thought of Charlotte showing up unannounced at Travis's doorstep. "She shouldn't go alone."

Kaitlyn frowned. "Yeah. Travis is a creep."

Charlotte flicked her hand in the air. "It's okay. I know how to deal with people like him. I'll just keep my head down."

Something hardened in Sam's dark eyes. "I can go with you."

"That's a horrible idea."

"I'll go with you then," I said, feeling an overwhelming need to help Charlotte, despite the pounding in my chest.

Charlotte tipped her head back. "Thanks, but I was thinking it might be better if we keep it low-key. We don't want to alarm him or make him think that we need his help. I'll tell Travis I need to call my husband—a family emergency or something. Then I'll call roadside assistance as soon as he leaves the room."

"What if he doesn't leave the room?"

"I don't know. I'll ask him for some privacy."

I thought about Charlotte's plan. The thought of Travis wandering over to our cabin again terrified me. "Yeah. Maybe you're right. We don't want to give him any reason to come back here."

"I'll be back in twenty minutes. Twenty-five minutes, tops. You guys can stay here and enjoy your coffee."

Jenna lifted her mug and made a face. "I don't see that happening."

Charlotte smiled. "Travis seems like one of those people whose bark is worse than his bite."

Kaitlyn fiddled with her necklace. "Are you sure?"

"Yes. Besides, if I'm not back in thirty minutes, you know where I am. Don't forget to bring a kitchen knife with you." Charlotte winked.

"Will do," I said.

Sam rubbed her forehead and sighed. "How in the world did we end up here?"

"I don't know," Charlotte said, "but we're never coming back."

Jenna cleared her throat. "Okay. So, Charlotte, when you get to the house, you'll call Megan's roadside assistance people and maybe also call Reed to let him know what's going on."

Charlotte nodded and I flopped back in my chair. Hopefully, we were only hours from getting the tires fixed and sipping fruity martinis in a hotel bar. A few geese honked in the distance and I gazed out toward the lake. The water had lost yesterday's brilliant blue sparkle and now looked more like an enormous, murky puddle.

"I can't wait to get to a real hotel," Sam said, mirroring my thoughts.

"Me too." Kaitlyn fluttered her pretty eyelashes and twisted her hair into a messy bun. "I need to talk to Derek. And the kids."

I noticed Jenna's frown. "How's your ankle feeling, Jenna?"

She bent over and rubbed it. "It still hurts like a mother. I need to take more ibuprofen."

It was just after 8 a.m. I complained about my sore muscles from yesterday's hike. The aches resulting from such an easy walk were embarrassing, considering I'd completed two marathons in the last three years. I'd stopped running a year ago, telling myself my priorities had shifted toward my kids and my counseling practice. In truth, between work, the kids, and sneaking around at odd hours to meet the second man in my life, there hadn't been much time for running. My leg muscles had atrophied from lack of use. Charlotte offered physical therapy advice, recommending some exercises to stretch out the soreness and others to rebuild my strength. Kaitlyn mentioned a Pilates class she attended every Wednesday morning. Jenna took over the conversation, telling us about a co-worker who was training for a triathlon. All the while, Sam sat without speaking, clutching her forgotten coffee and glancing toward the woods.

We carried our mugs of sludge back inside and prepared to activate our escape plan. I dug through my suitcase, selecting ankle jeans, sandals, and a fitted black tank top as I imagined a quick tire change, an hour-and-a-half drive to Wausau where we'd eat lunch in a homey restaurant, followed by an afternoon of browsing quaint shops.

I met the others downstairs. Sam rested her elbow on the windowsill, wearing jeans and a rose-colored shirt with delicate lace detailing around the neckline. Her hair was damp from the shower and her makeup freshly applied. Not surprisingly, she was even more eager to leave than me.

"We'll be out of here soon," I said.

She rubbed her forehead. "Thank God."

Charlotte stood next to her with her hair tied back in a braid and her face freshly washed. She appeared much younger without any makeup. I was suddenly nervous for her as I handed her my roadside assistance card.

She smoothed down her shirt and glanced toward the door. "Remember, if I'm not back in thirty minutes, send out a search party."

"We'll be ready."

Jenna smirked, nodding toward Charlotte. "It should be easy to find you in that shirt."

Charlotte glanced down at her orange-and-white striped T-shirt, then looked up and smiled. "At least no hunters will get me."

We followed her bright shirt out to the porch and watched as she trekked along the trail, disappearing over the hill and into the woods. My heart raced inside my chest. I closed my eyes, willing everything to go smoothly. I found a seat in the same chair where I'd been sitting earlier, the others filling in around me. The conversation returned to how desperate we were to leave the cabin. We could still salvage the weekend in a new location. The summer tourist season was over, and we imagined it would be easy to locate a couple of vacant hotel rooms or to secure lodging at a bed and breakfast. Barely twenty minutes had passed when footsteps sounded on the path. I looked up to find Charlotte plodding toward us with a blank expression on her face. I released a breath, relieved to see her unharmed.

She shook her head. "He wasn't home."

Sam tilted her head back.

"What?" Kaitlyn said. "Was his truck there?"

Charlotte approached the porch, breathing heavily. "No. It was gone. I knocked on the front door, too, but no one answered."

"Just our luck," Jenna said.

"I'll go back in an hour and check again. Maybe he had to run into town."

Jenna rolled her eyes. "For what? Live bait?"

Frustration glinted in Sam's dark eyes. I shifted in my seat as Sam glared at her phone, her lower lip quivering.

I leaned toward Charlotte. "Not to be a pain, but maybe one of us should go and check for Travis every thirty minutes. We're all anxious to get out of here."

Guilt washed through Charlotte's eyes. She laced her fingers together and glanced toward the path. "Yeah. Okay. I can do it. I feel like I caused this mess. I'll get us out of it. I promise."

I reached over and squeezed Charlotte's hand, letting her know I didn't blame her for any of this.

"Hey, I saw some board games in the living room," Kaitlyn said as she stood. "I'll bring a few out to help pass the time."

Jenna groaned. "You're such a mom."

A minute later, Kaitlyn returned with an armful of boxes, including Sorry!, Scattergories, checkers, and Uno. I usually found board games tiresome, but I was thankful for the distraction.

We settled on Scattergories, playing a few rounds and laughing once in a while. Charlotte checked her watch and set off on her mission again. She returned about twenty minutes later with a grim look on her face. We switched to Uno. Kaitlyn said the game reminded her of her kids. She was missing them, just like I was missing Wyatt and Marnie. Uno was one of their favorites. Sam opted to sit out, the light in her eyes dimming as she stared toward the lake. Soon, another thirty minutes had passed. Charlotte left and returned, shaking her head.

Sam paced across the porch and huffed. "Listen, guys, I'm not going to wait around all day for this guy to get back from his KKK rally, or wherever he went."

My shoulders tightened with the same anxiety that gripped Sam's face.

"He's gotta be back soon," Kaitlyn said.

"We don't know that. Charlotte can keep going back and checking, but I can't just sit here. I'm going to wander down by the lake and see if I can catch a signal."

"I'll come with you," I said.

Sam waved me away. "You don't have to. You'll hear me scream if I see bars on my phone."

Jenna yawned and pushed her chair back. "If you guys don't mind, I'm going to head inside and take a nap. I was awake most of the night."

My eyelids were heavy, and I also couldn't stop yawning due to my checkered sleep the night before. After I'd returned from my chat with Jenna in the kitchen, the musty pillow and screeches of nocturnal animals had woken me up throughout the night. "I might rest for a while, too," I said.

Kaitlyn nodded. "I'll stay here and play checkers with Charlotte until she has to leave again. Or maybe I'll take a turn hiking over there."

We went our separate ways. Jenna plopped on the couch and I headed up the stairs to my bedroom. I wasn't used to spending so much time surrounded by other women, and the thought of a few minutes alone was a welcome relief.

An hour later, I roused myself from the twin bed, rubbing the haze from my eyes. I'd passed out for a few minutes, but the cry of a bird pierced my sleep. The sandals I'd been wearing earlier were too tight, so I pulled on socks and sneakers instead. I skipped down the stairs, eager to learn about any progress made by Charlotte or Sam. Jenna was lying where I'd left her on the living room couch, her eyes closed and breath heavy. I tiptoed past her to join the others outside.

"Hey," I said, approaching their checkers game.

Kaitlyn lifted her eyes from the board. "Hi. There's an intense championship game happening here."

"Is Travis back yet?"

Charlotte flattened her lips. "No. I got back about twenty minutes ago. He still wasn't home. I'll go check again as soon as we're finished."

"Where's Sam?" I asked.

"She was here a few minutes ago. She couldn't find any reception."

I looked over my shoulder. "Where is she now?"

Kaitlyn followed my gaze. "She's probably taking a nap. I don't think any of us slept last night."

"I was going to tell Sam I'd walk back to the camp with her to find a phone. I'm pretty sure there was one in the office." I conjured up a vision of the desk I'd glimpsed through the dirty window and wished I'd paid closer attention.

Kaitlyn slid a chip to another square on the board, then looked at me. "Really? You're going to hike all the way over there again? Even if there is a phone in the office, it's probably disconnected."

"It's worth a try."

Kaitlyn glanced at her phone. "It's 11:35 a.m. already, almost lunchtime. I'll put together some food for us first. I brought bagels and cream cheese, plus some sliced turkey. I also have potato chips and apples. We should let Sam rest until I get it ready."

Charlotte contemplated her next move as Kaitlyn tried to remember the name of a hotel in Wausau where she'd stayed for a friend's wedding eight years earlier but couldn't come up with it. Without any phone reception or an internet connection, we couldn't look anything up.

"We'll figure it out when we get there," I finally said. "After this experience, I'll take any hotel that has two rooms available."

Kaitlyn turned toward the woods. "Sorry to ask, but do you want to head back to Travis's house again?"

Charlotte slid her chair back. "Yeah. I'll try again."

"Thanks. I'll go inside and get the food together."

"I'll help you with lunch."

My movements were slow as I stood. Charlotte hiked over the incline, her feet dragging with each step. Her orange shirt gradually disappeared into the horizon like the setting sun. I stared down the empty path. A better person would have insisted on going with her, but I couldn't stomach seeing Travis again. I wouldn't be able to hide my disgust, which could put us all in danger. We'd wasted the morning, and we hadn't contacted anyone about the tires.

"C'mon." Kaitlyn waved me toward the cabin.

I followed her across the deck and through the door to the kitchen, where she rummaged through grocery bags and removed a package of artisan bagels. I retrieved apples and a container of cream cheese from the fridge. I washed the fruit in the sink and set the apples in a large bowl I'd found in the cupboard.

"Hey."

Jenna's voice made me jump. I didn't realize she'd woken up. She stood in the doorway, towering over me.

"Can I help?"

"Maybe get some paper plates." I dried one more dripping apple with a paper towel and placed it in the bowl. Jenna nodded and searched through the bags as I slipped past her.

"I'm going to check on Sam." The stairs creaked beneath my feet as I climbed toward the landing. The door to Sam's room was half open. I inched forward, worried about scaring her if she'd fallen asleep. I pulled the door open wider, expecting to find her resting her head on the pillow. Instead, my stomach flipped. Her bed was empty.

I felt dizzy, panic surging through me. Still, I hoped there was an innocent explanation. Maybe Sam had switched to the other bedroom. I poked my head inside the room across the hall, finding it empty. Then I checked the bedroom where Charlotte and I slept. She wasn't in there either.

"Sam?" I said, in case she was in the bathroom. But as I moved to the hallway, I could see the bathroom door was open, and no one was inside. My feet tripped over each other as I descended the staircase. Kaitlyn and Jenna had moved out to the porch with the food.

"Sam isn't here."

Jenna stared at me. "What do you mean?"

My eyes landed on Kaitlyn. "Didn't you say she went inside to rest?"

"Yeah. That's what I thought, but…"

"But what?"

"Now that I think about it, I didn't see her go inside. Or maybe she went inside and came back out through the other door. I'm not sure." Kaitlyn waved toward the boxes of board games. "Charlotte and I were focused on our game."

Jenna's forehead wrinkled. "So, maybe she walked somewhere else to look for a phone signal?"

"Sam wouldn't head back to that camp on her own, would she?" I asked as a chill erupted across my skin.

"She's been gone a long time." Jenna peered toward the lake, her lips parting.

I searched the trees for any sign of movement. "Maybe Sam found reception and made a work call? Or called home to talk to Thomas?" But even as I said the words, I knew they weren't true. Sam was conscientious of others. She would never leave us waiting like this on purpose, especially not for this long. I couldn't believe how dumb we'd been, sitting here chatting, playing games, and making lunch while our friend was out in the woods somewhere. We'd left our dark-skinned friend to wander across the path of the neo-Nazi who lived next door.

My heartbeat accelerated. "We need to find her. Right now."

"Oh my God," Kaitlyn said under her breath. "What if something happened to her?"

Footsteps sounded in the distance, and I stretched my neck to see whose they were. Charlotte appeared from around the bend. She was alone, huffing along the path. A sheen of sweat glistened from her forehead as she neared and shook her head.

"So, Travis's truck was there this time, but he still wasn't home. I knocked on the door for about five minutes straight. He must have gone on a walk or left with someone else." Charlotte's breath was labored as she eyed the food on the table. "Thanks for getting the food together. All this walking back and forth is tiring."

Jenna's lips pulled back as she peered in the direction of Travis's house. "Charlotte, we can't find Sam."

Charlotte rubbed the back of her hand across her forehead as she looked toward the cabin. "Sam went inside to take a nap like an hour ago. Remember?"

I pressed my heels into the floor of the deck, struggling to anchor myself to something. "She's not in there."

Kaitlyn narrowed her eyes at Charlotte. "Did we see her go inside?"

"I think so. I mean, now that you mention it, I don't remember exactly." Charlotte's pale skin had turned the color of sour milk.

"We were wondering if Sam hiked off in a different direction to try to find cell reception."

Charlotte nodded. "Maybe she did. She was anxious about not being able to call Thomas."

Jenna squared her shoulders at us. "You guys should go look for her. I'll wait here in case she returns." She raised her ankle. "I don't want to slow you down."

"Okay," we said in unison.

"Let's follow the path toward the camp. I bet that's where she went." I locked eyes with the others. Kaitlyn nodded. Charlotte bowed her head. I turned and jogged toward the narrow dirt trail we'd traveled the day before. Kaitlyn and Charlotte flanked me.

"Sam!" we yelled as we trotted along the path. Kaitlyn was in front of me now. Charlotte's heavy breathing followed behind. My heart pounded in my ears as I stumbled forward in a frenzy. I worried another panic attack might be imminent. I focused on the trees and the sound of our footsteps as I pulled in air through my nose.

"Sam!" Kaitlyn screamed again. She looked back at me, worried. "What if that creep did something to her?"

I caught up to her and placed my hands on my hips, remembering the way Travis's hateful eyes had leered at my friend. Sam was the strongest person I knew. She could fend for herself. I'd seen her in action. Still, Travis had a gun, and the woods were remote.

"We can't panic," I said between jagged breaths. "Sam probably took a wrong turn and is making her way back to us. Or maybe she found someone to replace the tires. She wouldn't have been able to call us. Even if she found reception, we still don't have it."

The other two nodded but didn't say anything. Even to my own ears, the explanation sounded like wishful thinking. Still, it was crucial to stay positive. We skittered along the trail, eyes searching between the trees as we walked. I scoured the woods for any sign of our friend. Only birds and squirrels flitted near the deserted path.

"Sam! Are you out there?" I tried once more, hearing no response.

As we rounded a bend in the path, a flash of pink on the ground caught my eye, standing out against the earthy tones of the forest. My feet stuck in place. It wasn't any shade of pink; it was the color of rose petals, identical to the shirt Sam had been wearing this morning.

"Oh no!" Rows of tree trunks obscured my view. I couldn't see her face, but a rose shirt and two denim-covered legs lay motionless on the ground.

Kaitlyn froze and looked back at me, her mouth falling open. Charlotte stepped next to my shoulder and gasped. I shook my head in a moment of terrifying realization. The three of us raced toward our friend.

CHAPTER FOURTEEN

I sprinted toward Sam, my body quaking. Kaitlyn tripped on a branch and fell. I gripped her elbow and helped her up before we continued weaving through the trees.

"Sam!" Charlotte yelled.

The body's face came into focus as I neared. Just as I feared, the figure dressed in jeans and a rose-pink T-shirt was Sam. She lay sprawled on the ground. I only stopped when my toes were an inch from her splayed-out arm. Sam's shiny black hair fell past her shoulders and onto the moss. She could have been a doll, so perfect and still. My knees buckled, and I collapsed to the ground, gripping her cold fingers. Sam's unfocused eyes stared out, distant and vacant. I peered up at Kaitlyn's downturned mouth and Charlotte's bloodshot eyes. Charlotte shoved next to me and felt Sam's neck for a pulse, followed by a slight shake of her head.

"Oh my God! Sam!" My heart reached into my throat. A wave of nausea shot through me at the confirmation that Sam was dead. Everything felt wrong, especially my heaving body collapsing over Sam's lifeless one. "Oh no…" A thousand bombs exploded inside me as my chest caved and black spots swam before my eyes. The years of our friendship rushed over me—the tiny room we'd shared in the dorm, our long walks traversing the city sidewalks, our quest to find the perfect vanilla latte, our secret jokes, and our late nights spent studying in the library, or confiding our sorrows and our dreams in my cramped bedroom. "No, no, no."

Charlotte stood and kicked at the ground, her eyes searching the woods. "How did this…? Where did she…? Why would anyone…?" She couldn't complete a thought. Charlotte stumbled toward the trail but tripped over a fallen branch. Her face contorted. Instead of standing up, she curled into a fetal position and sobbed.

Kaitlyn wobbled in circles, using the trunk of a tree to keep herself upright. "NO!" Her drawn-out scream sounded more like a noise from a wild animal than a human.

"What happened?" I wanted to blame Sam's death on natural causes—a heart attack or a stroke. But fear blazed through me. A primal instinct deep within me knew something evil had taken place.

Kaitlyn tipped her chin toward the sky. "Help us! Someone, help us!" she screamed. There was no response. Kaitlyn fell onto her hands and knees as she struggled to catch her breath.

When I finally blinked away the terror, I leaned down and focused on an aberration on Sam's neck. Above the pretty lace collar of her shirt, there was a mark—a thin line of bluish-red bruising. Travis's twitchy eyes and crooked smile flashed in my mind.

"Look at her neck." My dry mouth felt filled with cobwebs. The others didn't hear me. I swallowed and tried again. "Look at her neck."

Tears streamed down Charlotte's cheeks as she uncurled herself and crawled over. "What is that?"

Kaitlyn lurched forward as her hands clutched her temples. "Did that bastard strangle her?" She shook her head. "Why would he strangle her when he carries a gun around all the time?"

I huffed a breath from my parched throat, a thousand scenarios swimming through my mind. "Maybe he didn't want us to hear the gunshot. Then we'd know it was him."

"I'm going to kill him." Kaitlyn kicked the nearest tree.

A vein pulsed down the center of Charlotte's forehead.

I wrung my hands and rocked side to side. "We need to call the police. We need to call 911 right now!"

"With what phone?" Charlotte bit her lip like she was trying not to cry again.

Kaitlyn stared in the opposite direction. "We could break into Travis's house. You said he wasn't there. Right, Charlotte?"

"Travis wasn't at his house because he was here, murdering Sam." I waved my hand toward our dead friend as another surge of hot emotion clogged my throat.

Charlotte clutched her head. "Kaitlyn, you want to break into the house of the guy who just murdered our friend? Yeah. That's really smart."

Kaitlyn scowled, her berry-stained lips turning thin and ugly. "Fuck you, Charlotte. None of this would have happened if it wasn't for you being so cheap. You couldn't spend an extra $200 dollars to stay somewhere decent?" She narrowed her jeweled eyes at Charlotte. "Well, this is what happens. *This* is the result. Great job."

Charlotte blinked rapidly. She covered her face with her hands, her shoulders shaking.

Kaitlyn lunged forward. "What were you doing in the woods, anyway?"

"Huh?" Charlotte dropped her hands from her face, her mouth hanging open.

"I saw something orange through the trees when I went down to the lake earlier. It was your shirt, wasn't it? What were you doing?"

"Nothing. I didn't do anything. I mean, I wandered around earlier looking for phone reception like everyone else, but I don't think I was even near here." Charlotte backed into a tree like cornered prey.

My heart splintered inside my hollow chest. I held up my hands, stepping between them. The therapist in me needed to take control and prevent the group from falling apart. "Kaitlyn.

Stop! You're out of line and not helping." Kaitlyn's angry words shocked me, but I knew she didn't mean them. People reacted to trauma in a variety of ways. Kaitlyn was merely displacing the blame she probably thought she deserved and shifting it to someone else. It was a common defense mechanism experienced by people who'd suffered a loss. I pulled a slow breath into my lungs, struggling for air. "Charlotte isn't responsible for this. I was over here earlier too. So was Jenna. We need to stick together. We're not breaking into Travis's house. We need to leave." The ground seemed to tilt beneath my feet, but I steadied myself. "Right now. Before he comes back." I turned toward the trail, ready to sprint as far away as possible. "Let's run to the camp. We can break into the office and call the police. I should have done that yesterday."

"What about Sam?" Kaitlyn's eyes had latched on to our friend's lifeless body. "We can't just leave her here."

Charlotte sniffled and motioned in the direction of the cabin. "And Jenna's waiting for us. We can't abandon her."

Terror ripped through me at the thought of Jenna sitting alone on the porch, her swollen ankle propped on a chair. My agitated state had jumbled my thoughts. Somehow, I'd forgotten all about Jenna. She wouldn't be expecting a surprise attack from Travis. She wouldn't be able to run from him. A wall of fear surrounded me. "Oh my God. She's all alone. What if Travis targets her next?"

"We'll have to come back later for Sam." Charlotte covered her mouth.

Kaitlyn's bony fingers grabbed my arm and squeezed. "We need to get back to Jenna."

We screamed Jenna's name as we raced toward her. My legs were shaky and unsteady beneath me, and a cramp stabbed at my side as I ran. I nearly collapsed with relief when I spotted Jenna lounging on the deck with her ankle propped up on a chair. She craned her neck toward us and set down a can of lemonade.

"What's going on?" My oblivious friend tilted her head and blinked.

A barrier broke inside me and a series of sobs flooded out. "We found Sam. He killed her," I cried between gulps of air.

"What? Why would you say that?" Jenna's eyes hardened as she looked at Charlotte and Kaitlyn who were both crying.

We climbed the stairs and surrounded Jenna. Kaitlyn placed her hand on Jenna's shoulder and sniffled. "It's true. Travis strangled Sam. She's dead. We need to get out of here."

"How? When?" Jenna buried her face in her hands. She stood up slowly, then sat down again, as if she didn't know what to do with her body.

Charlotte pointed toward the path. "Travis left her in the woods. There's a mark on her neck."

I gritted my teeth. "That piece of shit murdered Sam."

"Oh my God. Are you serious?"

Charlotte released a whimper.

"What is happening?" The muscles in Jenna's jaw pulsed as she slid back her chair, standing again. She picked up her can of lemonade and threw it at a tree. "What the fuck is wrong with this world?" she screamed, each word louder than the next. "WHAT THE FU—"

The fine hairs on my neck bristled, and I jumped toward her, cupping my hand around her mouth. "Quiet." My teeth clenched as I whispered the order into her ear, worried her screams were calling Travis directly toward us. Jenna's eyeballs bulged above my fingers, but her mouth closed. I lowered my hand. I pictured Sam lying in the woods. "We have to go back and get Sam. We can't leave her out there."

Jenna's breath seized as she pinched the bridge of her nose. "I want to go get her too, but maybe we shouldn't mess with the evidence. She's part of a crime scene now."

"What if Travis does something with the body when we leave." Charlotte paced back and forth, tugging at her braid. "We might never find her again."

We hovered in silence. Any move we made seemed to be the wrong one, as if booby traps loomed in every direction.

I raised my chin. "What if we wrapped Sam in a blanket and carried her to the minivan? We can hide her in the back and try to drive out again." My eyes flickered in the direction of the stranded vehicle. "It might work if a few of us push from the back. Once we get out of here, the police can tell us what to do."

Charlotte paced behind me. "Megan's right. Sam's family deserves to have her body returned."

"Oh, her poor boys," Kaitlyn said, fresh tears pooling in her eyes. "And Thomas. They'll be devastated."

I looked at my friends. Jenna bit her lip, Charlotte shifted her weight, and Kaitlyn nodded.

"Okay, yeah." All the color had drained from Jenna's face. "Screw the evidence. We don't have a ton of options."

"I'll get a blanket," I said, picturing the flowered polyester quilt from the twin bed in the upstairs bedroom.

I separated from the group, hiccupping as I forced my leaden feet up the stairs of the musty cabin. The faces of Sam's doting husband, Thomas, and the adoring eyes of her young boys, Leo and Brett, proudly displaying their Lego creations formed in my mind. Grief rose in me, but I pushed it back. *Don't think about it*, I told myself. *Not now.* The human mind had an unbelievable capacity to compartmentalize feelings. Someone had just murdered one of my closest friends in a hate crime, but I couldn't let anguish consume me now. Our lives were at risk. There was only one mission in front of me—getting the rest of us the hell out of here.

I yanked the quilt off the bed, Charlotte's sobs growing louder as I hurried downstairs. She was not compartmentalizing her emotions. She was falling apart.

"This is all my fault. All because I was trying to pinch a few pennies. Now Sam is dead because of this stupid place. Because of me." Charlotte's face crumpled as she spoke. Snot dripped from her nose.

I stepped toward her, laying down the quilt and hugging her. Charlotte's muscles quivered beneath my arms. "None of this is your fault," I said. "Kaitlyn was in shock. She didn't mean what she said. Every one of us agreed on renting this cabin. No one could have envisioned this outcome."

Charlotte gulped some air and wiped her nose with the back of her arm. I guided her over to a seat on one of the deck's metal chairs, where the others joined me in reassuring her.

Kaitlyn blinked her bleary eyes and touched Charlotte's arm. "I'm sorry, Charlotte. I shouldn't have said that to you before. I'm not thinking straight."

Charlotte nodded, her dazed stare holding on to Kaitlyn in a moment of forgiveness.

A few minutes later, Charlotte had collected herself and we decided to return the woods. I carried the quilt. Jenna limped along beside me, not speaking until she caught sight of Sam's body. She gasped as she covered her eyes with her hands to shield herself from the gruesome scene. Kaitlyn looped her arm around Jenna's shoulder to comfort her. I laid the blanket out next to Sam, not allowing myself to look at her lifeless face. Jenna and Kaitlyn stepped to the sides and grabbed the far corners. Amid sniffles and whimpers, the four of us shadowed each other as we moved around our friend's body, finding equidistant positions.

"Let's roll her over on the count of three," Jenna said without looking up. Her face was the color of ceiling paint and her lips turned down. "One, two, three."

I pulled Sam's limp arm over, pushing her shoulder as others struggled with her legs. She landed on the blanket. A leaf stuck to her hair and a twig clung to her shirt. Bile rose in my throat and I felt as if I might throw up. Just as I had the thought, Jenna lunged to the side and vomited beneath a tree. We waited for her as she coughed and spit. I averted my eyes, breathing in and out.

Grief pummeled each of us in turn, like a hurricane set on an unalterable path. Everything about the situation was surreal—the setting, the circumstances, and the agony. We sobbed and yelped and collapsed, all of us battered against the shore like wind-tossed boats. We did our best to comfort each other. As a therapist, I knew that grief wasn't linear; it surged and receded like a turbulent sea.

Finally, Jenna wiped the tears from her face and took charge. She wrapped the quilt tightly around Sam. "On the count of three, we'll lift her."

I stood across from Jenna, my insides hollow and shaky after the outpouring of emotion. Each of us positioned our hands under Sam's shoulders. Kaitlyn and Charlotte grasped the curves of Sam's legs and ankles through the blanket.

"One, two, three."

We heaved up Sam's dead weight. The bulk was awkward, and it took a few steps and several adjustments before we found the right position. Jenna winced and I wondered how much her ankle must be hurting. We moved Sam's body slowly but steadily toward the cabin, the threat of Travis's return lighting a fire under us.

We lowered Sam onto the dirt driveway when we reached the minivan. Charlotte's hands trembled as she opened the back and cleared a space. "We'll have to put our luggage under our feet." No one responded. Rearranging our luggage was the least of our concerns.

I helped hoist Sam's body into the back of the van, only vaguely aware of the hot tears streaming down my face. The door closed with a final click.

"Let's push this thing out of the pothole. Do you have the keys?" I looked at Charlotte, who felt her pocket and nodded. She climbed into the driver's seat. I motioned for Kaitlyn and Jenna to join me at the front of the van. The ignition turned and the motor hummed. "Put it in reverse," I yelled to Charlotte. "When I say 'go,' hit the accelerator, and we'll push."

Jenna and Kaitlyn braced themselves against the front of the minivan, knees bent and ready to push.

"Ready. Go!"

I strained against the metal so hard I thought my head would explode. Kaitlyn and Jenna grunted and pushed. Memories of survival stories of people facing imminent tragedies spun through my mind. Fueled by adrenaline and fear, these bystanders had suddenly found themselves infused with superhuman strength, able to flip over cars and trucks to rescue someone pinned underneath. I hoped the same phenomenon would happen here, but my weary body was no match for the stranded vehicle. The flat tires squealed, unable to spin themselves out of the pit. The minivan didn't budge. We repeated the process three more times, each effort unsuccessful. We switched to the back of the van and pushed forward. That didn't work either. The two flat tires and the pit were too much to overcome.

My toes dragged across the dirt and up the steps to the deck. I sat down, physically and emotionally drained. The others fell into their chairs and slumped forward, but we didn't have the luxury of waiting around.

Kaitlyn's mouth turned down. "How will we get out of here?"

I rested my elbows on the table and lowered my head into my hands. "Let's get some water and hike back to the camp. There might be a landline in the office."

"Are you sure?" Jenna asked.

"No, but I thought I remembered seeing a phone when I looked inside."

Charlotte bit her lip. "What if it's disconnected?"

I tipped my head toward the sky. "I don't know, Charlotte. It's worth a shot. It's better than asking the guy who killed our friend if we can use his phone to call for help." My voice had become frenzied.

Charlotte cowered away from me. "I guess."

I hadn't meant to yell, but the situation was desperate. I pressed the balls of my feet into the wooden deck and took a breath, remembering a professional seminar I'd attended a year and a half ago regarding how to help clients cope with trauma. Unfortunately, the course hadn't covered a situation like this, where the therapist herself had experienced the ordeal alongside her client. Still, I could recall useful bits and pieces—*Agony is temporary... A person's mood always returns to a baseline of normal... Loss is an expected part of life.* My job was to stay calm and separate myself from the situation, to keep my wits about me and my thoughts organized. I needed to offer hope and prevent my friends from falling apart so I could guide us all back to safety. My training had prepared me for dealing with catastrophes precisely like this.

"Megan's right. We should hike over to the camp phone," Kaitlyn said. "It's our best shot."

Charlotte looked at Jenna. "What about Jenna's ankle?"

"It doesn't matter anymore," Jenna said, shifting her leg. "We need to stay together."

I tipped my head back, relieved to have a viable plan.

Jenna peered toward the door to the cabin. "We should get our bags packed in the car and ready to go. That way, we can leave as soon as we find someone to replace the tires."

"They'll need to send a tow truck," Charlotte said, studying the minivan.

"Either way," Jenna said, "we'll be ready to get out of here as soon as help arrives."

Kaitlyn nodded. "Okay. Let's get our stuff. I'll gather Sam's things too."

We filed into the cabin, scattering like birds, and checking for any forgotten items, especially phones or purses. Grief filled my mouth as I joined Kaitlyn and forced my shaky hands to help pile Sam's belongings into her suitcase. When the upstairs was clear, I dropped the packed bags inside the kitchen door. The others languished near their suitcases. No one bothered to load up any of the food.

"Let's keep moving," I said, envisioning the long hike ahead of us. With my eyes stuck on the floor, I took a heavy step forward.

"Leaving so soon?"

A raspy voice cut through the subdued atmosphere. I spun toward its source as my heart reached into my throat. Travis rested his skeletal arm on the door frame, eyeing our packed luggage and blocking our escape route.

CHAPTER FIFTEEN

A dirty white T-shirt hung loosely from Travis's emaciated frame, untucked above his camouflage pants. A rifle dangled from a strap over his shoulder. Wherever he'd run off to after murdering Sam, he'd now returned.

I backed away from the menacing figure, glancing toward the tear-stained faces of my friends. Kaitlyn stepped toward me, fear flashing in the whites of her eyes. "He's going to kill us," she said in a voice barely above a whisper. Charlotte hugged her arms around herself and squeezed her eyelids closed.

My eyes darted around the kitchen. With as little movement as possible, I slid open the drawer behind me and located a butcher's knife, closing my fingers around the handle.

Travis moved toward us, his twitching body entering the kitchen. His ice-blue irises held the crazed stare of a killer. "You got a problem?" He squared his shoulders at Charlotte. "I got security cameras. Saw you at my door."

Charlotte shook her head but didn't speak.

"We needed to use your—" I began to say.

Before I could complete the thought, Jenna rushed from the living room. She raised an iron fire poker in the air, letting out a guttural scream as she swung it forward. The tip of the poker scraped across the ceiling. She lowered it and swung again, slamming it down on Travis's shaved head.

Travis toppled sideways, stunned. Blood glistened from his scalp, and he lifted his hand toward the gash. The gun slipped from his shoulder and dropped to the floor. Without thinking, I released the knife back into the drawer and rushed toward the rifle, snatching it up.

Travis moaned from the floor. His eyes flickered open. "What the—"

I pointed the gun at him, my heart thrumming against my ribcage. He was the one who'd extinguished Sam's bright smile and a lifetime of memories. He'd taken Sam from us, from her family. She'd never get to see her kids graduate from high school or college; she'd never help them plan their weddings or meet her grandkids. He'd snuffed out her education, knowledge, and compassion when he strangled her. He'd erased her accomplishments, destroyed the legacy of her business. All because she was born with more skin pigment than him. I hated him. I hated his ignorance. I cocked the gun.

"No, Megan. Don't." Kaitlyn lunged toward me, trying to pull the weapon from my hands. Charlotte moved in the corner of my eye too, but I couldn't focus on them. I was only looking at the disgusting man clutching his bloody head. Visions from years earlier surfaced in my mind—the other man in the mall who had blocked Sam's path and had practically accused her of not being American. I'd regretted staying silent back then. I should have joined Sam in standing up to him. I should have used my privilege to help her, but I'd only stood mute and dumb as she defended herself. I should have done a thousand other things since then. Now I had a chance to do something. My temples pulsed with pressure as the gun shook in my hands.

Jenna dropped the fire poker and it clattered against the floor. She pushed Kaitlyn away. "Do it, Megan," she said. "Kill the son of a bitch. Or I will."

"He murdered Sam," Charlotte said, standing like a statue. Her round eyes ricocheted between me and Jenna and Travis.

Travis's eyelids flickered as another moan oozed from his throat.

"No. Don't shoot, Megan. You don't want to live with that." Kaitlyn spoke quietly and widened her eyes as if she were talking to a child.

I swallowed, thinking twice about what I was about to do. My kids' pudgy faces and melodic giggles appeared before me like a vision—Marnie and Wyatt. They were my world, and I was their role model. I didn't want them to remember me as a murderer. I'd be no better than Travis if I pulled the trigger.

Kaitlyn inched closer to me and wrapped her slender fingers around mine, shaking her head slightly as if to say, "Please. Let it go."

Things were already bad. I didn't need to make them worse. I took a breath and exhaled, releasing my rage along with the air from my lungs. I lowered the weapon.

Just as I relaxed, Travis jerked forward. His eyes bulged and something resembling a growl unfurled from his mouth.

"Watch out!" Charlotte yelled.

Another wave of terror jolted through my veins. I yelped, raising the barrel of the gun in a knee-jerk reaction. Jenna and Charlotte lunged toward me, grasping for the gun. Kaitlyn was there too. Everyone grappled for the trigger. I wasn't sure if the others were trying to prevent me from shooting or struggling to defend themselves from Travis. It wasn't clear who squeezed. A grip tightened around my hand. The gun fired and its violent recoil threw us backward. The blast rang in my ears. The others stumbled away and my arm dropped to my side. I was the one left holding the gun.

"Oh shit!" Kaitlyn yelled.

Charlotte's hands clutched her head, horror stretching across her face. I looked up to see the cause of her reaction.

Travis's pale head slumped forward, hiding the knife tattoo on his neck. Blood seeped across his T-shirt. I hadn't meant to, but I'd shot him in the chest.

"Why did you shoot him?" Kaitlyn crouched down beside Travis as blood pooled on the floor.

Hot bile burned my throat. I raced toward the sink and vomited. My body couldn't contain the jumbled mix of emotions swelling inside me. I hated Travis, but I hadn't meant to shoot. I hadn't meant to kill. Someone had bumped my arm and squeezed my hand. It had happened so fast.

"It's okay, Megan. It was an accident." Kaitlyn crossed the room and rubbed my back.

Jenna huffed. "It was self-defense. Our lives were in danger. What were we supposed to do? Wait around for the neo-Nazi who killed our friend to murder the rest of us?"

Kaitlyn stood up and faced Jenna. "He didn't even have the gun after you hit him over the head! Megan had it. Now we'll never get any answers."

"The answer is obvious, don't you think?" Jenna leaned forward. "The only one of us who didn't have white skin was murdered in the woods. It just so happens this ex-con, neo-Nazi lived next door. There is no need to question anyone."

"Wow. Some attorney!" Kaitlyn said.

Jenna turned her back on Kaitlyn, looking from Charlotte to me. "We're going to say it was self-defense. The police will never doubt it as long as we all stick to the same story. This guy, who murdered our friend, barged into our cabin and pointed a gun at us. I whacked him over the head. Megan grabbed the gun. He lunged at us. Fearing for our lives, Megan shot him."

Kaitlyn jutted out her chin. "That's not what happened. I'm not going to lie."

Jenna tightened her fingers into fists, swinging her steely gaze toward Kaitlyn. "Are you serious? That's exactly what happened. Do you want to risk Megan going to jail over this?"

"Not Megan." Kaitlyn sucked in a breath. "You."

Jenna lifted her head. "What?"

"You were the one who tried to grab the gun, Jenna. You were afraid Megan was going to wimp out. Charlotte was grabbing for it, too, except she was trying to stop Megan from shooting. It was you. Or Charlotte. I'm not sure. One of you caused it to fire."

My body had gone numb, and I couldn't speak. I only stood in place, listening to my friends argue about the surreal events that had just unfolded.

Charlotte's mouth pulled down. "We were all struggling for it, Kaitlyn. It was an accident. No one is to blame."

"The only person we should blame is this piece of shit." Jenna motioned toward the dead man slumped against the kitchen wall. A crimson puddle had formed beneath him. Sweat reflected off his scalp, a sickly reminder of how recently he'd been alive.

My eyes darted away from the gruesome sight. I steadied myself against the counter. My thoughts were jumbled, my recollection of the shooting shifting like sand beneath the churning tide. "I need to leave. We all need to get out of here. Now."

"Are you going to the camp to call the police?" Charlotte asked.

I tightened my jaw. "Yes."

Jenna held up her hands and strode toward the doorway, blocking the opening the same way Travis had done moments earlier. "No one is going anywhere until we get our story straight. I'm not going to jail over this. I'm not losing my law degree. I'm sure we all feel the same way about our freedom and careers."

My kids' faces hovered before me, their laughter ringing in my ears. I thought about the years I'd spent in school to get my master's degree in psychology. All the training I'd done and the experience I'd gained over years of counseling clients at the clinic. Jenna was right. There was too much at risk.

"We should tell the truth," Kaitlyn said.

Jenna pressed her fingers into her temples. "We can't. This dirtbag was unarmed when we shot him. They won't consider it self-defense unless our lives were in danger. We need to bend the truth just a little bit."

Kaitlyn pressed her lips together. "I need some time. I can't think straight right now." Her eyes flickered toward the dead body. "Can we cover him up or something?"

"Maybe we can use Travis's landline now," Jenna said.

"What about that woman we saw?" I asked with a shaky voice. "She might live there, too. We don't want her asking questions."

"Oh no!" Charlotte's mouth fell open as she peered out the screen door. "What if she comes looking for him?"

My feet inched toward the puddle of blood. "Maybe we should hide his body. Move it down to the cellar or something?"

Kaitlyn shook her head. "Won't that make us look even more guilty?"

Jenna paced across the room. "Yeah. If our story is self-defense or an accident, we shouldn't hide him. It makes it look like we're covering something up." She inhaled and rolled her shoulders back. "Let's wait a minute and take a breath. We need to regroup. I'm completely overwhelmed right now." She motioned toward Travis. "At least the threat is gone for now."

Kaitlyn edged toward the doorway to the living room. "I'll get another quilt."

I gave her a nod. "Jenna's right. The immediate threat is gone. Let's think things through. Then we can make a plan to get out of here." My eyes found Kaitlyn. "We need to stick together."

Kaitlyn crossed her arms in front of her chest and looked at her feet.

"I agree," Charlotte said. She turned toward the stairs, and Kaitlyn followed behind her.

The walls of the small kitchen were closing in on me. My stomach turned every time I accidentally glanced toward the dead man. The image of Sam's lifeless body was etched in my mind. Now the feel of the trigger against my finger lingered, too. I wondered if I'd ever forget it. The air filled my throat like quicksand—an early indicator of a panic attack. "I'm going to sit by the lake for a couple of minutes," I said to Jenna. "I need some air."

"Mind if I join you?"

"Of course not," I said, although I craved a moment alone. I wanted to cry and breathe and focus on nothing but the sound of the water.

Relief loosened Jenna's features and I was glad I hadn't turned her away. She hobbled out the door next to me. We walked across the porch and on to a narrow dirt trail leading toward the lake below. The warm breeze against my cheeks felt refreshing, vital to my very survival. It had been difficult to breathe inside the dank cabin. I rubbed my fingers against my shirt as I followed the path, trying to erase the memory of the metal gun against my skin, of the sudden recoil against my torso when the shot rang out. Something in my brain wouldn't let me think about anything beyond that jerk of the gun. I witnessed the same phenomenon in my clients all the time. The mental blockage was a primal survival mechanism after experiencing trauma.

Leaves ruffled overhead, tinged with yellow and orange. The lapping waves lured me closer to the lake. I gripped my hand around a sapling to keep myself from sliding down the steep incline. I turned back toward Jenna. "Sit down here. It's steep. You can slide on your butt."

Jenna slid down after me. We trod through the sand and sat on the log near the water. Tears slid down my face, and I didn't make any effort to wipe them away. Now that I had a minute of quiet to reflect, the devastating truth hurtled into me like a rock flung from a slingshot. Sam—one of my best friends—was dead. I'd just shot a man. Now he was dead, too. It felt like the earth was falling away beneath me. I wanted to go home. I needed to hug Andrew and the kids, but they were unreachable.

I forced my heels into the rocky sand. The rippling waves sparkled under the sun. A group of seagulls flew near the surface and landed with a series of gentle splashes. The beautiful scenery didn't make sense. I wondered how something so dreadful could have happened here, how such a peaceful setting could be home to a loathsome person like Travis.

Jenna's sturdy arm looped around my body and pulled me into a hug. The tears flowed again. I looked up, finding that she was crying too.

"I'm sorry if I was the one who bumped your hand."

My shoulders caved. "I know."

"Poor Sam," she said. "How are we going to tell Thomas? Or her sweet kids?"

"I don't know." I blinked back the hot tears forming behind my eyes as I recalled the photo Sam had showed us the other night of Leo and Brett hiking up the mountain trail with their dad. She'd shown it to us right after "braggy time." Sam had always come up with funny phrases, ones that no one else used. Had that happened only two nights ago? It felt like two decades had passed.

Jenna picked up a stone and threw it into the water. "Remember the time Sam stole the neighbor's cat?"

I laughed through my watery eyes. "Yeah. We thought she adopted it from the Humane Society until we saw the 'Lost Cat' sign hanging on the tree out front."

"Didn't she name it Mr. Bojangles?"

"Yes. She did." I closed my eyes at the memory, savoring it.

"Remember how she wanted to start a cat rental business after she found out he belonged to someone else?"

"Yeah. She probably would have been successful at it, too."

Nestled shoulder to shoulder, we told stories about Sam and laughed through our tears. Finally, Jenna turned to me with solemn eyes.

"We need to get Kaitlyn on the same page. We didn't have a choice with that asshole. Travis's death was no one's fault but his."

I pushed my toe toward the water. "I think she'll come around."

"Hey guys. Let's talk up here. We need to keep moving."

We turned to find Charlotte standing at the top of the hill. Kaitlyn hovered behind her.

"Coming," Jenna said, raising her arm.

I supported Jenna's weight as we climbed the steep trail back to the porch. We found our seats. Sam's empty chair tore a hole through me, and I looked away.

Kaitlyn rubbed her forehead and sighed. "I've been thinking about it, and I'll agree with your story. It was self-defense. We were worried about our lives like you said." Her voice was flat, as if she was repeating words Charlotte had told her to say.

"It's important that we stick together," I said as my shoulders loosened.

Jenna nodded. "Good. Thanks. I know it seems hopeless right now, but we're going to make it through this."

"We should hike over to the camp now," I said. "We've already lost some daylight."

The others nodded, and I was thankful no one was suggesting breaking into Travis's house. We couldn't risk his girlfriend questioning us or finding his body.

Kaitlyn pushed a few foil-wrapped bars across the table. "Everyone grab a water bottle and a power bar. We need energy."

I had lost my appetite hours ago, but I took one anyway. Jenna swiped a bar, along with the bottle of ibuprofen. She popped another pill. We sat quietly for a minute.

"Let's go," I said, causing the others to push back their chairs.

As I stood, I gazed across the lake toward the abandoned beach. I told myself to focus on nothing but getting to the camp and making the phone call. But the more I struggled to ignore the images of Sam's body wrapped in a quilt in the back of Charlotte's minivan, or the bloody man slumped against the wall in the kitchen, the more the morbid visions wormed their way into my mind.

CHAPTER SIXTEEN

No one spoke for the first five minutes of the hike. The rubber soles of our shoes hit the earth, one after another. Air heaved in and out of my lungs in labored breaths. Camp Eventide loomed somewhere beyond the wall of trees and the winding paths. The landline phone I thought I'd glimpsed sitting on the desk inside the camp's office was our best chance to contact the outside world, our best chance to escape. If there was a phone there, the odds of someone having disconnected the line were probably at least fifty percent. According to the article Kaitlyn had read, Camp Eventide had shut down two or three months ago. Still, it was worth trying.

My stomach capsized as we approached the spot where we'd discovered Sam's body just a couple of hours before. Kaitlyn whimpered.

"It's okay," Jenna said. "Keep your eyes up and walk."

I followed her instructions, knowing she was correct. We had to compartmentalize our emotions if we wanted to make it to safety. I didn't allow myself to stare at the matted leaves or the puddle of vomit under the tree as we passed. My feet moved ahead on autopilot, one in front of the other. I kept my eyes on the trail. We had to get out of here.

Charlotte and I scurried ahead, walking side by side. When we were out of earshot of the others, I leaned toward her and whispered. "What did you say to Kaitlyn back there? She was quick to change her story."

Charlotte glanced at me but kept walking. "I reminded her of something she's always told us: sometimes it's better to be kind than to be right. Then, I reminded her of the car accident." Charlotte's eyes locked with mine. "I said we'd stolen enough from Jenna already. We didn't need to take her law degree too. Or her freedom, for that matter. After that, Kaitlyn stopped arguing."

I swallowed, tasting metal on my tongue. I wasn't the only one carrying the weight of that long-ago night on my shoulders.

*

"Who took my last Diet Coke?" I asked, peering into the barren fridge. It was late January of our junior year, and I was standing in the white kitchen of the house on 14th Street. Only a bottle of ketchup and a half-sandwich wrapped in foil languished on the frosty glass shelf. I didn't know who the sandwich belonged to, but it had been in the same spot for over a week.

Charlotte and Kaitlyn bantered behind me, joking about how they'd joined some other students in wrapping a blue-and-gold-striped scarf around the statue of Father Marquette as they walked home from their classes.

I turned toward them. "You realize he's made of stone, right?"

Kaitlyn gave me a playful nudge. "Oh, c'mon, Megan. Why are you so grumpy?"

"Someone drank my last Diet Coke. On top of that, we don't have any food in this house. Like, literally, nothing. We need to go to the store."

"She's right. I think we've put it off as long as possible." Charlotte nodded toward the stove. "I've been wanting to make my homemade spaghetti sauce."

Sam hurried down the stairs carrying a stack of books. She flopped them on the counter and sighed. "What's up?"

"We're going to the grocery store. I can drive us," I said.

Kaitlyn and I were the only two people in the house with cars. Leaving campus to go to a "real" grocery store was always considered a big outing. I tossed the forgotten sandwich in the garbage and closed the refrigerator door.

Kaitlyn pulled out a chair from the kitchen table, tossing her flowing locks behind her shoulder. "Jenna probably took your Diet Coke. You two are the only ones who drink it."

Sam made a face. "You shouldn't drink that stuff. It's all chemicals."

"No. It's good for you," I said, defending my favorite drink. "It doesn't have any calories. I can't believe Jenna took the last one."

"What did I do?" Jenna's voice bellowed from the living room. She stepped into the doorway, wearing athletic pants and a Marquette T-shirt, the same type worn by all the university's athletes. Tendrils of her dirty-blonde hair fell around her face, matted down with dried sweat. She'd already completed her nightly workout. Even though the soccer season had ended in November, she continued her exercise and practice sessions throughout the year.

Pete stepped behind her and offered a wave and a half-smile. "Hi ladies." He wore the same school-issued blue-and-gold athletic clothes as Jenna.

"Hey Pete." I raised my hand in a wave and refocused on Jenna. "My last can of Diet Coke mysteriously disappeared."

Jenna made a guilty face and shrugged. "Sorry. I needed my caffeine fix."

I forced a smile, secretly aggravated by her action. I'd been craving the cold bubbly liquid and the jolt of caffeine that came with it. I couldn't go a day without drinking it. The lack of caffeine was making me antsy. I pulled my car keys from the counter and jingled them in the air. "We're heading to the grocery store. We have no food. Come with us so we can stock up."

"Can't. I'm hanging with Pete tonight." Jenna gave her boyfriend a loving punch in his solid arm.

Pete grinned at us. "Order carry-out. That's what my roommates and I do when we run out of food."

"We've already done that three nights in a row," Sam said. "I need some fruit. Or anything that's not dripping in grease."

Charlotte opened a barren cupboard and frowned. "We don't even have any ramen."

"Can't you guys just pick up a few things for me?" Jenna asked, eyes pleading. "I'll pay you back."

I shook my head. "We shopped for you last time. Remember how long it took to figure out the receipt?"

"And you got mad at me for buying the wrong cereal," Kaitlyn said, frowning. "You can choose your own food tonight."

Jenna placed her hands on her hips and pinched her lips. She couldn't deny the issues she'd caused after our last shopping expedition when we returned with a few items she hadn't wanted.

"Come on, Jenna," Charlotte said. "Just ride along with us. Bring Pete, too."

Jenna shifted her feet and glanced toward Charlotte. "You wish."

We chuckled at Jenna's jab, but Charlotte only rolled her eyes. She'd learned to take our harassment in stride, maybe because she knew she deserved it.

Pete checked his watch, eyes darting away from us. "Nah. It's too cold out for me."

Through the window, the lights from the building next door illuminated falling snow.

Pete shoved his hands in his pockets. "You guys go to the store. Jenna, we'll hang out tomorrow night."

Jenna nodded, but her eyes pulled down. "Okay. I'll call you later."

Pete squeezed her around the waist and kissed her on the head. He zipped up his coat as he headed toward the front door.

I stepped next to Jenna and nudged her with my elbow. "Sorry if I ruined your plans, but we kind of need food."

"It's fine." Jenna grabbed her shoes. "Let's go."

We pulled on gloves and heavy coats as we exited through the door, shopping lists in hand. The frigid January air shocked my skin as we filed out of the warm kitchen, through the snow, and onto the driveway. My well-worn Honda Accord sat a few feet away, covered in a blanket of snow. The car had been a hand-me-down from my parents but was nothing short of luxury for a college student. Aside from gas and insurance, it was free, and that was good enough for me.

"I'll buy the veggies, and you buy the pasta and bread," Kaitlyn said to Charlotte as they negotiated splitting the ingredients for the spaghetti recipe.

"Jenna can sit in front because she doesn't want to go to the store." Kaitlyn pulled open the back door and slid into the middle seat.

"I don't think any of us want to go," I said, hiding the aggravation in my voice. It wasn't like anyone enjoyed grocery shopping. Jenna couldn't skip out every time. She acted so childishly sometimes, always so extreme in her emotions. She'd been a child actor before soccer had taken over her life and had never lost her flair for drama.

"I'll take what I can get." Jenna found her spot in the passenger seat.

I brushed the fresh layer of snow from my windshield and worked my way around the car.

My friends shivered as I started the ignition. I turned the heat on full blast, but my efforts to warm the interior failed. Freezing air blasted through the vents. Steam floated from my mouth as I backed out of the driveway.

Charlotte wiggled, struggling to adjust her seat belt.

I turned toward my passengers. "I guess it's a good thing Pete didn't come with us. We don't have enough seats."

Kaitlyn reached forward and touched Jenna's shoulder. "He seems like such a perfect guy, Jenna."

"He is. Don't tell him I said this, but…" Jenna paused, a dreamy smile spreading across her face, "I think he's the one."

I giggled, thankful for the sudden mood change. "Ooh! Jenna's in love," I said as I stopped at a frosty stop sign. In the back seat, Charlotte,

Kaitlyn, and Sam joined in with my playful chiding. There was no denying Jenna and Pete made a handsome couple.

"Imagine how good your kids will be at soccer," Sam said. "You'll have your own junior Olympic team."

My fingers fumbled with the temperature knob on the dashboard, turning up the fan.

"Why is it so cold?" Sam's teeth chattered from the back seat.

"How much would you pay to go on a tropical vacation right now?" Kaitlyn asked.

Chitchat about our hypothetical vacation destinations filled the car as I made my way down Kilbourn Avenue toward the two-lane highway that led to the grocery store several minutes away from campus. The night was black and my car beams lit the falling snow. The flakes landed on my windshield, dozens at a time, crystalizing against the glass as the wipers flattened them. My car's tires skidded through a turn onto a slick road. The snow thickened into a curtain. Visibility was poor, but that wasn't the type of thing that worried an indestructible twenty-year-old.

I approached an SUV covered in white and creeping along in front of us. The city had only plowed one lane of the road in the previous hours, and the slow vehicle blocked it. My speedometer read 25 mph.

"Ugh. We'll get to the store sometime next week at the rate we're going." I inched my car closer to the SUV, hoping the driver would get the message and speed up, but the SUV remained steady at 25 mph. "This guy is going like twenty miles under the speed limit."

Kaitlyn fiddled with her seat belt. "Can we get around him? I have so much reading to do tonight."

The snow fell harder, the flakes—almost as big as cotton balls— obscuring my line of sight. Still, I pressed my foot against the accelerator and swerved into the other lane as I sped around the creeping SUV. I didn't see a third car exiting the hidden driveway of a strip mall as I zoomed past. My foot slammed against the brakes, but it was too late in the wintery conditions. My battered Accord skidded and collided with the shadowy car that suddenly appeared in front of the windshield.

"Shit!" someone yelled in the second before impact. Metal scraped against metal. Glass shattered. An airbag inflated in front of me, the driver, but not for anyone else. That's how they'd designed cars back then, with only one airbag. The vehicle slammed to a halt, followed by a moment of stunned silence. The scent of burnt rubber and gasoline surrounded us.

Jenna screamed. "My leg! My leg!"

Jenna was sitting next to me, her face twisting in agony. The airbag suffocated me. I strained against the inflated bag toward her, but Jenna's right leg wasn't visible from the knee down. The car had crumpled around her, a metal monster consuming her limb. She wasn't faking any drama this time. She was trapped. I recognized the devastation in her eyes, the shrill terror in her voice; her injury was severe.

Black spots floated in front of my eyes. I looked down at my arms and legs, making sure they were still attached. Finding no marks on myself, I lifted my hand to help her, but I was unsure what to do.

"We've got you, Jenna." Sam's steady voice sounded from the back seat. I turned toward Sam, checking on her and the others. Shock stretched across their faces. A cut slashed across Charlotte's forehead and she cradled her head in her hands. Sam leaned forward and reached for Jenna, but her fingertips barely reached Jenna's slumped shoulder. Sam's skin was pasty in the dim light. Kaitlyn whimpered, her front teeth pinning down her lower lip.

"Ahhh!" Jenna screamed again.

A competing vision of Jenna tumbled through my dazed state— Jenna's muscled limbs sprinted across the soccer field on a brisk autumn afternoon. She waited for a pass, trapping the ball and swinging her foot back, shooting toward the corner of the goal. She raised her arms overhead, jumping up and down as we cheered in the stands at Valley Fields. Her triumphant teammates surrounded her.

Cold air speared through my lungs and snapped the memory from me. The chemical smell of the mangled car burned my nostrils. "Let's get her out of the car." I reached for the door handle.

"No!" Sam shook her head wildly. "We shouldn't move her."

"We need to call 911," Charlotte said. There was a cut on her forehead and a bead of blood dripped from it.

A knock rapped against my window and I jerked upright, my heart lurching into my throat. An older man in a thick black overcoat and a wool hat peered at us. He wore a dazed expression and, somehow, I knew he must have come from the other car. I opened my door.

"Everyone okay over here?" he asked, his worried eyes stopping on Jenna as she howled with pain.

"Our friend is injured."

"Oh boy." The man adjusted his hat. "Hold tight. I've already called 911. There's an ambulance on the way."

"Is everyone in your car okay?" I couldn't make eye contact as I asked the question. My teeth clenched, bracing myself for the answer.

"Yeah. My wife bumped her head, but she'll be fine. That SUV drove away like nothing happened." The man huffed and shook his head.

Guilt tunneled through me, my cheeks burning despite the frigid night. I squeezed Jenna's hand as she sobbed.

Minutes later, a siren blared in the distance, and an ambulance arrived. It took the EMTs several minutes to remove Jenna from the passenger seat, prying away pieces of metal and vinyl to free her leg. At last, they laid her on a stretcher and loaded her into the back of their vehicle. Another paramedic treated Charlotte's forehead on-site, affixing a bandage to the cut and assuring her that she didn't need stitches. Kaitlyn, Sam, and I were shaken but unharmed. A police officer arrived and took my information, offering us a ride to the hospital.

I hugged my arms around myself as the ambulance's flashing lights and whirring siren faded into the distance. My insides quivered, and the realization that the ordeal was only beginning tunneled through me. I feared for Jenna's leg, for the future of her soccer career. And I understood another crushing truth; the accident had been entirely my fault.

CHAPTER SEVENTEEN

It took another forty minutes of hiking and stopping while Jenna rested her ankle, but we eventually reached the bend in the trail where the path widened and led to camp property. I slapped a mosquito away from my arm. We traipsed past the trees and into the field, where the zip line loomed above us. The handlebars dangled near the far perch, directly above the spot where Jenna had fallen. It was impossible to believe her injury had happened only yesterday. It felt like years had passed since then. Sam had been with us, and now she wasn't. A hiccup formed in my throat.

Jenna grunted as we continued past the zip line and into the adjoining field with the archery targets. We kept walking, following the signs to the cabins. At last, the trail delivered us to the center of the camp. Six tiny bunk rooms stood in a line, watching over the main buildings. I picked up a jog, forgetting about Jenna's injury. The one-room building marked *Office* appeared in the distance. My feet moved faster.

I reached the camp's office before the others. Out of breath and cupping my hands to the side of my face, I peered through the window. Lightness flooded through me and I bounced on the balls of my feet. My vague and hopeful recollection had been correct. There was a phone sitting at the edge of a wooden desk. A curly cord extended from the receiver and plugged into the wall. I yanked on the door, but the metal handle stuck. It was locked.

Jenna leaned on Charlotte's shoulder as they hobbled closer. Kaitlyn reached me a few steps ahead of them, her face pink and slick with sweat.

"It's locked," I said loud enough for all of them to hear. I moved to the side of the door and jiggled the window. Someone had locked that, too.

Jenna removed her arm from Charlotte's shoulder and squinted into the sun. "We'll have to break the window. We need a rock."

We scattered in all directions, searching for a rock big enough to shatter the glass. I crouched near the perimeter of the building, finding nothing but pebbles and tall weeds.

"Got one!" Kaitlyn yelled. She heaved up a grapefruit-sized stone from the edge of an overgrown vegetable garden. She lumbered toward us, holding it with two hands. "Who wants to do it?"

Jenna lifted her hand. "I will."

Kaitlyn handed over the rock and waved the rest of us away. "Let's move back."

I stepped backward.

"Don't cut yourself, Jenna." I leaned to the side, hoping a broken window would be enough to gain entry.

"I won't." She stood a couple of feet from the window. She pressed her lips together and heaved the rock forward. I squinted as it crashed through and landed with a thud. I raised my eyelids and inched forward.

Charlotte frowned. "We have to push up the window and climb inside."

I looked from Jenna's ankle to the shattered window. "I'll do it." I reached through the opening, avoiding the shards, until my fingers found the metal latch. It took three tries, but I slid the lock to the side. "Okay. It's unlocked."

Kaitlyn stepped forward and we shoved up on opposite sides of the window. It slid open.

"Yes," Jenna said, a hint of a smile creeping onto her face. It was a small victory, but it was still a victory.

I motioned toward the open window. "Give me a boost."

Charlotte plucked a few loose shards of glass from the frame. Kaitlyn crouched next to me and laced her fingers together to form a step. "Put your foot in my hands, and I'll push you up."

I did as she said, reaching my arms through the window and pulling my body through. I balanced on my waist for a second then lifted my knee. With my other leg, I swung forward, toppling into the office.

"Are you okay?" Kaitlyn's voice was faint from outside.

"Yeah." I brushed pieces of glass from my shoe and leg. Somehow, I'd managed to land on my feet and knees. Other than a small cut on my forearm, I'd made it through unscathed. The air was hot and humid inside the enclosed space. My nose twitched at the musty smell. I unlocked the door and opened it for the others, who swarmed the desk.

My hand hovered over the phone. "Okay. Who should we call first?"

"Call 911," Jenna said. "We need to tell them what happened to Sam. And about the flat tires."

I lifted the phone. My hand hovered in the air as I anticipated the soothing sound of the dial tone. The connection was our lifeline. But when the receiver reached my ear, there was only silence. My chest heaved and I couldn't look at my friends. "It's not connected."

Jenna bent toward the outlet, unplugging the cord and plugging it back in. I held the receiver to my ear again, hitting the buttons, but the line was still dead.

"They must have canceled the phone service already," I said as my insides went numb.

Charlotte fell back against the log siding. Jenna scowled.

"Oh no." Kaitlyn leaned her weight against the door frame.

Charlotte stared toward the broken window, her cheeks flushed and full; her eyes were as glassy as the surface of the lake. "We walked all this way for nothing."

I kicked at the floor, swallowing back the sob expanding in my throat. "We had to try. We'll find another way."

"Hey, look." Jenna pointed to a door at the back of the office. A small placard hung from it: *First Aid.* Jenna hobbled over to the door, and I followed her through it.

The back room was the size of a large walk-in closet. A padded bench sat against the far wall. Most of the shelves were empty and covered with a dust layer, but three canvas storage bins remained. Jenna pulled two of them down. I grabbed the last one, finding a roll of white medical tape and dozens of Band-Aids.

"Look!" Jenna held up a beige bandage rolled into a neat ball.

I pointed to my bin. "There's tape in here."

Charlotte and Kaitlyn stood behind us now.

"I can bandage your ankle for you," Charlotte said.

"Okay. Thanks." Jenna sat on the bench and removed her shoe. She handed the supplies to Charlotte, who knelt in front of Jenna's ankle and began wrapping her foot.

"Wow, that's tight."

Soon, Charlotte taped the top of the bandage in place. "This should give you a lot more support."

Jenna stood and tested it out. "That's so much better. Thanks."

"At least we gained *something* from our trek." Sweat glistened across Charlotte's forehead, and I sensed her exhaustion. She'd probably walked at least fifteen miles today already, with all of the hikes she'd made back and forth to Travis's house in the morning, not to mention the emotional toll of Sam's murder and our shooting of Travis.

"Maybe we should dig through some other buildings." Kaitlyn drifted toward the door. "See if we find anything that can help us."

I nodded. "Yeah. We might as well, as long as we're here."

We wandered to the mess hall first, finding the doors locked. We peered in the darkened windows, where long wooden tables with benches sat empty. A sliver of a kitchen was visible through a doorway in the back.

"The camp's been closed for at least a couple of months," Kaitlyn said. "I'm sure they removed all the food."

Jenna made a face. "And if they didn't, we probably don't want to eat it."

We decided there was no point in breaking into the mess hall and moved over to the bluff overlooking the beach. Under different circumstances, it would have been a joyful scene. It was easy to envision kids in bathing suits clamoring down the uneven wooden steps and scrambling to jump in the water. I remembered the online photo of the colorful sailboat gliding across the glittering waves and realized the extent of Travis's false advertising. Only a desolate and foreboding vibe hung in the air.

Jenna, Charlotte, and Kaitlyn stood next to me with their eyes raised toward the lake.

"I don't see our cabin over there, do you?" Kaitlyn asked.

I peered across the water, struggling to catch a view of anything familiar, but the opposite shore was too far away. Nothing but the forest was visible on the other side.

Jenna shook her head, and Charlotte crossed her arms in front of herself. I turned on my heel and walked toward the arts and crafts building. Again, we took turns peering through hazy windows, finding empty tables and canisters of paintbrushes. The camp's owners must have cleared out everything else. We continued toward the far row of cabins. I tried the door on the first one, expecting it to be locked, but it swung open, revealing five sets of bunk beds with thin, dingy mattresses. I stepped inside and the others followed. The same oppressive air as the office surrounded me. An orange can of bug repellent lay in the corner. Otherwise, the cabin was empty. Someone had painted inspirational quotes in bright colors across the walls— *Be yourself. Everyone else is taken! You are special! Kindness matters! You are in charge of your destiny!*

Jenna blinked. "Wow. This is bright."

Kaitlyn made a face. "It's eerie, isn't it? Without any kids here."

"Yeah," Charlotte said, turning back toward the door.

We poked our heads into the remaining cabins, finding different inspirational quotes on every wall. The sleeping quarters were empty, except for the bunk beds. The camp had positioned a communal bathroom behind the cabins, but a metal padlock hung from the door.

Charlotte rested her hands on her hips. "Let's head back, guys. We need to come up with a new plan before it gets dark. Not to mention my feet are killing me."

I was about to agree when I noticed another path cutting through the trees. The route headed in the opposite direction, away from the lake. Overgrown limbs of a bush covered a wooden sign. I walked toward it and pulled away the branches to reveal the words: *Staff Quarters*.

"Wait." I lowered my chin toward Charlotte. "Let's go see this first. It will be quick." Curiosity drew me ahead even as guilt pulled at my gut. I knew Charlotte was exhausted, but the others stepped next to me along the trail, and Charlotte languished a few steps behind. A minute later, we rounded a bend and landed in a clearing filled with six more cabins. They were constructed in different configurations than the campers' bunk rooms. Each one had two entrances. One of the structures was larger than the others and sat further up the incline, but that wasn't what drew my eyes to it. That wasn't why I stopped short, my breath catching in my throat. I did a double take, confirming my eyes were not betraying me. A ribbon of yellow police tape encircled the cabin. It was a crime scene.

CHAPTER EIGHTEEN

A gust of wind chilled my skin, and the ground felt unsteady beneath me. I couldn't remove my eyes from the yellow tape as it fluttered in the wind.

Charlotte placed her hands on her hips as her mouth gaped open. "This must be where the counselor died."

"Oh my God." Kaitlyn covered her mouth. "She died here. In this cabin."

Jenna tilted her head toward the sky. "Just when I thought our weekend couldn't get anymore terrifying."

"If only the police were here now." My eyes searched the perimeter for any sign of movement. I hoped a cruiser with flashing lights would suddenly pull into the clearing. But only shadows stretched between the trees.

"That would be convenient. It looks like the police are long gone," Jenna said.

Charlotte hugged her arms around herself. "I don't feel good about this. We shouldn't be here. Can we please go back? I really can't handle anything else today." She motioned toward the cabins as tears streamed down her cheeks. "Plus, my feet are killing me."

"Charlotte's right." Jenna nodded toward the trail. "Let's head back. We shouldn't be messing around with a police investigation. Even an old one."

Kaitlyn tipped her head down and made the sign of the cross on her chest. "Lord, help us. This is too much."

I fought the urge to step across the police tape and investigate the cabin. Instead, I listened to my friends, hearing the anguish in their voices. We needed to head back to the rental and figure out a new plan for escaping to civilization. Besides, we'd already gotten some vigilante justice for the counselor if Travis had been the one who killed her.

Kaitlyn comforted Charlotte, who got her tears under control and hiked next to us. We retraced the path we'd taken earlier, passing the cabins, the mess hall, and more cabins. We cut through the zip-line area, archery field, and climbing wall until we were back on the narrow path through the woods. Hiking onward, I ducked and dodged through the gnarled branches that scraped against my arms and threatened to poke my eyeballs.

Jenna's ankle was sturdier with the bandage, and we only stopped once to rest. It was 5 p.m. by the time our decrepit cabin appeared through the trees on the hillside. Charlotte's red minivan drew my eye and I had to look away, knowing it doubled as Sam's coffin.

We collapsed into our usual chairs on the deck. My body was a shell of itself—the outside scraped and blistered, while the inside ached with sorrow and defeat. I balanced my elbows on the table, resting the weight of my pulsing head in my hands. I'd barely slept in two days. The only food and drink I'd consumed today was half of a muffin, a power bar, and some bad coffee. My throat was dry. I looked at my empty water bottle. Refilling it would mean entering the kitchen where I'd have to face Travis's body slumped against the wall in a bloody heap. I'd rather let myself be thirsty.

Kaitlyn pushed a lock of sweaty hair away from her eyes. "What are we going to do? What's the fastest way out of here?" Her voice cracked as she glanced around the table. A jagged scratch ran along her slender arm, no doubt a result of the thorny bushes and clawing trees we'd passed on the trail. The day's events had beaten her down, just like the rest of us.

"At least the immediate threat is gone." Jenna's eyes darted toward the kitchen. "Maybe we should try to rest tonight and hike out to the main road in the morning."

"Isn't it over twelve miles to the main road?" There was a hitch in Charlotte's voice like she might start crying again.

Kaitlyn nodded. "Something like that, but maybe we'll run into a car sooner."

Jenna rubbed her ankle. "Even with this bandage, I don't know if I can make it that many miles."

"Or we could use the landline in Travis's house." I crossed my arms in front of me, not believing the words coming out of my mouth. As much as I wanted to avoid any run-ins with the cabin owner's girlfriend, the thought of spending another night in this remote place made my stomach convulse. "We can knock on the front door first. If no one answers, we'll break in and call for help."

Jenna's shoulders straightened, a spark of hope igniting in her eyes. "Yeah. That's a good idea, Megan. We still have a few hours of daylight."

Charlotte leaned forward. "What about his truck? We should look for the keys. If we can't get to his phone, maybe we can drive to the police station."

Kaitlyn blinked. "Did anyone check his pockets?"

We glanced at each other, realizing how dumb we'd been to not think of that idea sooner. We scraped our chairs back and filed inside. Next to the kitchen wall, the quilt covered the nauseating lump of Travis's body. The tip of his hiking boot protruded from the covering. Splotches of crimson seeped through the blanket, adding grotesque blooms to the design. Jenna pressed her lips together and pulled back the cover, revealing the top of Travis's shaved head. Kaitlyn had returned the gun to his person, where it now lay diagonally across his lap.

Jenna looked at me, but I shook my head. "You do it."

Jenna inhaled a long breath as if she were about to dive to the bottom of a lake. She crouched down, her fingers poking into the pocket of the dead man's camouflage pants. She bit her lip and shook her head, hobbling over to the other side. Her face reddened as she held her breath. Again, Jenna reached her fingers into the pocket, feeling around. She stumbled away and shook her head.

"There's nothing in there."

I leaned my weight into the wall, pressing my forehead against the cold, flat surface. I wondered how many more blows we could take before completely giving up.

"Travis!" A woman's voice echoed from somewhere outside.

I froze, my heart reaching into my throat.

Jenna's eyes stretched wide. "Shit! It's his girlfriend. She's looking for him."

Kaitlyn covered her mouth with her hands. I grabbed a corner of the bloody blanket and threw it over the dead man.

Charlotte gently closed the sturdy wooden door behind the kitchen's screen door and waved us into the living room. "Hurry! We need to hide," she whispered.

We rushed into the darkened living room and crouched behind the couch.

"Travis!" the woman yelled, this time closer to us. I recognized her gravelly voice. Jenna was correct; she was the same woman who'd been at his house the day before. "You out here? You better not be standing me up again."

My heart pounded so violently I worried she might hear it.

Heavy footsteps sounded across the wooden planks of the deck. Four knocks cracked at the door leading to the kitchen.

Shit! Shit! Shit! Had I covered the whole body when I threw the blanket over him? Or was his foot visible, like it had been earlier? I couldn't remember. Regardless, the woman would see a bloody quilt draped over a human-like shape if she looked through the window.

More knocking. "Y'all in there?" Silence followed.

Kaitlyn perched on all fours next to me and stared at the floor. None of us breathed. My fingernails dug into my palms.

"Damn you, Travis," the woman muttered. At last, her footsteps crossed the deck, then faded.

Kaitlyn started to raise herself, but I held up my hand, signaling her to wait. We couldn't be too careful. Charlotte hugged her knees to her chest and hid her face. Jenna lay flat on her stomach and perched on her elbows. We looked at each other and waited. Five minutes passed. Then ten minutes.

"I think we can get up now," Jenna whispered. The rest of us nodded.

I stood slowly, peeking over the edge of the couch. I feared the woman would be standing in the window, waiting with a gun, and ready to get her revenge for the death of her lover. But no one was there. My lungs released a gulp of air.

Kaitlyn crept toward the kitchen and peered around the doorway. "I think we're clear."

"Holy shit. What else can happen to us?" Jenna paced around the room, removing her fabric headband and then sliding it back into place.

"I'm so tired," Charlotte said as she steadied herself against the couch. "And thirsty."

I sat next to her. "We're not safe. We need a plan to get out of here. Right now."

The four of us gathered around the couch, but no one spoke.

I picked at my fingernail, weighing our dwindling options. "I'll go scope out Travis's house."

"What about that woman?" Charlotte's nostrils flared as she faced me.

My body was rigid as I pictured the wild-eyed woman with the frayed hair. "I don't know. Maybe she'll realize Travis isn't around and leave."

Jenna frowned and shook her head. "I think she lives there."

"We don't know that for sure. Even if she lives with Travis, using that landline is our best shot at getting out of here tonight. Or at least by tomorrow morning."

Charlotte nodded. "We can all go."

"We'll have to stay hidden this time," Jenna said. "Remember, Travis saw Charlotte on his security cameras."

Kaitlyn scratched her forehead. "I mean, even if that woman is at the house, can't we just ask her to use the phone? It's not like she knows we shot her boyfriend."

Kaitlyn's idea made sense, but even the thought of speaking to the woman caused my insides to tremble. I shook my head. "We don't know how involved she is. It wouldn't surprise me if she helped Travis puncture our tires."

"Oh my gosh." Charlotte's lip quivered. "She probably knows Travis killed Sam. Megan's right. I bet she's been helping him."

The others looked at me, mouths falling open and eyelids twitching.

I continued, "What if she starts asking questions? None of us are great actresses."

Jenna jutted out her chin. "I'm pretty good. My rendition of Mary Poppins in my high school's production was second to none."

I stifled a smile, amazed Jenna had not yet lost her sense of humor.

Kaitlyn pinched her lips together. "This isn't a time for jokes, Jenna. Let's go and scope out the house. Then we can decide what to do."

"Yeah. Maybe she's not home," I said, hoping it was true.

Everyone agreed with the plan. We couldn't risk another nightfall without sending our SOS to someone in the outside world.

We waited inside the cabin for thirty minutes, hoping Travis's girlfriend would give up looking for him and leave the property altogether. After enough time had passed, we crept along the trail toward his house. I practiced a positive thinking technique I often suggested to clients—envisioning the outcome one wanted while simultaneously working toward the goal. I conjured up the image of Travis's vacant house, the front door unlocked. Jenna or Charlotte would slip inside and call the police while the rest of us hid in the bushes. We'd return to the cabin and wait for the comforting sight of spinning lights and patrol cars to whisk us away. The authorities would figure out how to get Sam's body back to her family. By this time tomorrow, I'd be back at home with Andrew and the kids, dealing with survivor's guilt and ready to re-evaluate my life.

I prowled along the narrow dirt road, my skin twitching with danger. After several minutes, Charlotte turned toward us and motioned for everyone to stop.

"Listen, there's a shed about fifty feet from the driveway with some big pine trees around it. I think we should hide behind the trees back there before getting any closer to the house."

Jenna nodded. "Yeah. We can see if anyone is home and come up with one of two plans. Either the woman is there, and I'll play dumb and ask her if I can make a phone call, or no one is home, and we'll break in and use the phone."

Both options terrified me, but none of us had a better idea, so we continued forward. Having already completed the trek so many times, Charlotte led the way. I brought up the back of the line, my heart pounding in my ears. A few minutes later, the path bent. Charlotte glanced over her shoulder, motioning toward the pine trees. I could see the outline of the shed through the branches. Up ahead, the run-down house sloped into a heap of white that reminded me of Travis's dead body. His pickup truck sat in the driveway.

Kaitlyn peered through the branches, standing on her tiptoes. "She's in there," she whispered.

Jenna closed her eyes. "Shit."

I edged next to them and looked for myself. Sure enough, the outline of a woman's head wavered in the front window as if she were standing at a sink, washing dishes.

Jenna sucked in a breath. "I guess I'll knock on the door and ask if I can use the phone."

"I'll do it, Jenna." Charlotte stepped forward. "It's my fault we're all here. It's my stupid minivan that has flat tires."

"No. It's my ankle that's keeping us trapped here. I'll go."

The rumble of a motor interrupted their debate. A familiar black pickup truck with a makeshift exhaust pipe protruding from the hood sped up the dirt driveway from the opposite direction, its sputtering engine polluting the tranquility of the forest.

My hands went limp. "Oh, great."

"It's the same guy who almost ran us off the road," Jenna said under her breath.

Charlotte glared at us, holding her finger to her lips. We bunched together behind the trees and watched as the truck lurched to a halt. A lanky guy dressed in head-to-toe camouflage jumped out, slamming the door behind him. He had shaved his black hair close to his head in a military-style crew cut, and his pale, veiny neck bore the same knife tattoo that Travis had inked across his skin—likely another symbol of their hateful group.

The front door of the house opened, and the woman we'd seen earlier stepped outside, squinting toward the trees.

"You seen Travis?" she asked.

The man rested his hand on his narrow hip. "No. Have you?"

"Nah. Piece of shit said he'd drive me home."

"It ain't like him," the man said, spitting on the ground. "Know where he went?"

"Don't know." She puckered her lips. "There might be a problem with the renters. They weren't around when I checked before."

"Let's have a look around. I'll get my gun."

My breath lodged in my throat, the words "*renters*" and "*gun*" sending lightning bolts through me. I turned to face Jenna, whose eyes practically popped from her head.

"Oh no," Kaitlyn whispered.

I envisioned Travis's bloody body slumped against the wall of the kitchen. His friends didn't seem like the type of people to forgive an accidental shooting. My feet felt like they were melting into the ground, my legs rubbery. "We have to move the body." My voice was so low even I could barely hear it.

Charlotte looked at me and swallowed, offering a slight nod.

We crouched low and skittered along the path back toward the cabin, knowing a few minutes' head start could mean the difference between life and death. As soon as we rounded the bend, we ran. I stayed next to Jenna, making sure she could keep up. Her stride was wild and lopsided, and she winced with each step, but she didn't slow us down. I remembered her comment after she fell from the zip line: "*Great. Now I have two bum legs.*" Adrenaline could do powerful things, but still, my chest swelled with admiration for her determination to battle through the pain. I gulped in oxygen and kept running. Fear prodded me forward, even when a cramp twisted at my side. I tried not to think of Travis's armed friends following a few steps behind.

By the time we reached the cabin, my jagged breath splintered from my lungs. Jenna lumbered ahead of me. Kaitlyn waved us into the kitchen, panting.

"Should we put him in the back with Sam?" Jenna motioned toward the minivan outside.

Kaitlyn shook her head, her cheeks flushed. "No. The cellar. Hurry." She lunged toward a tiny door with a wooden handle at the edge of the kitchen. The cupboard-like door was painted the same cream color as the wall and blended in. Kaitlyn's fingers grasped the knob and she yanked it open. Inside, a string hung from an exposed light bulb. She pulled it, illuminating the cramped space. "I looked in here yesterday. It's empty. Just a dirt floor and lots of spiderwebs."

I bent forward and peeked into the opening, finding a root cellar with a low ceiling. Cold, damp air seeped around my face. I stepped back, hugging my arms in front of me.

"Come on. Grab his legs." Jenna stood next to Travis, gripping one of his forearms. His head hung forward, and I was grateful not to have to see his face. Charlotte hovered opposite her. They had removed the bloody quilt and tossed it next to the wall. The rifle lay nearby. I stepped toward them and gripped the dead man's bony ankle as Kaitlyn took the other leg.

"One, two, three," Jenna said.

Sadly, we knew what to do because we'd followed the same routine to move Sam's body from the woods. Only, this time we couldn't lift the skinny man's dead weight. I wasn't sure if Travis was heavier than Sam, or if we were struggling because we were all physically drained and exhausted. We tried a second time, but only Jenna was successful in lifting a limb from the floor. Travis's body wouldn't budge.

"Drag him," I said.

Kaitlyn nodded. We pulled and strained as the body slid across the linoleum floor toward the cellar door. We lined him up, head-first, and shoved him through the opening. He fell three feet to the ground, landing with a nauseating thud.

Kaitlyn grabbed the quilt and threw it on top of him. Charlotte clicked the light bulb off and began to shut the door.

"What about the gun?" Jenna asked. "Should we keep it?"

"No." Panic flashed across Kaitlyn's face. "What if they see it? Then they'll know something's off."

Voices sounded from outside. They were faint, but we knew whose they were. I grabbed the gun and dropped it into the cellar. Charlotte closed the door and pulled a kitchen chair in front of it.

A man's voice reached us from somewhere down the road, followed by a woman's muffled response. We scattered around the room.

A puddle of smeared blood marred the floor. Another stain spread across the wall. Splatter fanned out above it. I grabbed a handful of paper towels and mopped up the areas that were still wet. Jenna retrieved a bottle of cleaner and a stack of rags from under the sink and sprayed the dried blood, scrubbing furiously. Everyone helped as we discarded the bloody towels and repeated the process. The voices outside grew louder. I shoved more dirty towels into the garbage bin. After a couple of minutes of frantic work, the floor was hazy but clean. All visible signs of Travis's death had disappeared.

Footsteps clomped across the porch. "Hello?" the woman said, followed by three knocks. The man grunted.

"Try to act casual," Jenna whispered. Sweat glistened from her upper lip.

Kaitlyn forced her mouth into a smile, even as her bloodshot eyes betrayed her. She stepped toward the door, grasping the handle and pulling it open. "Hi."

My eyes flew from the matted waves of Kaitlyn's wind-blown hair to a dark object on the floor. I blinked as panic exploded inside of me. My hand covered my lips to stop the scream from leaving my throat. In our haste, we'd missed a spot. Near the leg of the kitchen table, two crimson drops of blood glistened against the yellowed flooring.

CHAPTER NINETEEN

"Can I help you?" The metal spring creaked as Kaitlyn opened the kitchen door.

The woman cast a shadow through the opening. "Yeah. I'm Marlene and this here is Ed. My boyfriend, Travis, owns this cabin. He said he seen you ladies the other night." Her eyes buzzed around the kitchen like a fly. I prayed they didn't land on the floor.

Kaitlyn nodded. "Yep. We did meet him."

Marlene poked her finger through her crispy hair. "We can't find him. Thought you might know something."

I crossed the kitchen, my heart slamming against my ribcage with every beat. Charlotte rested against the counter in front of the sink. Her eyes followed mine toward the floor, her mouth dropping open when she realized what I was doing. I lowered my sneaker on top of the two drops of blood.

The woman peered over Kaitlyn's shoulder, eyeing the rest of us. "Any of you seen him around?"

I glanced toward the wall, hoping the dim kitchen would hide my fearful and guilty eyes. I refocused on Marlene's carved features and nest of bleached hair. I weighed her question, wondering if she knew about Sam's murder. Had she been involved in some way? Or had Travis kept quiet and acted on his own?

Jenna stepped next to Kaitlyn, stretching her shoulders back. "We saw him Thursday night. Right after we arrived. That was the only time."

Kaitlyn nodded. "Yeah. He stopped by when we were sitting out on the deck. He wanted to make sure we were settling in okay."

"That's the only time we saw him," Jenna said, repeating the lie.

"You ain't see him walk by or nothing?" Ed stretched his neck, peering past Jenna and Kaitlyn to look inside at Charlotte and me. "None o' ya?"

"No," Charlotte said.

I swallowed against my dry throat and shook my head. My foot pressed into the linoleum, hiding the evidence.

Kaitlyn smoothed back her hair with her free hand, exposing her bleary eyes and a pink nose. "To be honest, we haven't been inside the cabin the whole time. We've gone out on a few long hikes. He might have passed by when we were gone."

Marlene stared at Kaitlyn but didn't say anything. The woman's small eyes crawled around the room. She pointed at the ceiling. "What's that?"

I followed the direction of her finger up to the ceiling. My heart somersaulted. A black line screamed out from the white paint. It was the spot Jenna had scraped with the iron poker before she smashed it over Travis's head. We hadn't looked up since it happened. We hadn't noticed the mark.

"I don't know," Jenna said with a shrug. "We saw that when we got here. No worries, though. It doesn't bother us."

Jenna's acting experience was paying off. She lied like a champ, and I could have hugged her.

"Yeah. It's no problem," Charlotte added.

Marlene's features tightened as if she was working out a math problem in her head. She lowered her gaze and stepped back.

The man clutched his rifle. "I guess we'll keep lookin' for him."

Kaitlyn smiled. "I'm sure he'll turn up."

The man grunted and turned away, and the woman followed. I thought they were leaving, but Marlene flipped around and peeked through the doorway again. "Wasn't there five of you staying here?"

"Huh?" Kaitlyn said.

"Travis said there was five females renting this cabin, but I only see four. Where's the other one?" Her tone was challenging, and I couldn't tell if she was baiting us or merely searching for information.

Jenna waved toward the window. "Oh, yeah. Sam went for a hike. I'm sure she'll be back in a few minutes."

"Huh." Marlene kicked at something. "Is that right?" Her lips peeled back into a smile that sent a thousand spiders crawling up my spine. "Ask her if she's seen Travis. Will ya?"

I nodded, but my mouth had filled with cobwebs.

"Yes. We will." Jenna let the screen door slam shut.

We watched the woman turn away from us and follow her companion down the steps. They headed down the trail toward the lake as we perched in silence.

Kaitlyn placed her hands on her forehead and closed her eyes. "Oh my God. Do you think they knew we were lying?"

"No," Jenna said, shaking her head. "They have no reason to think that."

"Did you see the way they were looking at us?" I asked. "It's obvious we've all been crying. And that scrape." I motioned toward the ceiling. "How did we miss that?"

Charlotte raised her eyes toward the mark. "I don't know. It didn't seem like they knew anything about Travis *or* Sam."

My teeth clenched. "No, Charlotte. Did you hear what Marlene said when you said Sam would be back in a few minutes? *Is that right?*" I said, imitating the woman's sarcastic voice. "She knew something."

Kaitlyn tugged at the ends of her hair. "You're reading too much into it, Megan. I agree with Charlotte. I don't think they know anything."

"It was hard to tell." Jenna grasped her elbows. "They're definitely creepy, but I got the feeling they're clueless. At worst, they're just beginning to suspect something."

My palms were sweaty. I wiped them on my shirt, realizing my friends might be right. I tended to overanalyze the tones of people's voices and their facial expressions. It was an occupational hazard.

Charlotte hurried toward the window, peering out. "We should ask them to call roadside assistance for us. Before they leave."

"Won't they think it's odd we didn't mention it before?" Kaitlyn asked.

"They don't strike me as deep thinkers." I lifted my foot from the blood spatter and joined the others near the window. "And it's not like we have a lot of options."

Jenna touched her forehead. "What if they start checking out the minivan on their own? They might see Sam's body in the back."

"The back windows are tinted," I said. "And we wrapped Sam in a blanket."

"Whether we like it or not, those two people are our best shot of getting out of here right now." Charlotte stood on her tiptoes and looked outside. "They're about to turn down the trail toward the camp. I'll catch up with them and give them the card. We know they have access to a landline."

Nobody argued with Charlotte's plan. She rushed toward the door, but Jenna grabbed her arm. "Don't sneak up on them, Charlotte. That guy will shoot you."

Charlotte dug the card out of her pocket and held it in the air. "It's okay. I'll yell from a distance. I'll ask them to wait."

I edged toward her. "Do you want me to come with you?"

Charlotte waved me off. "No. It's fine. You can watch me from the deck."

I exhaled, relieved not to have to face them but scared for Charlotte.

Jenna stepped outside, opening the door for us. "Thanks, Charlotte. My ankle is wrecked."

We filed out onto the deck as Charlotte threw a nervous glance over her shoulder and clamored down the trail. I was happy to be out of the kitchen and into the fresh air. Still, I held my breath. Travis's friends were no longer in sight.

"Hey, Marlene!" Charlotte called as she made her way through the trees. "Marlene!" Charlotte had changed out of her orange shirt and now wore a moss-colored tank top that wasn't as easy to track through the green-brown forest. When she reached the bottom of the incline, she looked up at us. "They went this way," she said, pointing toward the trail that veered to the left.

I stood and gave her a wave. She followed the bend in the trail, her body blending into the trees. My fingers tightened around the wooden porch railing as I lost sight of her. Crooked Lake stretched beyond the trees, its opaque surface undulating like a mouth waiting to swallow us.

"I can't see her," Kaitlyn said.

I held up my hand. "Shh! Wait."

Voices murmured through the leaves.

"Charlotte's talking to them."

Marlene's gravelly voice sounded through the lapping waves, followed by a man's mumbling.

"Okay. Thanks." It was Charlotte's voice, and I could barely make out her words. She wasn't visible, but the upswing in her statement sent a ripple of hope through me. Seconds later, she emerged onto the trail below us, her step carrying a bounce that hadn't been there a few minutes ago. She gave a thumbs up and a nod.

I let my weary body collapse into the chair behind me. Was it possible our nightmare was finally coming to an end? What were the odds that those two misfits would be the ones to rescue us? As long as they didn't find out what we'd done to Travis, this could work.

Charlotte's breath heaved as she trudged closer. "I gave them the card. They said they'd make the call for us when they got back to the house."

Kaitlyn flopped her head forward on the table. "Oh, thank God!"

"Did they ask anymore questions about Travis?" Jenna paced along the railing, eyes flickering toward the lake.

Charlotte's face brightened. "No questions asked."

I slapped my hand on the table. "Good job, Charlotte. We'll be out of here soon."

Kaitlyn leaned forward, a spark in her eyes. "It's possible a tow truck could get here tonight."

"It's already seven o'clock," Jenna said, checking her watch. "Do you think they'd go out that late?"

"The card said twenty-four-hour service."

"What should we tell the driver?" Kaitlyn asked.

I looked at her, my muscles constricting at the thought of being left here again. "We need to ride out with him. All of us. We'll call 911 as soon as we have cell-phone reception."

Jenna fell into a chair across from me. Her eyes traveled around the table and landed on each of us in turn. "There's going to be no mention of Travis until we get to the police station. Understand? Then we all remember the story, right? We didn't have a choice. It was self-defense."

Charlotte frowned. "But now we've moved his body."

"We can tell the truth about that," I said. "We were scared of how armed members of a hate group would react to finding their friend's dead body in our kitchen. Any reasonable person would have acted the same way we did."

Everyone mumbled agreement and nodded. Not knowing how long we'd be waiting for roadside assistance to arrive, we decided to put together something to eat. We were dehydrated and hungry. Thankfully, Kaitlyn had brought enough groceries to feed a small army.

Twenty minutes later, we'd returned to our seats on the porch, picking at an assortment of cheese and crackers, strawberries, raw vegetables, and tortilla chips with guacamole. A glass of water and a glass of wine sat in front of each person. Our empty wine bottles from the night before lined the wall next to the door.

"My feet are killing me," Charlotte said. "I wonder how many miles I walked today."

"At least ten or fifteen," I said, thinking of all the hikes she'd made back and forth to Travis's house this morning, not to mention the long treks that followed.

"If nothing else, maybe I burned some calories." Charlotte lowered her gaze to her midsection.

My half-chewed food sat in my mouth. I wondered how Charlotte could worry about her physique at a time like this when she should have been grateful just to be alive.

Kaitlyn scoffed. "Stop putting yourself down, Charlotte. We're too old for that bullshit. We're beautiful just the way we are. All of us."

Charlotte raised her eyes. "Easy for you to say, Nicole Kidman."

My disgust at Charlotte's previous concern faded, and I smiled at her jab. Kaitlyn had always stolen the show as far as guys were concerned. There wasn't a single party or bar we'd ever entered with her where at least one eager young suitor would ask her if anyone ever told her she looked like Nicole Kidman. As the rest of us rolled our eyes, Kaitlyn would flash a bashful smile in response and say it was the first time anyone had ever told her that.

I bit into another chip as my eyes gravitated toward the empty chair—the one where Sam had been sitting less than forty-eight hours ago. I felt someone staring and looked up.

"It's surreal without Sam here, isn't it?" Jenna pulled her eyes from me and lifted her wine. "It doesn't seem possible that she's gone." She sniffled and rubbed the back of her sleeve across her eyes.

The weight of my grief expanded in my chest. "I miss her so much."

Kaitlyn massaged her temples, water pooling i
her eyes. "It's going to be so horrible when Thoma
find out. I can't even let myself think about it."

"I know." I envisioned the heart-wrenching tears oi
who'd lost his soulmate, and the sobs of children who'd
mother. There'd be funeral arrangements and counseli
nannies and maybe even a stepmother in their future. Bu.
now, they were blissfully unaware. Hot tears built behind
eyes again, and I couldn't blink them back. The wine was mak
everything worse, yet it dulled the edges of my pain. I poure
myself another glass but stopped halfway. There would be plenty
of time to mourn for Sam and her family once the rest of us were
safe. I needed to keep my head clear and make sure my family
didn't have to endure a similar tragedy.

"Do you think Marlene and Ed called for help yet?" Kaitlyn's
head rotated toward the minivan.

Jenna surveyed the trees. "I didn't see them pass by here again,
but I'm sure they know a different route back."

We waited on the deck, listening for any sign of an incoming
tow truck—tires cracking along the gravel or the murmur of an
engine. Instead, we heard only the steady lull of the water lapping
against the rocky shoreline, the drawn-out chirps of crickets, and
the occasional cackles of crows. Dusk fell around us and bats
flitted overhead as the sky turned the color of gunpowder. Our
conversation turned back to Sam. We took turns sharing our
favorite memories, remembering her kindness and humor, her
down-to-earth view of the world, her silly, made-up phrases, and
her decision to see the best in others. I silently forgave her for
making me keep the secret about Jenna's broken mug all those
years ago. I no longer cared whether she'd shattered it by accident
or on purpose. We had all done things we regretted.

I told the others how I was awestruck by Sam's ability to build
MedTech—a multimillion-dollar corporation—from the ground

And it wasn't just any company that she'd created. It was
e that helped people. She had saved countless lives by making
escription drugs available to those who couldn't otherwise afford
1em. We remembered how happy she'd been at her wedding, how
:cstatic she'd been to become a mother. The laughter and tears
morphed into each other, as fluid and natural as a lake freezing
and thawing. When the memories finally ran out, my insides
ached, empty and raw.

I got up to use the bathroom, realizing I could barely see my
feet. The night had turned black. "What time is it?" I asked.

Jenna lifted her wrist toward the light of the flickering candle.
"Almost ten thirty. I hate to say it, but I don't know if the tow
truck is coming tonight."

"We don't know what time they called." Charlotte's eyelashes
lowered. "Maybe help will arrive in the morning."

"Are you sure they promised to call?" I asked.

"Yeah," Charlotte said, her eyes round and unblinking. "They
said they would do it as soon as they could."

Kaitlyn tipped her head back, her wavy hair hanging behind
her. "I'm so tired, guys. How about I sleep on the couch tonight?
I'm a light sleeper. If the tow truck arrives in the middle of the
night, I'll hear it and wake everyone up."

"Thanks Kaitlyn," I said. "I guess the truck could still show
up tonight."

Everyone stood and gathered their glasses and paper plates. I
placed another empty wine bottle near the door as we filed into the
kitchen to throw away plates and napkins. My eyes darted toward
the tiny door in the wall, and I noticed the others eyeing it too.

Kaitlyn motioned toward the cellar. "How long do you think
we have until... you know?"

"What?" I asked.

"The smell," her feet shuffled sideways, "of the dead bodies."

I pinched my lips together. I'd been wondering the same thing.

"It takes three days for putrefaction to set in," Charlotte said matter-of-factly. She raised her chin when she noticed us staring at her. "It's one of the things you learn as a pre-med student."

Jenna pulled at the ends of her chin-length hair. "It's only been a day. We'll get out of here before then."

"Yeah," I said, my molars grinding together. We had to get out of here before then.

Several minutes later, I was lying in the twin bed across from Charlotte, hugging the musty pillow to my cheek. A sheet and a thin blanket were draped over me, but I was cold without the quilt. Charlotte shifted on her mattress. Her quilt was missing too. I squeezed my eyelids closed, not letting myself envision the current locations of the bedspreads. Of course, the more I tried not to think about the flowered quilts wrapped around the dead bodies, the more vividly the images etched themselves into my mind.

I rolled to my other side but couldn't calm myself. Exhaustion consumed me. My eyelids hung heavy, and my muscles ached with weariness. My head was hazy with grief and alcohol. Still, dread trickled through my veins, keeping me awake. Even though I'd used the bathroom less than twenty minutes ago, that second glass of wine was hitting me. I couldn't ignore the acid in my stomach and the growing pressure in my bladder. Charlotte's breath sounded evenly from across the room. She was already asleep.

I slipped from the covers and tiptoed down the dark hall to the bathroom, returning a minute later, relieved. The door creaked as I closed it behind me and climbed under the cold sheets again. My stomach churned. Charlotte's breath puffed in and out. I wished I'd thought to bring earplugs. I told myself roadside assistance would arrive in the morning—or maybe even tonight—but something deep within me felt hollow and hopeless. I feared the worst. It was possible Marlene and Ed had lied to Charlotte about making the phone call. What if my initial assessment had been correct—that they either knew Travis had murdered Sam, or they suspected we'd done something to Travis? What if they were the ones who'd helped Travis slash the tires and kill Sam in the first place?

I shivered and told myself to shut up. My mind was spiraling downward without any proof to backup my paranoia. Few things could comfort me now. I imagined Andrew lying next to me, his sturdy arm holding me close, the heat of his body warming me. But my legs kicked back and forth under the scratchy sheets. The vision didn't soothe me the way I'd hoped it would. Andrew didn't know I'd cheated on him. He would hate me if he knew. There was a space between us filled with lies and guilt, and I couldn't find a way to bridge the gap. Maybe this weekend was karma returning for me, the universe making me pay for my sin. I could almost see a giant finger reaching down from the sky and wagging at me, saying, "You didn't appreciate what you had, Megan. Maybe now you will."

Still, out of exhaustion and desperation, I leaned into my betrayal. Andrew's face blurred and dissolved until it transformed into someone else. My husband became the other man, the one I'd been sneaking off to meet at hotels and restaurants and the back seats of cars. As much as I didn't want it to be, it was his flexed arm I felt around me, his oaky aftershave I smelled, his lips brushing against my earlobe and whispering, "Everything's going to be okay." My head sunk into the pillow. Before I knew it, I was asleep.

CHAPTER TWENTY

I woke early, the morning sun prodding my eyelids open. A yawn forced its way out of my mouth. I sat up, finding Charlotte still sleeping in the other twin bed. My eyes squinted toward the brightening sky and then toward my useless phone charging on the nightstand. I angled the screen toward me—7:08 a.m. The wine had knocked me out and I'd slept through the night. But the realization was bittersweet because Kaitlyn hadn't woken us up. That meant the tow truck had not arrived to rescue us.

Charlotte turned over and rubbed the weariness from her eyes. Her brunette hair sat tangled on her shoulders and poofed up on one side. "Hi."

"I finally got some sleep," I said. "The wine hit me hard."

"Yeah. Me too. I was so exhausted."

"I guess the tow truck didn't show up." I pulled on a sweatshirt over my T-shirt and pajama bottoms.

Charlotte swung her feet off the edge of the bed, her mouth turning down in the corners. "I don't get what's taking so long."

"Maybe the roadside assistance place isn't really open twenty-four hours. I bet they'll show up this morning." Even as I said the words, panic tunneled through me.

"Yeah," Charlotte said, her voice flat.

Water splashed in the sink down the hall. I shoved my feet into my flip-flops and wandered into the hallway, finding the bathroom door ajar. Jenna turned off the faucet, then patted her face with a towel. She limped toward us, raising her hand in a half-hearted wave. Purplish bags were visible beneath her sunken eyes. "I guess we didn't get rescued last night."

I sighed. "That's what we just realized. Did you get any sleep?"

"It wasn't the greatest. I'm so tired." Jenna tipped her head toward the stairway. "Should we let Kaitlyn sleep or go make some horrible coffee?"

"Coffee."

Charlotte nodded. "Yeah. Coffee."

Jenna led the way downstairs, favoring the leg without the ankle bandage. She wore running shorts and a turquoise athletic top. Jenna stopped short and I bumped into her.

"Sorry," I said, following her gaze toward the couch, which lay empty. Only a dingy blanket and a pillow rested on top of the cushions. I could see partway into the kitchen at the bottom of the stairs, but there was no rustling of grocery bags or opening and closing of cupboards like I'd heard the previous mornings.

"Kaitlyn?"

There was no reply.

"Where is she?" Jenna asked.

My eyes flickered toward the window, my chest lightening with hope. "She might be outside. Maybe the tow truck is finally here."

We followed Jenna as she double-timed it down the steps, through the kitchen, and onto the deck. But my shoulders sank as I stepped into the chilly morning air. The red minivan remained in the same spot on the dirt driveway, melting into its deflated front tires. There was no tow truck.

"Oh man." Charlotte dropped her head into her hands and let out a shriek. "That's what I get for getting my hopes up."

Jenna looked at her fingernail, then down the dirt driveway. "Do you think she went with them?"

Charlotte narrowed her eyes. "Marlene and Ed?"

"No. The roadside assistance people. Maybe they drove a car or a van instead of a tow truck. Kaitlyn probably didn't want to wake us up. Maybe she went with them so she could call the police and rescue us."

I shifted my weight to my other foot. "I don't think she'd leave without telling us."

"Yeah," Jenna said, her hands dropping to her sides.

"I'll check the house again. Maybe she's in the downstairs bathroom." Charlotte turned toward the door.

Fear gripped my throat and I couldn't respond. My spine went rigid as I scanned the trees for any sign of Kaitlyn's auburn hair and slender frame. I listened for any sound of her sing-song voice. I tried to remember what she'd been wearing when she went to bed but couldn't. I cupped my hands to my mouth and yelled over the railing. "Kaitlyn!"

Only birds chirped in response.

"She wouldn't have walked over to Travis's house on her own, would she?" Jenna bit her lip. Creases of worry formed across her forehead as she gazed down the narrow dirt road.

"No. Kaitlyn wouldn't be that stupid. With everything that's happened, she wouldn't go anywhere without telling us first. Especially to Travis's house."

Jenna rubbed her forehead. Her usually vibrant skin was dry and leathery, her hair uncombed and stringy. I touched my face, realizing I probably looked even worse. I paced across the deck, hoping Charlotte would pop her head through the door and tell us Kaitlyn had been inside the house all along. Instead, the door creaked open and Charlotte edged her way into the gap, alone. "Kaitlyn's not in here." Charlotte waited, but we didn't respond.

A nagging in my gut told me something wasn't right. My eyes searched through the trees and drifted over the smooth water. The lake had transformed again—a deep-blue mirror reflecting in the morning sun. My vision snagged on an imperfection in the glassy surface. I leaned against the railing, letting the length of wood press into my ribs. A log floated near the shore, but the trees obscured my view. I stepped to the side, noting a curved object rising from the flat surface. It wasn't a log. There was something animal-like about the mass. I wondered if Ed and Marlene were so deranged that they would shoot a deer and throw it into the lake just to scare us. I stretched my neck to the side, getting a clear view around a tree. An auburn tendril floated on the water like seaweed, something pale and slender bobbing next to it. My heart pounded, and my blood rushed through my veins, threatening to burst through the vessels.

"Oh no." My teeth clicked as my mind caught up to my internal alarm.

Jenna looked at me, then followed my line of vision toward the lake. She yelped, throwing her hands over her mouth.

I jumped off the deck and stumbled down the hill toward the rocky beach, feeling like I was going to throw up. The metal door slammed shut from the kitchen, and footsteps rushed behind me. I didn't turn back. My legs spun faster, even as my limbs went numb and black spots danced before my eyes.

"Please, no! Please, no!" As I neared the water's edge, my feet stepped onto rocks and plunged into the frigid liquid. My stomach turned inside out. It was Kaitlyn. Her hair fanned out across the bobbing waves. Her willowy body floated face down on the surface. A sob heaved from my chest, echoing across the lake. "Who did this?" I screamed.

Jenna and Charlotte were next to me, up to their knees in the water. They were sobbing and screaming, too. My ears throbbed as my blood pulsed inside my head.

We splashed through the water toward her. I grabbed Kaitlyn's shoulders and with the help of Jenna and Charlotte, we flipped her over. I stumbled backward at the sight of Kaitlyn's face. Her mouth was open as if she'd been screaming underwater or struggling for breath. Her eyeballs bulged, staring upward at nothing.

"Oh, God." Jenna turned away at the gruesome sight.

Charlotte whimpered and hid her face in the crook of her elbow, shoulders shaking.

"Let's drag her to shore and do CPR." I hooked my hands under Kaitlyn's armpits and pulled, splashing backward through the water. My foot hit a rock and I fell back with a splash. I struggled to my feet and kept tugging.

Jenna covered her mouth with her hand and shook her head. "We're too late."

Charlotte lowered her eyelashes and nodded. "Jenna's right. It won't do any good."

I ignored them. I hadn't even had time to process Sam's death yet. I refused to believe another of my friends was dead. I pulled her onto the rugged shore, desperate for a miracle. A purplish line encircled her neck, similar to the mark we'd found on Sam's neck. I felt for a pulse, but only cold skin met my fingertips. My body doubled over, my head falling onto Kaitlyn's silent chest. Charlotte's hand pressed against my back as I cried.

Jenna kicked a stone, her facing twisting in disgust. She jutted out her chin and stared up the hill and into the woods. "Those fucking bastards. Marlene and Ed never called for help. *They* did this!"

Charlotte chewed on her lip, making no effort to stop the tears streaming down her face. "They lied to me. They must have figured out we killed Travis. I'm so stupid."

I fell back on my butt, jagged rocks poking through my thin pajama bottoms. "Marlene must have seen the blood on the floor. She knew we made that mark on the ceiling."

Jenna stared across the lake. "Wouldn't they call the police if they suspected us?"

"Travis must have told them what he did to Sam," Charlotte said, her face crumpling.

"I bet they helped him kill her. Kaitlyn has the same mark on her neck." I spat the words from my mouth.

Charlotte's eyes widened. "They probably assumed we got back at Travis after he murdered our friend. Of course, Ed and Marlene wouldn't call the police because it would expose their hate crime."

"Oh my God. You're right," Jenna said. "They're out for revenge."

I released my grip on Kaitlyn's limp hand, trying not to think about her girls and her husband and her parents. Kaitlyn was one of the good ones. She'd lived a charmed life in her upscale suburb, more than comfortable in her luxury home inside her gated community. Life had come easily for her. Kaitlyn had never wanted for anything—not looks, or friends, or money, or a devoted husband, or loving children. An outsider might have been jealous, but I knew her better than that. She'd never taken her good fortune for granted. She'd known how lucky she was. Many women in her position hid behind their privilege, safeguarding their lifestyle at the expense of others. Not Kaitlyn. She had made it her life's mission not to forget her obligation to her community. She went out of her way to serve others because she could and because it was the right thing to do. She'd gladly skipped dinners at the country club in favor of distributing food at the soup kitchen or accompanying a recent immigrant to the Secretary of State to fill out his paperwork or organizing the fundraisers for her kids' schools. She had witnessed people in the most desperate of situations, yet she always offered them hope. She was one in a million, and now she was dead.

"Why Kaitlyn?" I asked, my voice breaking.

Jenna huffed. "Probably because she was sleeping on the couch. She was the first one they saw."

"Or maybe they knew about her charity work helping immigrants," Charlotte said. "That would piss them off."

I placed my palm on the sand, steadying myself. "How would Marlene and Ed know about Kaitlyn's charity work?"

"I don't know. We emailed Travis our names. He could have googled us before we got here."

"Oh no." Jenna's eyes flickered. "What if they know about my Jewish heritage?"

"You guys. Stop!" I leaned forward, clutching my head. "Those two idiots aren't doing any research on us. I bet they barely know how to read. They're probably picking off whoever is the easiest target."

Jenna glanced at her ankle before her eyes darted toward the woods again. "Great. So I'm next, either way."

"No," I said, raising myself off the sand. "We're not going to let that happen. We need to get out of here before anyone else dies."

Charlotte pushed a damp clump of hair away from her face, then straightened her shoulders. "Let's hike out along the road. It's over fifteen miles to the town, but only twelve or so to the main road. We'll probably spot a car before then."

Jenna's shoulders slumped. "There's no way I can go that far on my ankle. You guys can leave without me." She motioned toward the cabin. "I'll hide in a closet or something."

I stepped toward her. "No. We shouldn't split up. And no one's staying in this murder cabin alone."

Jenna pointed to my foot. "You're bleeding."

I slid my foot from my flip-flop, noticing a line of blood stretching from my big toe to my ankle. Something had sliced my skin and I hadn't even noticed. I had the sensation that someone else was occupying my body.

Jenna frowned. "Did that just happen?"

"I guess." I looked away, suddenly noticing the line of pain stinging across the top of my foot. My cut only needed a Band-Aid or two. It was nothing compared to what had happened to Kaitlyn and Sam.

Jenna stared at the fresh cut. "You might have to hike out on your own, Charlotte."

Charlotte's dark eyes hardened above her round cheeks. "I can do it. You guys can stay here together with Travis's rifle. I'll send help as soon as I can."

"What if Marlene and Ed are hiding out there, waiting for you?" I asked. "I mean, isn't it obvious we would walk along the road to get help?"

Charlotte scowled and rubbed her temples. "I don't know. We're running out of options, especially now that both of you are injured. I'm not going to sit around and watch us all get killed."

I blinked, considering Charlotte's plan. I looked at Jenna's hunched shoulders and then toward the stinging gash on my foot. It was risky to separate, but the payoff would be worth it. All Charlotte had to do was find a car that was willing to stop or make it within range of a cell-phone tower. "Okay. Charlotte's idea might be our best bet." My eyes drifted back to the ground, toward Kaitlyn. For a split second, I'd forgotten what had happened to her. My stomach convulsed at the sight of her bluish skin, but I closed my eyes and tightened my jaw. "We need to carry Kaitlyn up to the cabin."

"Should we put her in the minivan with Sam?" Charlotte asked.

I pressed my lips together, not knowing the answer.

Charlotte and I heaved Kaitlyn's waterlogged body inch by inch up the hill. Jenna hovered on the beach, keeping a lookout for Ed and Marlene. She wiped tears from her cheeks and muttered profanities under her breath. Without a hand up, Jenna couldn't make it up the hill on her weak ankle. After we laid Kaitlyn's body on a flat stretch of gravel near the minivan, I returned for Jenna, extending my hand and letting her lean against me as we climbed the incline. We retrieved the charcoal-colored blanket Kaitlyn had used the night before from the couch and wrapped it carefully around her. The covering was a few inches too short. The sight of Kaitlyn's manicured toes protruding from one end caused my breath to catch in my throat. Jenna gasped, and Charlotte covered her mouth with her hand.

Don't think about it, I told myself, over and over again. *Don't process the enormity of this loss until we are safe.* Assuming the role of a therapist offered me a speck of comfort. I needed to bury my agony in a temporary grave. I had to keep my wits so that I could guide my friends through this crisis and back to safety. My schooling had trained me to remain calm and focus.

"Let's get Kaitlyn into the van." I put my hand on Jenna's shoulder, then moved to Charlotte. "Everyone, take a breath. We're going to get through this, but we need to stay calm and keep moving."

Charlotte blinked and nodded. Jenna inhaled a loud breath, followed by an exhale. I opened the back of the minivan, where Sam's body already lay in a neat roll. We gently slid her further inside to make room. Operating with the mindless efficiency of three robots, we hoisted the gray bundle next to the other one. Charlotte closed the door and locked the van. I thought I might vomit. We faced each other, forming a circle.

Charlotte rubbed her hands together. "I'm going to get dressed and brush my teeth. Then I'll pack some food and water and start walking."

"We need to get the gun from the cellar," Jenna said, her jaw set.

"Yeah. I was thinking the same thing," I turned toward Charlotte. "We won't go anywhere until you get back."

"I'll return as soon as I can. With help."

Jenna frowned, lifting her foot. "I'm sorry about my ankle. I should have listened to everyone about the zip line."

"It's not your fault." Charlotte's eyelids closed. "No one could have foreseen this."

A silence as thick as lake water filled in around us. I had the feeling my feet were stuck in the mud and I couldn't move. My friends also remained motionless. At last, Charlotte turned and dragged her soaking legs toward the cabin. I scanned the horizon for any sign of movement, for any warning that Ed and Marlene had returned. Those evil people were killing my friends. There were no other suspects.

A gust of wind whipped from the lake and blew across my cheek. A nearby branch groaned and cracked. The air was colder than expected and sent a chill traveling over my skin. Somewhere inside my mind, the picture shifted. Doubt poked at my resolve. The tiny hairs on the back of my neck bristled as I watched Charlotte scurry behind the door. Jenna stared toward the cabin with a blank expression. I had no idea what she was thinking. A repulsive thought formed slowly, dark and discolored like a bruise. Travis and his friends weren't the *only* suspects. Travis's words from the other night floated past my ears along with the wind: "*Same as the last time you stayed here.*" Had he been mistaken, or had one of my friends been to this place before? I thought of the long history with Charlotte and Jenna—the lies, the slights, the betrayals, and the five-year gap since our last get-together. Five of us had arrived at this desolate cabin. Now, only three of us remained. I pinned my lip under teeth, drawing blood. This shocking alternative was almost too terrifying to consider, and yet the horrible question forced its way into my mind. *What if one of us was the killer?*

*

I deposited Jenna's assignment from her Nineteenth-Century Women's Literature class on the bed next to her. The warmth of the room soothed my numb fingers after my trek across the frigid campus. It was a relief to have Jenna back in the house on 14th Street. It had been too quiet without her. The day after the car accident, we'd learned the crash's impact had fractured her femur in two places, and a metal pin had been inserted in her leg. The hospital required her to stay for a week after the surgery, but now she was on bed rest. Because Jenna couldn't walk to class, Sam, Kaitlyn, Charlotte, and I took turns visiting her professors and collecting assignments.

I patted the stack of books, several printouts of questions tucked inside. "Don't worry. You'll have plenty of reading to keep yourself busy."

A smile tugged at Jenna's lips, but her eyes had lost their usual glimmer. Her constant talking and chiding had dried up. I knew why she didn't feel like cracking jokes. Yesterday, Jenna's doctor had told her that her leg would require another surgery in six months. The implication was painfully clear: Jenna wouldn't be playing soccer during her final year of school. Her soccer career was over.

"Is there anything else I can get you?" I asked. "Are you thirsty? Or hungry? I can run out to Campus Café and get you a frozen yogurt with Oreos mixed in? Or a hot chocolate?"

Jenna pursed her lips. "No. I'm good. Thanks for bringing these books over for me."

The guilt gnawed at my insides. All at once, I was grateful the enormous room had gone to Jenna. I almost wished she would yell at me and tell me I'd ruined her life, rather than sitting quietly and pretending like she wasn't mad. I sat down on the edge of the bed and squeezed my hands together. "You know, I just wanted to say, again, that I'm really sorry we made you come to the store with us. And I'm sorry I tried to pass that car. It was so stupid of me. I should have been more careful."

Jenna blinked and lowered her gaze. "It was an accident. You couldn't have known."

"Is there any chance you can forgive me?" Hot tears welled in the corners of my eyes.

Jenna reached over and squeezed my hand. "Megan, I promise there's nothing to forgive. It's not like you crashed your car on purpose. Life just sucks sometimes."

I couldn't stop the tears from streaming down my cheeks, but I smiled. "Thank you. You're such a good friend."

A week later, I exited Jenna's bedroom, carrying her dirty plate and glass down to the kitchen. She'd started some light physical therapy and was able to move around on her own a little more now, but I insisted on helping her with many of her everyday tasks whenever I could. I turned the corner on the narrow staircase, nearly running into Pete's bulky frame.

"Oh. Hey Pete."

"Hey," he said, looking away.

"How's it going?" I asked, searching for his usually friendly demeanor. He didn't respond. He only shoved his hands in his pockets and stepped past me up the stairs, refusing to make eye contact. Something wasn't right. My stomach turned as I wondered if Pete blamed me for the accident. I wouldn't hold it against him if he did. I continued down to the kitchen, telling myself that he was probably just having a bad day.

I scrubbed Jenna's dishes by hand and then moved on to some dirty pots and pans I'd left on the stove the day before. As I dried a spatula with a dish towel, heavy footsteps clomped down the stairs behind me. I turned to glimpse Pete disappearing out the back door. He hadn't bothered to say goodbye. My jaw tightened at his rude behavior as I returned the spatula to its place in a drawer.

A moment later, a squeal of anguish sounded from upstairs. I paused, hoping I'd imagined it. The noise pierced through the air again. I dropped the dish towel and bounded up the stairs toward Jenna's room. As I got closer, I peeked through the narrow gap between the open door and the wall. Jenna hadn't re-injured herself as I'd initially feared; she was sitting in bed, exactly where I'd left her, except her shoulders slumped forward, her face hidden behind her hands. She sobbed.

Jenna prided herself on her tough exterior. Although she could be loud and dramatic, I'd never really seen her cry before, except when her mom died. I froze in the doorway for a second, unsure what to do.

"Jenna," I finally said, pushing the door open wider and stepping closer to her. "What happened? Are you okay?"

She shook her head and raised her bleary eyes to meet mine. "Pete broke up with me."

I rolled back on my heels, stunned. My jaw tightened as I remembered the cold vibe I'd gotten from Pete when we'd passed on the stairs and the way he'd slipped out the back door. What an asshole!

"Why?" I asked through gritted teeth.

She hiccupped and glanced toward her leg. "Apparently, we don't have anything in common anymore." Jenna's eyes connected with mine as my stomach dropped to the floor. She didn't say it outright. Of course, she was too kind to place that kind of blame on a friend. But I saw the flash of hate in her eyes, the way her pupils dilated and expanded in an instant, and I knew what she was thinking—that it was all my fault.

CHAPTER TWENTY-ONE

"What are you thinking about?" Jenna's voice tore me from the distressing memory. She'd caught me staring, and I shifted my feet. The warmth in her pale eyes and the curve of her cheekbones was familiar and safe. Even with our long history, it was ridiculous to think either she or Charlotte was capable of anything as sinister as murdering their closest friends.

"I was going to ask you the same thing," I said, blinking away my suspicions.

Jenna exhaled and sat on the nearest step. "I was thinking that I'm glad Travis is dead, even if it was an accident. I hope Ed and Marlene get what's coming to them, too."

I slid my palms together and looked away. I'd never witnessed this vengeful side of Jenna before, but her feelings made sense. She was careening through the stages of grief, and she'd landed on anger. A part of me agreed with her. Still, I didn't want to kill anymore people, even if they had stolen my friends' lives. "Let's settle for life in prison."

"Fine. I'll take that."

My thin pajama bottoms and T-shirt were wet and stuck to my skin. I shivered, finding my body shaky and hollow. "Let's go inside and change our clothes. We can get the rifle and help Charlotte pack some things."

I stepped past Jenna. She stood and followed me into the kitchen. The room held the chemical odor of the cleaner we'd used the day before to spray the floor and walls. At least the stench of Travis's decaying body hadn't yet leeched into the cabin.

Charlotte hurried down the stairs, wearing leggings and an army-green zip-up hoodie. Her dark hair was smoothed back in a ponytail. She carried a dry pair of sneakers in her hand and draped a black backpack over one shoulder. We turned into the kitchen, where she sat on a chair, put on her sneakers, and tied up her shoelaces.

I tipped my head toward the tiny door in the wall. "Should we get the rifle?"

We looked blankly at each other, no one jumping to volunteer. Bile rose in my throat at the thought of viewing Travis's decomposing body.

Jenna cleared her throat. "I guess I'll do it."

I exhaled, but my shoulders tightened as Jenna approached the small door and crouched down. Charlotte and I wavered a few feet behind her as she pulled at the wooden knob. The door stuck and Jenna yanked harder, causing the swollen piece of wood to fling open. I jerked backward, afraid of the smell that would meet me, but only a musty odor seeped into the air. Jenna turned her face away from the darkened opening as she squinted at the ceiling. She reached her arm inside the cellar and pulled the string. The light bulb clicked on.

I flattened myself against the wall, afraid to catch sight of the dead body. Travis had been a horrible, ignorant person, but he was still a human being. I'd killed him.

"What the…?" Jenna gasped. She leaned farther into the cramped space.

Charlotte stepped closer to her. "What's wrong?"

My heart thrummed against my ribcage.

"The rifle isn't here," Jenna said, swinging her head back into the kitchen.

"What?" I forced myself to inch toward the opening, my hands anchored to my sides. I peered into the cellar where Travis's body lay face down in a mound. A quilt with patchworks of blood covered his torso. Everything appeared just as we'd left him, except the rifle we'd set on top of him was gone.

"What the hell is going on? Who would have taken it?" Charlotte's face stretched with fear, her eyes flickering between Jenna and me.

I stepped toward the window, squeezing my hands. "Maybe Kaitlyn grabbed the rifle when Marlene and Ed broke in." Even as I said the words, they didn't make sense. Kaitlyn would have been able to defend herself if she'd gotten to the gun in time. Instead, someone had held her head under the water and strangled her.

Charlotte bit her fingernail. Jenna massaged her head and sighed.

I swallowed. "So, none of us took the gun. Right?"

"What?" Jenna scratched her eyebrow. "Are you saying you think one of us—"

"Of course, we didn't!" Charlotte's mouth gaped. "Don't you think we would have shared that information?"

I hugged my arms close to my chest, averting my eyes from the friends I'd all but accused.

Charlotte glared at me. "Maybe *you* took it, Megan? Did you steal the rifle and hide it somewhere? I heard you get out of bed last night."

"I went to the bathroom!"

Jenna stepped forward and held out her arms, creating a wall between us. "Come on, you guys. Turning on each other isn't going to help. Obviously, none of us took the gun."

I pulled at the hem of my shirt, feeling a quiver in my lip. I focused on taking a breath and pressing my feet into the floor to center myself. The rush of emotion passed as quickly as it had overtaken me, like I'd been caught in a riptide but had made it to shore. "I didn't mean to accuse you, Charlotte."

Charlotte wiped the back of her hand across her eyes and nodded.

"So, who took the gun?" Jenna turned to the side and looked out the window.

"It had to be Marlene and Ed," I said. "They're the only other people around."

Jenna lowered her chin, a dazed look floating in her eyes.

Perspiration dotted my face. We had locked all the doors, and I wondered, again, how Ed and Marlene had entered the cabin without us hearing them. Then again, we'd been exhausted and had drunk too much wine. They must have used Travis's key.

Charlotte frowned. "They could have swiped the gun last night when they attacked Kaitlyn. I bet she told them where we hid his body."

The horrifying theory made sense. Ed and Marlene would have discovered Kaitlyn sleeping on the couch when they entered the cabin. Fearing for her life, she must have come clean with them and told them about Travis's location in the cellar. A tremor traveled up my spine and into my throat, making my next words almost impossible to spit out. "That means Ed and Marlene know we killed Travis."

Jenna's swayed to the side. "And that we don't have a gun."

Fear stretched through the air, making it difficult to breathe. The mission to find help became even more urgent.

Still, I wondered why Ed and Marlene hadn't killed all of us when they had the chance. Why was Travis's body still in the cellar? Maybe his friends had only meant to scare Kaitlyn, not kill her. My thoughts were splintered. I couldn't piece it all together.

I looked at Charlotte's backpack. "Maybe we should all go for help. Or all stay? It doesn't feel right to split up."

"We already talked about this." Charlotte shook her head. "Jenna can't make it on her ankle. Now you have a gash on your foot too. I'll be able to get to an area with cell reception faster on my own." She reached over and squeezed my arm. "I'll send help right away. I promise."

"Okay," I said, but the word tasted sour on my tongue. "At least eat something before you go."

Charlotte pressed her lips together. "I'm not hungry. I'll take an apple and a couple of power bars with me."

I didn't argue with her because my appetite had disappeared too, my stomach churning with grief and worry. I scrounged through Kaitlyn's grocery bags, locating the box of granola bars and setting them on the table in front of Charlotte. I opened the refrigerator and clutched a shiny apple, trying not to envision how Kaitlyn must have carefully selected it from the fruit stand at her local market only a few days earlier. I handed the fruit to Charlotte. Jenna refilled Charlotte's water bottle at the sink.

"What's in your bag?" Jenna asked.

Charlotte unzipped the backpack and peered inside. "My purse, with my phone and credit cards. Sunscreen. Sunglasses. A phone charger just in case my phone battery died." She lifted the apple and box of granola bars and dropped them in the bag. "Now I have snacks and water, so I think I'm ready to go." Charlotte lowered her thick eyelashes and stood up.

I imagined her hiking through the woods and along the backcountry roads, exposed and alone.

Jenna gazed toward the window, wringing her hands. "Be careful. Go as fast as you can. Wave down any car you see, as long as it's not Ed and Marlene."

"I will."

I swallowed, hugging my elbows. Suddenly this plan didn't seem like the best idea. My heart couldn't endure losing another friend.

Charlotte tightened a strap on her backpack and turned toward us. Her brown eyes reflected a sheen of determination. "Stay calm. There's bound to be a car on one of these roads. I'll find help really soon. Make sure you wait here. Don't go anywhere."

"We won't leave." I spread my arms and stepped into her with a tight hug. Jenna did the same.

"Stay safe, Charlotte. Keep yourself hidden until you get out to the road. You don't want Ed and Marlene catching sight of you."

"I know. I'll stay behind the trees."

"Good luck." Jenna stepped back, looking at the floor.

Charlotte hoisted the backpack onto her shoulders and slipped out the door. Jenna and I watched from the porch as Charlotte power-walked across the gravel driveway and took a right down the narrow lane that would eventually lead her out to the never-ending dirt road.

Jenna slumped into a metal chair and buried her face in her hands. The fear and grief swirling in my stomach now radiated into my chest and out through my limbs. A whimper escaped my mouth. I couldn't help but feel we'd sent Charlotte on a death march.

Jenna looked up. "She'll be okay. This will all be over soon."

"I hope so."

Jenna snapped out of her trance and studied me. "Let's go inside. We can barricade the doors. You can take a shower and change into dry clothes." She eyed my foot. "I have extra Band-Aids." Jenna scooted her chair back and held the door open for me.

Once inside, we dragged chairs from the kitchen table toward each of the two doors, propping them under the handles. We double-checked all the windows, making sure we'd locked them. Jenna limped around the kitchen, where she rummaged through a drawer. She pulled out a butcher's knife and a smaller paring knife meant for slicing fruit. She held them up.

"We should keep these with us. It's better than nothing."

I agreed and gave her the one with the bigger blade because she would wait downstairs while I was in the bathroom.

A minute later, I set the paring knife on the edge of the sink and peeled off my wet pajama pants. Stepping under the steaming water was a relief. Tears slid down my cheeks, along with the streams of water. I was trapped inside a living nightmare. Sam and Kaitlyn were dead, gone forever. Only a day or two had passed since we'd been sitting on the deck overlooking the lake, joking and laughing. I couldn't wrap my mind around the concept. Despite the hot water blasting against my skin, coldness dripped through me. The three of us who'd survived wouldn't be safe until we escaped this place. I prayed that Charlotte would be able to find help before Ed and Marlene returned.

CHAPTER TWENTY-TWO

I wasn't sure how much time had passed when I finally shut off the water and wrapped a thin towel around myself. The cabin was quiet as I pulled on my dry clothes and combed the knots out of my hair, the wet ends resting on my shoulders. I almost didn't recognize my face. My skin was colorless. The wrinkles around my eyes and across my forehead appeared deeper than they'd been only a few days ago. The emotional turmoil was taking a physical toll.

I found Jenna on the couch in the living room with her foot propped up on the table. The blade of the butcher's knife glinted from its position next to her heel. She'd changed into gray sweatpants and a clean white shirt. Jenna's head rested on a cushion and her eyes popped open as I stepped down the stairs with the compact knife clutched in my fingers.

Her hand raised to stifle a yawn. "I haven't gotten any real sleep since we've been here."

"Yeah. I don't know how I slept last night. Exhaustion and wine, I guess."

Jenna straightened up, making room for me on the couch.

I lowered myself onto the cushion, setting the knife on the table and pushing my wet hair off my shoulder. "So, did you hear anything when you were awake last night?"

"I was trying to remember." Jenna closed her eyes and slowly opened them. "I think I heard footsteps in the hallway at one point, but I assumed it was one of you going to the bathroom."

"What time?"

"I don't really remember."

"It might have been me. I used the bathroom sometime before midnight."

Jenna stared blankly.

"Can you remember anything else?"

She tipped her head back. "No. I wish I did."

My eyes flitted toward the window, where clouds gathered outside. "How do you think Marlene and Ed got Kaitlyn down to the lake?"

"They had a gun, remember? Probably two guns, after they took the one from the cellar. All they would have had to do was point it at Kaitlyn and tell her not to scream."

I crossed my legs at the ankles, then uncrossed them. "Yeah, but the weird thing was, they didn't shoot Kaitlyn. It looked like she was strangled just like Sam."

Jenna leaned forward, studying her hands. "Maybe they didn't want to wake the rest of us up. Their goal is to terrorize us, picking us off one by one because they know we're trapped. It must be their way of getting revenge for Travis."

I clenched my teeth. The wind rattled against the window outside. I wondered how far Charlotte had gotten and if she'd found someone to help us yet.

Jenna yawned again. "I'm so sorry, but do you mind if I take a nap upstairs? I'm not feeling so great, and I can barely keep my eyes open."

A gust of wind rattled the windowpanes, and storm clouds darkened the sky. The thought of sitting in this room alone terrified me, but Jenna looked drained and unwell. I'd been so tired the day before after two bad nights of sleep. I could only imagine how miserable Jenna felt trying to function after three sleepless nights.

"I'll leave the bedroom door open," she added.

"Go ahead. I'll wake you up if anything happens."

"Thanks. I owe you one." Jenna patted the handle of the butcher's knife. "I'll leave this with you." She gripped the handle of the smaller weapon and plodded up the stairs, favoring her healthy ankle. The footsteps stopped halfway up. "Megan, don't leave the house."

The fear cracking through her usually steady voice made me sit up.

"Don't worry. I'll keep a lookout."

Jenna gave a nod. Her footsteps creaked up the stairs and into her room. I heaved myself up from my seat, checking the locks on the doors and windows yet again and confirming they were secure. I paced toward the window across from the couch. Menacing clouds had gathered above the lake in dark shades of purplish gray. Although it was mid-morning, the light in the cabin was dim and dreary. I could have flipped on a lamp but doing so felt as reckless as shining a spotlight on myself. I huddled close to the wall, staring outside.

Without internet access, we hadn't been able to check the weather forecast since we'd arrived. A storm was forming outside, and I wondered how severe it would be. The lake had turned black and angry. White-capped waves traveled across the surface and crashed to the shore. I ran through the items Charlotte had packed in her backpack and clenched my teeth. She hadn't taken an umbrella.

I hovered at the edge of the window frame, scanning the wooded cliff leading down to the lake and searching for anything suspicious. I looked for any reason to crouch in a shadowy corner with the blade pointed upward, any excuse to wake Jenna. Only a gust of wind blew past, causing branches to groan and leaves to rustle and spiral to the ground. Even Marlene and Ed weren't crazy enough to hike through the woods on a day like this.

I rolled back my shoulders, feeling lightheaded and unsteady. Although I had no appetite, I needed to eat something to keep up my strength. Making my way to the kitchen, I opened the refrigerator and found the bag of blueberry muffins Kaitlyn had brought. My fingers touched the sticky surface of the baked goods. I lifted the top one, placed it on a paper plate, and poured myself a cup of orange juice. My throat was dry and my blood sugar low. My eyes crept toward the tiny door in the wall. Behind it, Travis's body lay in a rotting heap. The disturbing vision repelled me away. That horrible man was the reason all this had happened.

I hurried into the living room and set my plate on the table. The orange juice slid down my throat in gulps. I took a few bites of the muffin, realizing how famished I was. As I finished the food, the corner of Kaitlyn's canvas tote caught my eye from beside the couch. I wiped my fingers on a napkin and retrieved the bag, which was heavy because of the photo album inside. It was the album we'd all been laughing over the other night.

I sat back down and opened the book on my lap. Sam and Kaitlyn stared back at me from a photo, their arms looped around each other, and the whole world laid out in front of them. My chest heaved. No one could have imagined their lives would be cut short. No one expected to die at age forty. But I was thankful they hadn't known. That kind of knowledge would have been too devastating a burden for any of us to carry.

The rows of pictures caused tears to swell in my eyes. A painful realization seared through me—perhaps the best part of my life was over. I swiped away the wetness with the back of my hand and continued down treacherous memory lane. In the next photo, the five of us—me, Kaitlyn, Sam, Jenna, and Charlotte—stood shoulder-to-shoulder at a party, blue cups in hand and fists pumped in the air. Hope had filled our eyes back then. Life hadn't smacked us down yet and shellacked us with the standard layer of cynicism that developed in one's thirties.

I turned the page, finding photos from one of our many house parties on 14th Street. Some women I didn't recognize stood in our living room with their arms around Jenna. It was early in the school year—a few months before the car accident. Judging by their tall statures and athletic builds, I guessed they were her soccer teammates. In another photo, Charlotte's freshman-year roommate, Frida, hovered in our kitchen behind others who played beer pong. Frida seemed unaware someone was taking her picture. She wore her trademark expression—a frown pulling down her lips and a shadow of disapproval in her eyes. Charlotte and another guy who looked vaguely familiar made faces at the camera. Charlotte had dated him for a few weeks, and I tried to remember his name. *Phil? Fred?* No. That wasn't right. It was hard to keep track of all the men Charlotte had dated, most of her relationships had been short-lived. I wondered where all these people were now.

Another group photo showed my housemates wearing skimpy clothes and overdone makeup, getting ready to head out somewhere. Maybe a party or a bar. I must have taken the picture because I was the only one who wasn't in it. Those were the days before cell-phone cameras and selfies. Sam's bright smile and Kaitlyn's classic beauty struck me again. I tried not to think of the rolled-up blankets in the back of the minivan.

The page crinkled as I turned it again. I blinked at the image in the top row. I leaned close to my former boyfriend, Dan, who I'd dated for over a year. He'd dumped me a few weeks after Jenna's accident, complaining I was too preoccupied. Dan had been handsome though, with thick, dark hair, kind eyes, and a rugged voice. He'd been an English major, and I wondered what he was doing now. How would my life have been different if the accident never happened? If I'd married Dan instead of Andrew? Thinking about a parallel universe where Dan and I were madly in love with two kids who weren't Marnie and Wyatt made both my head and my heart hurt.

I moved to another photo across the page, where Kaitlyn and Derek held up enormous ice-cream cones. They'd met junior year. Love at first sight. My chest caved for Kaitlyn's husband, for the family man who hadn't yet received the devastating news that the love of his life was dead. I remembered so clearly the night he and Kaitlyn met. It was at the same October house party I'd been thinking about yesterday.

I flipped the album's page, pulling my thoughts away from the night Kaitlyn found true love. The scene should have been happy, but the vivid memory felt devastating instead. I forced my eyes down the page, seeing a photo of Jenna and Charlotte dressed in sleeveless Hawaiian-print shirts, with bright plastic flowers tucked behind their ears. I'd gone to that luau party, too. It had been at a fraternity and I vaguely remembered snapping the photo before we left. A page later, a close-up of Charlotte wearing black from head-to-toe stared back at me. A metal piercing looped through her nostril, and a thick layer of charcoal eyeliner rimmed her eyes. She puckered at the camera with inky lips. Her boyfriend of the month had broken up with her days or weeks before, but I couldn't recall if her new look was the cause or the effect of the breakup. Her eyes were empty and unfocused like someone faking happiness. Nothing like the Charlotte I knew today. Thankfully, her morbid phase had been short-lived. She had spent the following summer interning at a physical therapy rehab center in Madison. By the time we'd all returned for senior year, Charlotte was back to jeans, colorful shirts, and glittery eye shadow that highlighted her flirtatious glances. Jenna didn't live with us anymore by then, although we saw her often. She'd opted for the privacy of a one-bedroom apartment.

I flipped back to the front of the album, finding a snapshot of Charlotte, Kaitlyn, Sam, and I. We sat in the stands at the soccer complex, holding a giant poster board sign that read: *Go, Jenna #22!* I smiled at the image of Sam—the peace sign on her tie-dyed T-shirt and the failed attempt at dreadlocks in her stringy hair. I studied my young face, which still carried baby fat. My eyebrows were thicker and my hair shinier. Pure joy lit my eyes. I'd been so carefree then, my biggest worry whether or not to skip a few hours of studying to enjoy a night out with my friends.

The next photo showed Jenna on the field in her blue-and-gold uniform, rushing toward the ball with single-minded determination. Her blonde hair had been longer then and pulled back into a sporty ponytail. We'd gone to a few of her home games at Valley Fields that year, but I remembered this one in particular because the weather had been perfect that fall night, and Jenna had scored two goals. After the game, we'd celebrated with pizza at Campus Café, making fun of Sam and her sad dreads. I still remembered the smell of the vinyl leather booth and the way my stomach ached with laughter. In so many ways, that night could have been yesterday. In others, it felt like twenty lifetimes ago.

A gust of wind blew past the cabin and an object hit the window, causing my body to go rigid. Something had moved outside, although I didn't know if it was a person or a swirl of leaves skittering past. Crouching forward, I slid the album from my lap and resumed my post next to the window. I didn't see anyone, but that didn't mean anything. Anyone outside who wanted to harm us would probably be hiding. My fingers trembled, fumbling through the air as if searching for the missing rifle. I scurried back to the table and grabbed the knife.

CHAPTER TWENTY-THREE

Unable to identify the noise from outside, I leaped from my crouched position and took the stairs two at a time to wake up Jenna. But with each step I took toward my sleeping friend, an alternate version of events edged into my mind. Halfway up the staircase, my feet stopped, my shoulders suddenly weighed down with dread.

I thought again about how Kaitlyn had ended up floating lifeless in the lake. What had led to her murder? Questions I'd previously answered and tucked away had now dislodged, flitting around my head like bats emerging at dusk. When Ed and Marlene discovered Travis's dead body in the cellar, wouldn't they have yelled or screamed at the shock of the sight? Wouldn't they have wanted to remove their friend's body from the dank space? They could have killed us all as we slept if they wanted us dead, but they hadn't. The tiny door to the cellar was wedged shut and clamored when it opened. I wondered, again, how Jenna hadn't heard any commotion last night if she'd been awake.

The picture in my mind tilted, turning my world on its head. A warning pressed against my chest, two cement blocks pushing me away from the upstairs bedroom where Jenna napped. I backtracked down the steps and fell into the couch, pulling the photo album close to me. My fingertip quivered as I ran it over the photos.

I studied Jenna's soccer picture a second time, noting the look of freedom on her face. It was a few months before the car accident destroyed her dreams. Jenna had had hopes of playing professionally, and she'd been talented enough to do it. But after the accident, her soccer career was over. The car crash fractured her leg. Then Pete shattered her heart. The university honored her scholarship for senior year. Still, Jenna turned inward toward her studies in our final year of school, opting to live by herself. I met her once or twice a week for lunch or dinner that last year of school, so I knew that her nearly perfect grades had soared even higher. She graduated with honors and continued on to law school. Despite her dramatic tendencies, I'd never seen her sulk or look back. She must have realized what she'd lost, though. Or had she been repressing her grief and anger all these years?

Jenna's comment from the other night replayed in my mind: *"Looks like everyone's life turned out rosy and perfect, except for mine."* It hadn't been the words themselves, but the bitter edge to her voice that made my stomach lurch. My head had snapped toward her like the sail of a boat caught in a shifting wind.

Was it possible Jenna still harbored anger and resentment about the car accident so many years ago? On top of that, there'd been Sam's confession about the mug, Jenna's most cherished relic of her deceased mom. Sam admitted to lying about having broken it. The deception might have been less devastating if Sam had owned up to the truth a week or a month after it happened. But twenty years had passed since she'd first told Jenna the lie. The rest of us had kept up the story about the missing mug, covering for Sam. Jenna must have felt betrayed the other morning. Less than twenty-four hours after Sam revealed the truth about the mug's ending, someone strangled her to death.

Suppressed feelings were dangerous. I'd seen it in my clients many times. The longer a person pushed back their emotions, the more intensified those feelings became, multiplying and expanding over time until they had nowhere to go but outward, sometimes violently. I'd practically forced Jenna into the car that wintery night twenty years ago. I wondered how often she thought about the accident and my negligence. Her assurances of forgiveness had sounded sincere. But, then again, Jenna was a terrific actress. She'd lied flawlessly to Marlene and Ed. Jenna had studied acting in her younger years when drama had been her second love behind soccer. She'd even appeared in a handful of commercials as a child, moving on to numerous high school productions, including *Mary Poppins*, just as she'd mentioned yesterday. Could she be putting on an act now?

My eyes landed on another photo next to the one of Jenna on the soccer field. *Jenna and Pete.* The golden couple. They wore matching athletic clothes, maybe just returning from a workout. Jenna's teeth flashed white in the light of the camera as Pete leaned close to her, his blue eyes shining. I perched on the edge of the couch, running my fingertips over the scratchy fabric as my body filled with dread. The glassy eyes of the deer head watched me from the far wall, conjuring up the same lifeless look I'd witnessed in Jenna's eyes after Pete had dumped her. He'd left her stranded in her bed with a bum leg.

I tried to push away the notion of Jenna as a threat, but more troubling facts emerged from the dark corners of my mind. Jenna had barely slept this weekend. Maybe she'd been awake last night because she was luring Kaitlyn down to the lake and drowning her. A forty-year-old attorney killing her friends seemed dubious. Yet here I was, with two of my closest friends lying lifeless in the minivan and another corpse in the cellar. Unlikely things happened sometimes.

I could think of plenty of reasons for Jenna to want to kill me, but I struggled to come up with why Jenna would want to kill Sam or Kaitlyn. Revealing the truth about a broken mug didn't seem like enough of a motive. But maybe I'd overlooked something. Maybe something had happened between them years earlier that had only just resurfaced.

"Looks like everyone's life turned out rosy and perfect, except for mine."

What if Jenna had simply snapped? Everyone had a breaking point. She could have been jealous of the full lives Kaitlyn and Sam had built for themselves. Her resentment could have been accumulating for years, violently bursting forth once she had us trapped in this remote location. I remembered how Jenna had pushed for a rental that was "off the grid," how she'd encouraged me to pull the trigger on Travis and then grabbed my arm. Had she made the gun go off on purpose? Was this all part of her sick game?

I thought back to the morning Sam lost her life. Jenna had been napping on the couch while I'd slept upstairs. But had anyone actually seen her there? The board games on the deck had absorbed Charlotte and Kaitlyn's attention. Jenna could have followed Sam into the woods and returned before anyone knew she was gone. The former soccer player would have been plenty strong enough to overtake her unsuspecting friends.

And this morning, something else had bothered me. Jenna had raced down the hill behind me to get to Kaitlyn's body. How had she done that with her injured ankle? I'd been too overwhelmed with grief to question her. Was it possible Jenna had faked her injury from the zip-line fall? Was her bad ankle a ploy to distract us? Maybe she was using her injury to make us think we couldn't hike out from this place. As long as Jenna couldn't walk long distances, at least one of us was trapped here with her. It was a perfect cover.

Rain pelted against the window, and I thought of Charlotte burrowing through the downpour. I touched the photo with my finger, telling myself that my theory of Jenna murdering her friends was absurd. If Jenna was out for revenge, wouldn't she have killed me first? It was my negligent driving that changed the course of her life. I'd betrayed her after that too. My actions had been more devastating than Sam's lie about the mug.

I gripped my hands together, digging the edge of my fingernail into my skin. This dreadful weekend was making me crazy. The stress was causing me to invent stories that weren't true. Jenna wanted to get out of here just as much as Charlotte and I did, maybe even more so. Jenna was a successful attorney who lived a glamorous life in New York City. She wasn't married with kids like the rest of us, but she was happy with the life she'd built. That was more than I could say for myself most of the time.

Footsteps creaked from upstairs and plodded toward the bathroom where water splashed into the sink. A minute later, Jenna hobbled down the steps, her short blonde hair matted to her head. She spotted me as she descended, the paring knife dangling from her fingers. I reached for the handle of the butcher's knife, reminding myself she was the same Jenna I'd always known. A loyal friend of over twenty years. Still, a sliver of doubt nagged at my insides. I hated myself for not being able to shake away the lingering suspicion, but after recent events I'd be stupid to trust anyone too completely.

"Did you sleep?" I asked.

"Kind of. Somehow, I feel even more tired now." She stepped into the kitchen and removed a can of soda from the refrigerator.

As she walked back into the living room and joined me on the couch, I searched her face for any sign of guilt, but her dazed eyes stared blankly toward the window. "Wow. It's really raining out there. I hope Charlotte is okay."

The sky had darkened and rain pelted against the roof. I pictured Charlotte trudging through the downpour over the muddy dirt road, all alone. "I'm worried about her."

Jenna's fingers tightened around her drink. Her lower lip twitched, and I thought she might start crying. I hadn't seen my strong friend so vulnerable since the days following the accident, and I realized she was just as terrified as me.

I shifted toward her. "I was looking at the photo album when you were sleeping. You were really an amazing soccer player."

Jenna pressed her lips into a smile.

I swallowed away the dryness in my throat. "There's something I've meant to tell you, and I just wanted to say it now because, well, let's face it. Who knows how much time we have left?"

Two uncomfortable seconds ticked by before Jenna responded. "Yeah. Especially if help doesn't show up soon." She snapped out of her trance, raising her eyebrows at me. "What is it?"

"The car accident. Back in college. It stole so much from you, and I'm sorry. We shouldn't have made you come with us to the store that night. I wish I could go back in time and not pass that car. I know your injury was my fault and I'm so sorry. It's my fault Pete broke up with you."

Jenna shook her head. "Like I told you back then, there's nothing to apologize for, Megan. It was an accident. I made my own decision to go to the store that night. No one forced me. End of story."

"Really? I mean, you're not even a little bit mad at me?"

"No." Jenna set down her can of soda and rested her hands on her knees. "Okay, maybe for a week or two after it happened, I was a little bit mad. But you felt so horrible about the whole thing. You must have apologized to me a thousand times. I knew you didn't do it on purpose. And Pete was bad news anyway. What kind of guy dumps his girlfriend right after she gets seriously injured? Even if we had ended up together, I'm sure we'd be divorced by now. The accident forced me to move on and focus on my studies. I might not have gotten into law school, otherwise."

I nodded, relief swimming through me because she hadn't mentioned the other thing. Or was she leaving it out on purpose? Was it possible she was acting again? My reckless driving hadn't been my only betrayal of my friend's trust. I'd lied about the mug, and I'd made other mistakes, too—errors in judgment I'd never been able to forget, no matter how much I tried.

*

It was early March, over a month since the car accident that shattered Jenna's leg. I blew out a puff of air as I languished in the library flipping through pages of my Abnormal Psychology textbook. There were only two days until the second-to-last exam and so much material to cover. My back pressed into the hard chair as dusk descended on the other side of the wall of windows. Jenna wasn't the only one whose boyfriend had dumped her. Last week, Dan had shown up to my bedroom door, shoved his hands in his pockets, and asked if we could talk. I knew right then it was over. He said I'd changed, that I was preoccupied. He couldn't see our future together. I didn't know what that meant, but it sounded like a cop-out.

When I'd told Sam and Kaitlyn about the breakup, they had ordered a pizza and insisted the five of us watch Kaitlyn's well-worn VHS tape of Titanic *together. We'd all been single for a brief moment in time, and our solidarity was comforting. I spent the days that followed struggling to banish Dan from my thoughts.*

Now, though, I was distracted as I sat in the library and reread the highlighted paragraph in my psychology textbook. I was unnerved to find Jenna's ex, Pete, sitting one table over, diagonally across from me. I'd accidentally made eye contact with him three times already, each time looking away as quickly as possible and swearing under my breath on Jenna's behalf. My uncooperative eyes bounced toward him again. Pete was staring at me and a smile twitched in the corner of his lip. He stood up and came over.

"Hey." He hiked the strap of his backpack further onto his shoulder and motioned toward the empty seat next to me. "Mind if I sit?"

I shrugged. "Sure."

He pulled out the chair and sat down, setting his books and pen in front of him. "How's Jenna doing?"

I raised my chin, my skin bristling. "How do you think she's doing?" Jackass.

Pete scooted forward and rested his forehead in his hand before looking at me. "Listen, I know you probably think I'm a jerk."

I focused on a barren tree outside the window, unwilling to disagree. A woman sitting a few seats away cleared her throat and glared at us.

Pete lowered his voice to a whisper. "I just. It's just that..." He stopped talking and ran his fingers through his hair, leaving it standing on end. "Things weren't that great between Jenna and me. She's a lot to handle. I was already planning on breaking up with her even before the accident. Once she was injured and stuck in bed, I felt even more trapped."

"You could have waited."

"Yeah. I know. It was selfish." He lowered his head and faced me, forcing me to look at him. "I'm not a bad guy. I want you to know that." He straightened his muscular shoulders. Pete was much taller and sturdier than Dan. "I've always liked you, Megan."

I stared at Pete, not sure what he was getting at. I got a weird feeling he was flirting with me. His sea-blue irises shone in the overhead lights. Movement rippled through my chest, and I instructed myself to ignore it.

"What are you studying?" he asked.

"Abnormal Psychology."

"Me too."

"Shh!" The woman a few seats down frowned at me.

Pete shook his head. "Do you want to grab some coffee with me? We can review the materials together?"

My fingers tightened around the edge of the hard chair. Going out for coffee with Jenna's ex-boyfriend felt wrong, but it wasn't a date. Pete and I were in the same class and had an exam in two days. It would be a relief to get away from the disapproving woman at the other end of the table.

"Okay. Sure."

A few minutes later, we found a corner table inside a brick-walled cafe. The lights were dim and jazz music floated through the air. Pete bought me a vanilla latte. We covered most of the course material by asking each other questions and recounting various experiments, chapter by chapter. We joked about our tendency to self-diagnose each one of the mental illnesses as we studied them. Pete had an easy way about him, and I could suddenly see how he might have felt diminished by Jenna's need to be the center of attention. I laughed more during that study session than I ever had with Dan. Once or twice, Pete's eyes hung on to mine for a second too long. I could understand how Jenna had fallen for him.

It was nearly midnight when we left the cafe. Pete insisted on walking me home. The city streets were dark, and there'd been a recent rash of late-night muggings near campus, so I didn't object. After several minutes of strolling and talking, we approached the front door of the house on 14th Street. Later, I would wish I'd kept my voice down.

"Thanks for walking me home. And studying for the exam with me."

He smiled. "We're going to kill it."

I raised my hand in a goodbye wave, hoping he'd get out of there before anyone caught us together. Instead, Pete stepped forward and pecked me on the cheek. He paused, locking eyes with me. My cheeks flushed and I couldn't help grinning. He turned on his heel, practically skipping down the sidewalk.

I shuffled backward, stunned by the kiss but also thrilled. My sudden attraction to Pete was confusing. Electricity traveled through my veins, but guilt drew my eyes upward toward Jenna's bedroom window. My knees almost buckled when I spotted a shadow behind the dark glass, her pale face peering down at me like a ghost.

"Shit." The sight of my friend extinguished any euphoria I'd felt at the unexpected kiss. I fumbled for my keys, unlocked the door, and raced up the stairs to explain myself. The hallway was dark, and a muffled conversation seeped from Sam's room, but Jenna's door was closed. I paused outside her bedroom. "Jenna?" My knuckles rapped against the wood. "Jenna?" There was no answer.

I turned the handle and peeked through the crack. Jenna sat on her bed with her arms crossed and a scowl on her face. Her bedside lamp cast long shadows across the room.

"It wasn't what it looked like."

"What the hell, Megan?" Jenna's icy stare speared through me. "Haven't you done enough?"

The loaded question sent another dagger through my heart. I balled my clammy hands into fists and steadied my voice. "I ran into Pete by chance. At the library. He's in my Abnormal Psych class, so we reviewed some stuff for the exam on Friday. That was it."

"Ha." Jenna turned away from me.

"I'm sorry. I made a mistake. I wasn't thinking." I lowered my eyes toward Jenna, but she wouldn't look at me. "There's nothing between us. I promise."

Jenna bit her lip, then sneered at me. "You and Charlotte can fight over Pete, for all I care. He's a complete asshole. He's dead to me."

I shook my head. "I don't want him. Not after what he did to you. I'm sure Charlotte doesn't want him either."

Jenna arched an eyebrow at me at the mention of Charlotte, causing us both to chuckle.

"I'm so sorry, Jenna." My eyes traveled over her bandaged leg. "For everything. I've been such a crappy friend. Can you forgive me?"

Jenna released a breath and closed her eyes. The tense muscles in her face softened. "Let's forget about it."

I sat down and hugged her. I'd been stupid to fall victim to Pete's boyish charm, to let him put a wedge between us. The fleeting attraction had been nothing more than a childish reaction to Dan dumping me. I pulled away from Jenna, feeling both relieved and jittery as if I'd narrowly missed being run over by a train.

On Friday, I turned in my exam and exited the auditorium. I'd seen Pete sitting on the opposite side of the room when I'd arrived and had purposely avoided him. Still, I couldn't deny the fluttering of my heart when he raised his eyes toward me and smiled. He'd been hunched over his paper when I'd left. Now, I hurried down the sidewalk, happy it *was 5 p.m. on Friday. Hunger gnawed at my stomach, and I debated whether to run into Campus Café and grab a chicken sandwich and some fries. I deserved a treat after all the studying I'd put in.*

"Megan, wait up."

My feet stopped at the sound of Pete's voice. I cursed under my breath, wishing he would forget about us. A mixture of annoyance and yearning rushed over me.

Pete jogged up next to me. "How'd it go?"

"Pretty well, I think."

"Yeah. Me too." He matched my pace.

I kept walking, gluing my eyes ahead as Friday traffic lurched beside us.

"Want to get something to eat?"

"I shouldn't," I said, although I was starving. "Jenna is one of my best friends."

He hurried along next to me, touching my arm. "You don't have to tell Jenna. It's only a meal to celebrate our test being over."

"It's not a good idea."

"Have you ever been to The Old Cantina? It's downtown, just a few minutes away. Best enchiladas you'll ever eat." Pete grinned. The stubble on his square jaw was rugged and handsome. I paused. Before I knew what was happening, Pete raised his arm and flagged down a cab. He opened the passenger door.

"Get in. My treat."

My stomach rumbled again.

"Come with me just this once and I'll never bother you again. I promise. No one will ever know."

I realized Pete might be right. A dinner with him wasn't going to hurt anyone. We'd be downtown, across the highway from campus. The chances of running into anyone I knew, particularly Jenna, were slim.

"Okay. Fine. Jenna can never know about this, though." I ducked into the taxi, feeling guilty but enjoying the heat of Pete's body next to mine.

The restaurant was dark and loud, but a hostess seated us right away. Mariachi music echoed through the cavernous room, where every nook and cranny housed another table. We sat in a booth in the corner. I was thankful for the secluded location but couldn't stop myself from scanning the faces at nearby tables. We spent over an hour at the restaurant, eating chips and salsa and drinking margaritas before ordering the main course. Our conversation quickly turned from the exam to other things, like our families and funny people we'd known in high school. When the food no longer looked appetizing, Pete ordered another round of drinks and gazed at me. "You're too far away." He got up and walked around to my side of the booth, repositioned himself next to me. His arm slid around my back and he kissed my lips. My body stiffened at first. I knew it was wrong, but I didn't stop him. The margaritas had impaired my judgment and lowered my inhibitions. I liked the warmth of his lips on mine and I kissed him back. I didn't think about Jenna.

The waitress neared our booth, and Pete and I pulled away from each other, pretending we'd only been sitting there. She set down our drinks and walked away. A strange sensation tingled up my neck and over my scalp. I scanned the room again, my gaze snagging on a dark pair of eyes leering from a booth in the opposite corner. My mouth went dry as my stomach turned. I'd been caught.

Frida stared at me from across the room, her unflinching eyes surrounding me like a net. She was with someone unfamiliar, a lanky guy with acne scars across his cheeks. A basket of chips rested between them. Frida frowned, her pale face pinching in disapproval; she made it clear that she'd witnessed the kiss. I worried she would report back to Charlotte, who would then tell Jenna. Jenna wouldn't be so quick to forgive me this time. My secret was exposed, and this second betrayal would be the end of our friendship. I wanted to look away from Frida but couldn't. The grip of her stare felt like hands around my windpipe.

"We should leave." The words stuck in my throat as I struggled to turn away from Frida's lurking silhouette. Instead, I glimpsed *something dark and unsettling behind the strange woman's eyes, like two stones sinking into the mud.*

*

Jenna tapped her fingers on the photo of herself on the soccer field as I smothered the memory of my betrayal. The photo was the same picture she'd been staring at the other night.

"You looked so happy," I said.

"I was. I'm still happy." Jenna waved her hand in the air. "Or, at least I was before we arrived here."

I registered Jenna's words, hearing the authenticity behind them. If she was acting, she deserved an Oscar.

My mind tumbled back to my betrayal that night at the Mexican restaurant. As far as I knew, Jenna had never discovered the illicit date, but I could still feel the burning judgment from Frida's stare.

I pressed my palms into my thighs. "Who else knows we're staying here? I mean, besides our families."

"Huh?"

"What if Marlene and Ed didn't kill Kaitlyn? What if Travis didn't kill Sam?"

Jenna's jaw slackened. "I don't understand. You think one of us—"

"No." I held up my hand. "Not one of us. Someone who wanted to *be* one of us."

"I still don't follow."

I stared at Jenna as the memory of Frida's knowing eyes burrowed through me. "Frida King."

A spark of understanding flickered in Jenna's pupils, but she didn't speak.

"Charlotte said she posted our weekend reunion plans on Facebook. She and Frida are Facebook friends. She would have known exactly where to find us."

"You think Frida followed us up here after twenty years to murder us? That's a little far-fetched, don't you think?"

"I don't know. We always excluded her from our group. I didn't give it much thought back then, but that must have been painful for her. Maybe her life has gone downhill. Maybe she saw the Facebook post and snapped."

"I just don't see it. None of us have even spoken to Frida since college. Even Charlotte said they'd lost touch after Oliver was born." Jenna shook her head and thumbed toward the window. "The terrorists next door seem much more likely suspects."

I stared through the glass at the thrashing tree branches outside. "Yeah. I guess you're right. It sounds crazy now that I said it out loud."

My suspicions of Frida and Jenna had all but eroded. My eyes stuck on the door Charlotte had exited hours earlier, and I couldn't stop another treacherous thought from leaking into my head. I pulled the album closer and examined the photo of Charlotte dressed in black, in what we referred to jokingly as her "morbid phase." Was it possible Charlotte had a hidden dark side that was now surfacing? She and Reed were having marital problems. While it seemed that Charlotte had gained confidence in herself after her first divorce, she'd always had a habit of pouring her self-worth into the hands of men. Maybe her marital issues with Reed were having a more severe effect on her than I realized. Then there'd been Charlotte's insistence on driving all of us to the remote cabin. A cabin she wanted to rent because of her supposedly tight financial situation. Then again, I hadn't offered to drive, and Charlotte was the only one of us with a minivan.

It was risky to share my theory with Jenna, but I couldn't keep the troubling suspicion contained. Still, if there was ever a time to think outside the box, it was now. I leaned forward, softening my voice. "What if Charlotte planned this?"

Jenna's eyes popped. "Are you insane? Strait-laced, church-going, doe-eyed, girl-next-door Charlotte who has never spoken a swear word in her life and is trudging through the forest in a thunderstorm to find us help?"

I bit my lip as I felt my cheeks redden.

"Why would Charlotte suddenly decide to kill her friends?" Jenna asked.

"I don't know. She and Reed are having problems. Charlotte thinks he's lost interest in her."

"Wouldn't she go to marriage counseling or file for divorce from Reed, then, and not murder two of her closest friends?"

I aimed my eyes on the floor, acknowledging my flawed logic. I couldn't think of any reason Charlotte would want to harm Sam or Kaitlyn, much less kill them. "Yeah. You're right. Being cooped up in this wooden prison is messing with my head."

Jenna's eyes tightened on me. "I know this whole thing sucks, Megan, but I don't get you sometimes. How could you even think that one of us is capable of this? You must have a pretty low opinion of your friends."

Her words felt like a slap in the face. My mouth pinched closed, and I couldn't form a response. I'd offended her. Jenna didn't want to consider the idea the killer could be someone other than Travis, Marlene, or Ed, but I hadn't expected such an extreme reaction. I blinked my eyelashes. When I looked back at Jenna, the disdain on her face pinned me to my seat.

In my attempt to talk things through, I'd made the situation even worse. Jenna's features appeared altered in the shifting light. Shadowy flecks in her eyes had risen to the surface, and a tendon strained along her neck. For a second, I didn't recognize her at all. I shuddered and gulped for air, feeling as if I'd been thrown in the lake. My loyalties shifted again. Now I wasn't sure if a hell-bent murderer was locked inside the cabin with me while Charlotte lay somewhere in a ditch. My gaze traveled back to the deer head on the opposite wall. I wondered if the peaceful animal had known it was going to die in the moments before it was shot.

CHAPTER TWENTY-FOUR

Morning turned to afternoon. I perched on the couch and then paced the perimeter of the living room before returning to the flattened cushion again. I kept Jenna in my sights and the knife in my grip, just in case she was someone other than the loyal friend I wanted her to be. The darkened sky made it difficult to gauge the time. Rain hammered against the window, interrupted by occasional flashes of lightning and booms of thunder. When Jenna complained about the surging pain in her ankle, I studied her face and weighed the intonation of her voice, struggling to determine whether she was faking the injury. She gave nothing away. I left her only briefly and occasionally to use the bathroom or skitter into the kitchen to gather drinks or snacks. We flipped through the pages of the photo album and relived our favorite memories of Sam and Kaitlyn. The knowledge of the grief awaiting their families made my chest ache. After reaching the end of the album, we sat motionlessly and waited for help to arrive, trying not to think about Charlotte sopping wet and huddled under a tree somewhere or splashing through the downpour exposed to a lightning strike.

By the time my watch read 4:15 p.m., the air inside the cabin was damp and thick. I felt like crawling out of my skin. "Do you think Charlotte has found help yet?" I asked, raising my voice over the pelting rain.

"I don't know. There probably aren't many people driving around in this storm."

"I wonder if Andrew is worried that he hasn't heard from me? Or if Reed and Derek and Thomas are trying to reach us? Maybe someone has called the local police."

"Didn't you tell Andrew that you'd have spotty reception at the cabin? I thought the others warned their husbands too."

"Yeah." I covered my eyes with my palms. "I really wish we hadn't done that."

Jenna rested her foot on the table and popped another ibuprofen. She made a face and shook the empty bottle. It was the last one. "I really messed up my ankle running down the hill this morning." She touched the bandage.

"Do you want me to rewrap it for you?" I asked.

Jenna swung her leg away from me. "No. Thanks. It's good."

I glanced at the wall, wondering why Jenna didn't want me to see her ankle. I rubbed my elbow, reining in my suspicions. Wouldn't Jenna have attacked me by now if she'd wanted to? Reassured, I approached the empty stairway. "Charlotte mentioned she might have a couple of leftover pills. I'll go check in her suitcase."

Jenna nodded. I headed to the upstairs bathroom where I searched through Charlotte's toiletries. There was no ibuprofen or aspirin. I moved into our shared bedroom and found Charlotte's suitcase shoved into a corner and covered with a heap of her dirty laundry. I rifled through the clothes, searching for a small plastic bottle or a travel-sized packet of pills. The lining of the suitcase hid a zippered side pocket. I opened it, expecting to find money, feminine products, or medicine. Instead, I found a plastic sandwich bag filled with quarters and a metal container of peppermint breath mints. Behind the random items, the white corners of a stack of papers poked out. Curious, I pinched the bundle and lifted it.

The first sheet was a printout of the cabin's vacation listing, the same one I'd viewed online before we agreed to rent this place. I scoffed at the photos of a pristine log house overlooking a crystal-blue lake, a shiny, rainbow-sailed boat gliding over the waves. I wondered how many years ago someone had taken that snapshot. I flipped to the next paper, finding a receipt of payment. I'd seen this document before, too. Travis had emailed the confirmed reservation to Charlotte, which she had then forwarded to all of us. My thumb flipped behind the receipt, and my eyes did a double take. It was another receipt, but this one was of a payment made to Charlotte. It was dated two weeks earlier and showed that Charlotte had received a check for $932 from the State of Wisconsin Office of Unemployment. I turned the paper over, looking for an explanation, but it was blank on the other side. I looked around the room, confused.

Charlotte had been talking non-stop about her tireless work as a physical therapist and her long hours. She'd described the medical center's bustling atmosphere and the constant demands of her supervisor. *Had Charlotte been lying to us?* Maybe she was ashamed of being out of work, especially if the hospital had fired her. My arms flopped to my sides as I imagined how difficult it must have been for her to keep up that lie in front of us; it was upsetting that she felt she needed to lie about having lost her job in the first place. I skimmed through the last two papers, finding nothing of any significance. Then I replaced them in the secret pocket and went downstairs, taking a seat next to Jenna.

"I didn't find any medicine, but I discovered something else."

Jenna turned toward me, the knife still resting at her feet. "What?"

"I think Charlotte lost her job. There was a receipt from an unemployment check in her suitcase. It was mixed in with some other papers."

Jenna's eyes narrowed. "Are you serious? Why would she lie about that?"

"I don't know. Maybe she was embarrassed."

"Maybe it wasn't Charlotte's check. It could have been Reed who lost his job."

I considered the possibility but shook my head. "The payment was made to her name. It was dated two weeks ago."

"Man. I feel so bad." Jenna massaged her forehead with her fingertips. "No wonder Charlotte wanted to rent this cheap, run-down cabin."

"In her defense, she didn't know it was run-down—and terrifying—until we got here."

"I don't think we should mention anything about this when she comes back," Jenna said, followed by a sigh. "She clearly didn't want us to find out."

"Yeah, you're probably right. Charlotte's going through enough. There's no need to make her feel worse." I laced my fingers together, the edge of a jagged fingernail scratching my skin. "On the other hand, it might help her to talk through her feelings."

"Yeah, but not with us. She doesn't want us to know."

I picked at my fingernail and stared toward the floor. Charlotte's dark eyes flickered in my mind. She'd been so eager to leave this morning. I pressed my weight into the cushion, feeling as if I was stranded on a sinking raft, as if I'd glimpsed a sea monster gliding just beneath the surface of the rippling water but couldn't see its face. Was Charlotte hiding more than an unemployment check from us? A job loss could have devastating effects on a person. I'd seen it first-hand in a former client, Annie Linderman, who'd driven her car into a lake while her kids slept in the back seat. I'd counseled Annie only five days earlier. She'd shown no signs of violence then. But that was three days before her advertising firm had let her go with no warning. Thankfully, a bystander had intervened before the car was submerged and Annie hadn't injured anyone in that incident. Law enforcement had charged her with reckless driving and child endangerment but had ultimately released her under the supervision of a psychologist capable of administering medication and monitoring her more closely.

A job loss plus marital problems could change someone. Two tragedies back to back could alter a person's view of the world, cause them to blame others, and lash out in violence. I rubbed the top of my nail, smoothing out the craggy edge and wondering if Charlotte was lurking somewhere outside the cabin, planning a surprise attack on Jenna and me. I held my breath, listening for any clues, but only rain pelted against the windows.

My eyes squeezed closed, my brain struggling to banish my wild theories. Maybe Jenna was right about me. I was a horrible person for suspecting a friend of murder, especially when two armed suspects seeking revenge lived just down the road. Charlotte had seemed fine at the start of this weekend. Happy, even. She had probably been relieved to get away from her home life for a few days. It was a stretch to assume she was capable of such horrific acts toward her closest friends. I hugged my arms in front of me, no closer to figuring out the truth.

The cabin was humid and warm. Traces of Travis's decaying body clung to the air and I gagged. I didn't want to make things worse by mentioning the odor to Jenna. Instead, I walked to the window and cracked it open. Rain spattered through the opening.

"I should go over to Travis's house and break in to use the phone."

Jenna's lips flattened. "No. We can't separate. It's bad enough that Charlotte's out there on her own."

"You can come with me."

Jenna pointed to her ankle. "I can barely walk. I wouldn't be able to run if we needed to. Plus, Ed and Marlene are probably at the house, lying in wait. Those two would be happy to have any excuse to shoot us."

"What if I just scope it out from a distance to see if they're there? I'll stay hidden behind the trees. I'll be back in twenty minutes."

Jenna set her chin. "No. Neither of us should be alone. It's not safe." Her gaze landed on the two knives on the coffee table. "Especially without the stupid rifle."

My mouth was dry and pressure built up inside my chest. I paced over to the couch, realizing Jenna was probably right. It was safer to stay together. Still, things were desperate. The path forward was murky. Maybe a risk was necessary.

"Anyway, Charlotte might have found help already," Jenna said, sitting up straight. "There could be a police car on its way to us right now. It's only been a few hours. This rain probably slowed her down. Let's give her a chance."

I wished I could collect the crumbs of hope Jenna was throwing my way, but my limbs felt heavy and useless. I sank into the couch next to her and waited.

"You should eat something." I set two paper plates with leftover pieces of cold pizza on the coffee table.

Jenna sniffled. She flopped back, wiping the tears from her eyes. "Where's Charlotte?"

I gazed toward the window, where the rain still fell in sheets. It was almost 9 p.m. "I don't know." Heat climbed up my neck and over my cheeks, but I quieted my face. Jenna and I couldn't fall apart at the same time. We needed to support each other, to hold each other up.

I edged the plate toward her. "Try to take a few bites. We need to keep up our strength." I picked up my flimsy piece of pizza and bit into it, leading by example. Jenna lowered her chin and copied me. Her movements were mechanical, the mannerisms of someone who'd lost hope.

"Jenna, we're stronger than we know. We're going to get out of here."

Her eyelids lowered as she gave a slight nod.

I finished most of my slice and stepped toward the shelves. "Do you want to play a card game? It might make the time go faster."

"Okay."

I grabbed Uno, returning to the couch and dealing the cards.

Another hour passed as we played several rounds, not caring who won or lost. Jenna barely talked. Her sense of humor had vanished along with her words. There was still no sign of Charlotte. Jenna pushed the cards away and hobbled toward the window.

I stood up and followed her. "Maybe we should take turns sleeping tonight, so one of us can keep a lookout."

"Yeah," Jenna said, turning toward me. "That's a good idea. Do you want to go first?"

I checked my watch as my jittering insides competed with my heavy eyelids. A refreshing sleep wasn't likely to happen, but it would be good to lie down and gather my thoughts. "Okay. Wake me up at 2 a.m., or earlier if you can't stay awake. And come get me if you hear anything."

"I will." Jenna wobbled back to the couch and squeezed her arms around herself.

"Jenna," I said, and she looked up at me. "We're going to be okay."

She forced a half-smile. Her eyes were illuminated in the lamplight, their color now pale and sharp like shards of glass. She didn't believe me. Or maybe she knew something I didn't.

I dragged my feet up the stairs, paranoia needling through me. The four walls of my small bedroom provided an illusion of security, and I closed myself inside it, moving a wooden stool in front of the door. The seat wasn't tall enough to reach the doorknob, and I pulled it away. Opening the door again, I paced down the hallway and into the bathroom, where I splashed water on my face and focused on breathing. As I stepped into the hallway, every shadowy doorway loomed like a waiting predator. I couldn't shake the feeling that I was missing something, that things weren't as they seemed. Instead of going back to my room, I tiptoed into Jenna's darkened bedroom. Using the flashlight on my phone, I peered under the bed, searching for the missing rifle. It wasn't there. My trembling hands lifted the messy covers, finding nothing underneath. I tiptoed to the closet and opened the door, flashing my light into the space. A wire hanger and a spare pillow were the only things inside. I lunged toward her suitcase and sifted through her clothes. No gun. Jenna's extra pair of running shoes sat next to her luggage. My hand flew to my mouth as I noticed one of the shoes was missing its laces. I thought of the thin, purplish strangulation marks across Sam and Kaitlyn's necks and tried not to scream. *Did Jenna use her shoelace to strangle them? Was this evidence?* I closed my eyes, desperate for another explanation. The laces were missing from her left shoe, the same side as her ankle injury. Jenna's ankle and foot were probably so swollen that she couldn't get her foot into the shoe. That was a reasonable explanation that made more sense than the murderous alternative.

I tipped my head toward the ceiling and huffed out a breath. Again, I silently scolded myself for suspecting my friend of such gruesome acts. I slid through the doorway and into my bedroom. A stubborn pebble of determination formed in my chest, along with a new plan in my head. It wasn't wise to trust Jenna completely, but I'd found no convincing reason not to trust her. I would attempt to get some sleep if my body allowed. When it was Jenna's turn to rest, I would wait until she fell asleep, then sneak out and break into Travis's house to call the police. Even if Ed and Marlene were there, they'd likely be asleep by then. It was risky, but we were desperate.

With my clothes still on, I laid on the bed and let my head fall into the pillow. I listened to the steady drumming of the rain on the roof. The churning in my gut told me what my mind already suspected—Charlotte wasn't coming back. At least, not tonight. For all we knew, Marlene and Ed had already gotten to her. I was done waiting around for someone else to save me.

I closed my eyes, craving sleep. Instead of falling into the soothing blackness of my dreams, only visions of Marnie and

Wyatt scampered through my mind. Panic gripped my throat at the thought of never seeing my kids again. It was as if I was reaching over the edge of a cliff trying to grasp their hands, but I couldn't hang on. Their sticky fingers were sliding through mine. I was desperate to be near them, to hold them tight and smell the fruity scent of their hair after a bath, to dance in the sound of their laughter. I imagined Marnie's sandy-brown curls under the palm of my hand. I pictured her devious grin as she plucked an extra chocolate-chip cookie from the box when she thought I wasn't looking. A memory surfaced of Wyatt with his chest puffed out and holding up a watercolor painting of our backyard bird feeder in his pudgy fingers. I smiled, remembering how the birds in the picture were so out of proportion, almost as big as the house he'd drawn across one side. Wyatt had scrawled words in the corner: *To Mommy. I love you and birds.* It had been a perfect piece of art, though, and I told him as much. I wouldn't have changed a thing.

A sob choked my throat. I wouldn't lose my kids. I had to find a way to return to them. And I wouldn't stop at that. This nightmare of a weekend had forced my life back into perspective. Marnie and Wyatt deserved to have happy parents—honest parents—who loved each other. It was time to come clean with Andrew. I could only hope he'd forgive me and be willing to go to marriage counseling. Hopefully, we could find a therapist who was better at her job than me. Suddenly, I wanted to work things out with Andrew more than anything in the world. What an idiot I'd been to turn away from him.

It hadn't been that long ago when Andrew and I had been madly in love. I thought back to the first night we'd met. A mutual friend had introduced us at a charity event. I was twenty-seven then. An urgent magnetism had surged between us, apparent from the spark in his eyes and my tingling skin. The feeling had been impossible to ignore. I hadn't been able to take my eyes off Andrew or leave his side for the rest of the night, and it was obvious he felt the same way. We'd migrated to a private table in the hotel lobby and forgot about mingling with others. We talked about everything. The conversation was easy, like we'd known each other for years. Andrew was smart, funny, and handsome in a nerdy kind of way that was utterly endearing. He'd left with my number and called the next morning. He hadn't played it cool, and that attracted me to him even more. Three years later, we were married.

Years of holidays, trips, early mornings, yard work, diaper changes, dirty bathrooms, missed dinner dates, and work meetings spun through my mind as I tried to pinpoint the moment things went wrong between us. Our marriage hadn't collapsed in an instant, like a house destroyed by an earthquake. It had eroded over time, a brick here, a shingle there, until it was too late. One day the foundation wasn't strong enough to support me, to stop me from falling for the advances of a charming and handsome stranger. After I escaped from this place, my only mission would be to rebuild our house.

I closed my eyes. The next thing I knew, Jenna was leaning over me, squeezing.

CHAPTER TWENTY-FIVE

My eyes popped open, my muscles coiling. Jenna released her grip on my shoulders. The glowing numbers on the bedside clock illuminated her shadowy outline as she stood next to my head, peering down at me. It was just after 1 a.m.

"Sorry," Jenna said. "I can't stay awake. Can you take a turn on the lookout?"

I sat up and exhaled. For a fleeting moment, I feared Jenna had been doing something else. Her hands had tightened around my shoulder. I'd been vulnerable lying there. *Had I felt her fingers squeezing my throat? Had I stopped breathing for a second? She hadn't done that, had she...?* I touched my neck. *Of course she hadn't.*

"Yeah. I'll take over." I swung my feet over the side of the bed and laced on my sneakers with fumbling fingers. "Did anything happen?"

"No. Nothing. Just rain. The knife is downstairs."

I pointed to the small knife on the bedside table. "I'll leave this one here. Get some sleep. I'll wake you up at the first sign of daylight."

Jenna picked up the paring knife. Her shoulders sagged as she plodded across the hall with the blade pointed down. She closed her bedroom door but then opened it a crack, the same way my kids did to feel safe at night. Her mattress creaked as I stepped down the stairway. My feet rushed to put space between us.

A haze of exhaustion and fear clouded my brain. I moved into the kitchen, rinsed out the coffee carafe, and started brewing a fresh pot, averting my eyes from the tiny door in the wall. As soon as enough dark liquid dripped into the carafe, I poured it into a mug and carried it into the living room. The bitter coffee jolted my insides as I sipped. I gulped another mouthful of the dregs. I didn't care how bad it tasted anymore. I was after the caffeine. Full alertness was required for what I was going to do next.

After twenty-five minutes of waiting on the couch, I tiptoed back up the stairs and paused outside Jenna's room. Her breath sounded in even puffs. She was asleep. I crept into my room and removed a windbreaker from my suitcase. Then I inched my way down the stairs, swiping the key to the front door and an old flashlight from the side table. The knife balanced in my hand. It would be cumbersome to carry, especially with the flashlight, so I slid the weapon under the couch's middle cushion. I removed the chair from underneath the kitchen door, aware that I might be putting Jenna at risk. I added my actions to my growing list of betrayals.

Pulling the hood of my jacket over my head, I stepped into the black night. My body stiffened against the rain. The key shook in my fingers as I closed the door and locked it from outside. Someone could find a way into the rickety cabin if they wanted to, but a locked door would slow them down. Besides, I wouldn't be gone long.

With my circle of light shining across the soaked ground, I leaned into the rain and jogged ahead. My feet slopped through the mud. The pelting drops made it impossible to hear if anyone else was nearby. I followed the same narrow road that led us to Travis's house two days earlier. The path angled away from the lake, deeper and deeper into the woods. My hood obstructed my peripheral vision, and my head darted from side to side, searching the shadowy surroundings for attackers as I ran. My toe hit a protruding rock, and I tumbled forward but caught my balance before hitting the ground. Strangled breath gurgled from my lungs, and I slowed to a fast walk, afraid of suffering from another panic attack.

I concentrated only on my breath and my footsteps as I hurried along the path for several more minutes. Travis's statement about seeing Charlotte on his security camera played in my ears. I worried about Marlene and Ed spotting my approach. It was nearly 2 a.m., though. Even if they were inside, they were likely asleep. I wove between the trees, staying hidden near the edge of the woods as I approached Travis's house. I ducked behind the shed and surveyed the scene.

Travis's pickup truck remained in the same spot it had been the other day, but Ed's monster truck was gone. Hopefully that meant Ed and Marlene had left, but I couldn't be sure. Ed might have gone away on his own, leaving Marlene inside. Through the curtain of rain, I made out a security camera holding watch above the front door. Entering through the front was too dangerous. I would have to sneak around the house and search for a back entrance or an unlocked window. I craned my neck toward the roof of the shed, blinking my eyes against the rain and searching for more cameras but I didn't see any others.

I took a few deep breaths, ignoring my instinct to run. Marnie and Wyatt's faces flashed before me, just out of reach, urging me forward. I had to figure out a way inside. There was a working phone on the other side of those walls. It was the fastest way back to them. I crouched low, skittering along the edge of the woods. My feet angled across the clearing toward the rear of the house. A low window lured me closer, but I worried it might be a bedroom. Marlene could be sleeping in that room. Then again, she could be waiting inside any room. My stomach heaved at the enormous hole in my plan, at my lack of forethought. Still, my best chance to escape was to reach the phone sitting within those walls. I pressed ahead, my feet squishing into the mud with every step.

I bypassed the window and darted toward the back door, which sat a couple of feet above the ground. The step leading up to the entry was missing. Only weeds reached up along the raised cement slab. There was no security camera like at the front. My arm quivered as I lifted it and closed my fingers around the metal handle. I prayed someone had left the door unlocked. Something clicked beneath my index finger. I pulled, and the door drifted toward me. It was open.

My mouth gaped at the easy access, but there was no time to celebrate; the fear of Ed or Marlene lying in wait pressed in on me. I took a giant step into the house, finding myself in a cramped mudroom that smelled of garbage and cigarettes. My light scanned across the back of a person and I jumped, thinking it was Ed. I looked closer, realizing the human form was merely a coat piled on top of other coats and hanging from a hook, bulky hiking boots set below it. I swallowed, trying to stop my heart from beating so loudly.

My eyes flickered toward an open doorway leading into a larger room. I stepped forward, where a couch and two armchairs materialized through the shadows. An opening to the kitchen lay beyond the dark living room. Deer heads like the one in the rental cabin lined the walls above me, their deadened eyes following me as my light passed over them. I released a breath. Marlene wasn't in this room, but there was another door opposite me. It was partially open, and I wondered if that was the bedroom and if Marlene was sleeping inside. I crept around the perimeter of the living room, searching for a phone with a cord. A computer sat on a table in the corner, and I remembered that Travis had internet access. Maybe I could access a police website and send a request for help. Or I could log into my email account and send a message to Andrew, urging him to call 911.

I tapped the keys, hoping to wake up the device without causing any loud beeping noises. The screen flickered and brightened. A white box appeared in the center, asking for the security code. My head fell forward. Of course, the computer required a password. I could guess ten thousand times, and I still wouldn't know what it was.

I inched away from the glowing screen, resuming my search for the phone. I expected to find the phone next to the computer, but it wasn't there. The kitchen pulled me toward it. My feet stepped from the spongy carpeting onto a linoleum-tiled floor. A weak ring of light guided my way. Empty beer cans covered the counter next to the refrigerator, and dirty dishes filled the sink. The stench of forgotten garbage surrounded me.

I breathed in shallow breaths as I circled the room, searching for a lifeline. The kitchen was small and my search didn't take long. There was no phone in this room either. My blood dripped through my veins, thick and cold, as I tried not to lose hope. Travis had no reason to lie about having a landline in his house. I hadn't checked the bedroom yet.

I exited the kitchen and tiptoed across the living room toward the door that sat ajar. As I approached, I angled my flashlight away. My face edged into the narrow opening, and I slowly raised the light, illuminating a bed and a nightstand. A curved, white object on the nightstand caught my eye. It was the phone. I clapped my free hand over my mouth and rolled onto the balls of my feet.

A breath heaved and sputtered from somewhere inside the dark bedroom. I froze, aiming the light at the floor as my heart exploded in my chest. Someone was in there. My instinct was to run, but I didn't dare move. I stood, motionless, and waited. A body rolled over. A sigh escaped a mouth, followed by even breathing. My hand shaking, I raised the flashlight, catching a glimpse of bleached hair peeking out from a mound of covers. It was Marlene. She was sleeping directly next to the phone. There was no way I could call for help without waking her up.

My legs wobbled beneath me. I'd been so close to saving us, only to fail. Waking up Marlene would be a death sentence for me. I supposed threatening her was an option, but I'd already killed one person this weekend, and I didn't want to add another body to my conscience. I could hardly claim self-defense this time.

Not to mention, I didn't have a gun. She probably slept with one under the covers.

My eyes flitted around the dim room as I debated what to do next. I searched for a misplaced gun but didn't see one. I bet Travis stashed his extra guns on a closet shelf or under the bed. I backed away from the bedroom door, blinking away my tears. I refused to give in to defeat. I had to figure out another way.

I thought of Travis's truck sitting outside. We'd checked his pockets for keys to his vehicle the day I'd shot him. The keys hadn't been on him. That meant they were probably somewhere in this house. I scurried back toward the kitchen, opening any drawers that might hold odds and ends, but finding only silverware and cooking utensils. I returned to the computer area, scanning over some odd office supplies. Then, I crept back into the mudroom, searching for a bag or purse that belonged to Marlene. There was no purse there. Not in the living room either.

I stepped forward, cursing the creak of a floorboard beneath my feet. My eyes snagged on a cardboard box underneath the computer table. I hurried toward it and crouched down, shining my light on the papers inside. There were several sheets of printed emails regarding the cabin rentals and receipts of payment, including a duplicate of the most recent one I'd found in Charlotte's suitcase. I dug through the papers behind it, not sure exactly what I was looking for.

More receipts surfaced with the names, phone numbers, and email addresses of seven or eight renters who'd stayed at the cabin before us. I flipped back one more page and blinked, seeing Charlotte's last name again. *Leeman*. No first name had been included on the earlier receipt, but the address field matched the city where Charlotte lived, Hartland, WI. Below that, *Paid in Cash*. I wondered why there was another receipt for Charlotte buried behind all the previous renters. My eyes scanned the page, stopping on the date—June 13. It was now mid-September. June was three months ago.

"What the…" I said under my breath, recalling the night Travis startled us on the deck. He'd mentioned that we'd stayed at the cabin before. We'd been quick to correct him, and he hadn't bothered to argue. Now it seemed Travis had been telling the truth. Charlotte had rented the cabin back in June. Had she come up here with her family? Or different friends? My chest heaved. Why would she lie about having been to the cabin, on top of lying about losing her job?

Frantic for an explanation, I dug through more papers, finding nothing of any relevance at first, but finally I landed on a folded section of a local newspaper. The headline and date of the article made me pause—June 15: *CAMP EVENTIDE SHAKEN BY DEATH OF OWNER. FOUL PLAY SUSPECTED.*

My teeth clicked as I read the headline a second time. *Foul play?* Kaitlyn had told us as much in the car on the way up, but she'd gotten the facts wrong. She said a counselor had died in some sort of accident. I thought of the bruising on Sam and Kaitlyn's necks. Two more suspicious deaths. I remembered the staff cabins we'd stumbled across on the other side of the lake; specifically, the larger cabin encircled with yellow police tape. My eyes swam across the page, taking in the information as fast as I could. I pulled in a breath, not wanting to believe the words in front of me. As the headline stated, it hadn't been a counselor who'd died at Camp Eventide; it was the camp's owner—a social worker named Frida King.

My teeth clicked, my body feeling like it was levitating in disbelief. *Frida King.* Her name sent a cold wind through me. A black-and-white photo of the murdered woman stared back at me, the same woman who'd watched me from across the Mexican restaurant years ago. Frida had aged like the rest of us—her hair cut shorter and her eyes set deeper—but I remembered her features. The newspaper photo showed a happier-looking version of the woman I'd known in college. I'd thought of Frida only sporadically over the years but looking through the images in Kaitlyn's album had uncovered so many painful memories, like ripping scabs off of wounds.

My stomach dropped to the floor as a terrifying realization spread through me—Frida's death occurred the same weekend Charlotte had rented Travis's cabin three months ago. The timing couldn't have been a coincidence. I forced my eyes to retrace the details in the article.

> *Camp Eventide serves teens from troubled, sometimes violent, backgrounds… The police are actively questioning all campers… Medical Examiner stated that the victim suffered a fatal blow to the back of the head… extensive loss of blood…*

A fatal blow to the back of the head? As convenient as it was to pin Sam and Kaitlyn's deaths on Travis and company, my terrible suspicion that they might not have been the ones killing my friends grew stronger. What if Charlotte had chosen this location because she knew that the sleazy cabin owner and his friends were easy to condemn? Could she have killed her former roommate, Frida, who had owned the camp across the lake? But why? I couldn't think of a viable motive. Charlotte had been such a loyal companion to Frida back in college.

I didn't have all the information, but a rock turned over in my gut. Charlotte had deceived us. She'd lied about renting the cabin. The previous dates she had stayed at the rental matched Frida's untimely death. It was too much of a coincidence to ignore. As much as I resisted the truth, it ripped through me as sudden and painful as a bullet. Charlotte had set a trap for her closest friends, and we'd stepped directly into it.

CHAPTER TWENTY-SIX

The newspaper shook in my hands. I choked on my breath as I gulped for air. I tried to move, but my feet weighed a thousand pounds. The truth felt like a straitjacket tightening around me. Charlotte had murdered Sam, Kaitlyn, and Frida. *Why?*

"Someone out there?" Marlene's angry voice sounded from the other room. "I got a gun."

Her words snapped me from my frozen state and propelled me forward; Marlene had plenty of reasons to shoot me. I raced to the front door, still holding the newspaper and the flashlight. I slipped outside and closed the door.

A scream formed in the back of my throat, but I swallowed it down and sprinted into the trees. I hoped Marlene hadn't spotted me. Suddenly, I was thankful for the cover of the darkness and the rain. The disturbing revelations reeled through my mind as I ran. I'd been so stupid. Charlotte had never left to find help. She'd never asked Marlene and Ed to call roadside assistance. She must have punctured the tires on her minivan to keep us here. It now seemed Marlene and Ed weren't the ones who had confiscated Travis's rifle from the cellar. Those two might not have even been near the cabin the night Kaitlyn died. Charlotte had probably taken the gun. She had orchestrated this whole weekend so she could trap us in this isolated location and murder us.

My breath came quicker, panic ripping through me. I'd left Jenna alone in the cabin. She was asleep and vulnerable. I'd known locking the door wouldn't keep anyone out, yet I'd left anyway.

Even if Jenna woke up in time, she couldn't outrun Charlotte on her injured ankle.

"Please, please," I said as I stumbled over the uneven earth, the rain mixing with the tears on my face. I needed to make it back to the cabin before Charlotte. I couldn't fail Jenna again. The weight of her death on my conscience after everything I'd put her through back in college would be too much to bear. I wondered if Charlotte had been watching us from the woods the whole time, just waiting for me and Jenna to separate from each other. *Or was she following me now?* My eyes searched the dark gaps between the trees but couldn't detect anything more than five or six feet away.

I wasn't sure how long I'd been running when the crooked outline of the cabin emerged in the distance. The upstairs windows were dark, and a lamp glowed from within the living room, just as I'd left it. I pulled air into my lungs as my step lightened. Maybe I'd beaten Charlotte to the cabin and arrived in time to save both me and Jenna. I turned off the flashlight before emerging from the shelter of the woods.

The rain had let up by the time I crept past the disabled minivan, my eyes ricocheting around me in search of Charlotte. The forest sat dark and hooded like a reluctant witness, revealing no secrets. Only the rhythm of water lapping against the shore sounded from the bottom of the hill. I unlocked the door and eased into the kitchen, remembering the butcher's knife I'd hidden under the cushion. With my back against the wall, I stood still for a few seconds, listening for any sign of movement. There was nothing.

I slunk into the living room, finding it empty. My feet edged toward the couch, and I lifted the cushion. The knife was there, and I grabbed it. I hurried up the stairs, eager to wake up Jenna. We had to make sure Charlotte couldn't get into the cabin. Either that, or we had to run. But with Jenna's injury, running would be difficult.

"Jenna," I said in a loud whisper as I reached the landing. I shouldered the door open. "Jenna."

There was no response. I flipped on the light as my body recoiled. My trembling fingers tightened around the handle of the knife. The sheets lay tangled at the foot of the bed. She was gone. "Jenna!" I screamed. I spun on my heel, ready to fight. I lunged across the hall into my bedroom, flipping on the light and turning from wall to wall. The room was empty. I repeated my actions in the third bedroom and then the bathroom, finding them vacant.

"Jenna!" I yelled. "Make a noise so I can find you." I stood at the top of the stairs, listening for any sign that my friend was nearby—a bang, a knock, or a yelp. Only silence surrounded me. With the blade pointed in front of me, I crept down the stairs into the living room. The Uno cards sat in a neat pile on the coffee table, exactly as we'd left them. I willed the deer on the wall to speak to me, to tell me what it had seen. Charlotte must have forced Jenna outside. I hoped Jenna was strong enough to fight back or smart enough to figure a way to escape.

With my clothes dripping, I hovered next to the couch, debating whether to barricade myself inside the cabin or run toward the road. Not searching for Jenna was unbearable. I hurried back to my bedroom to gather a few supplies. The numbers glowed from the alarm clock—2:49 a.m. Daylight was still a few hours away. It would be dumb to stay here alone. I'd be a sitting duck for Charlotte when she returned. She would anticipate me running toward the main road to look for help. I imagined her waiting in the woods, ready to pounce.

Several terrible options spun through my head as I thought of the abandoned summer camp across the lake. I could hide out in one of the cabins for the remainder of the night, then head toward the road in the morning. Hiking over to the camp in the dark would be treacherous, especially with the muddy conditions. I remembered the first morning when we hiked down to the desolate beach below the cabin. I'd discovered a rusty old canoe hidden under the brush—a new plan formed in my head. I grabbed my nylon backpack and shoved a couple more pairs of dry socks inside. I rushed downstairs, filling my water bottle and dropping the last few power bars inside the pack. The newspaper lay on the floor, and I stuffed that inside my bag too in case Charlotte returned. It was better if she didn't know I'd discovered the truth.

I escaped from the cabin with the pack on my back and the knife and flashlight in my hands. The rain had let up, but darkness swallowed me when I clicked off the light. Not even the moon was visible behind the blackened clouds. Quietly, I stepped across the deck and down the steps, pressing myself against the wooden siding. I craned my ear toward the woods, listening for a struggle between Charlotte and Jenna. Only the screech of an owl and the lull of the waves interrupted the silence. I gritted my teeth and stumbled down the cliff toward the lake. I fell twice, sliding through the mud down the slippery incline until I could grab onto a tree. At last, my foot sunk into the sand as I reached level ground.

The lake stretched out before me like a black hole. I fumbled for my flashlight, turning it on and hoping the vegetation hid me enough that the light wouldn't draw Charlotte's attention. I edged along the shoreline and aimed my light at the overgrown brush. Thorns punctured my skin as I yanked back a branch, revealing the dull metal siding of the canoe. I exhaled. The boat was still there. My shaking fingers released the flashlight and the knife. I used both hands to grip the aluminum edge and pull. The canoe slid forward across the wet sand, and the corner of an oar poked out beneath the boat. I gasped. In my desperation to get to the canoe, I hadn't considered how I would paddle. Thankfully, whoever had abandoned the canoe here had thought it through. Once away from the brush, I flipped over the boat and loaded my meager belongings inside, ignoring the spiderwebs clinging to my arm. I grabbed the paddle and pushed off, soaking one of my shoes again.

The water felt thick as oil as I propelled through the darkness. I couldn't see to the other side of the lake, and I hoped I had aimed toward the camp's beach. I dipped the oar into the lake, again and again, pulling with all my strength and occasionally switching sides. A brisk wind brushed against my cheeks as the water churned and splashed around the canoe. I moved my foot, causing an even closer sloshing noise. My eyes adjusted to the night. I looked down, finding a puddle of water surrounding my shoes. The liquid hadn't been there a few minutes ago.

"Shit! Shit! Shit!" I said under my breath as my muscles seized. There was a hole in the boat. I paddled faster. A faint wall of trees appeared on the lake's far side, slightly blacker than the sky above them. The foreboding sensation of watching eyes sent a shiver across the back of my neck. Wherever Charlotte was, I hoped she couldn't see me. Coyotes yipped in the distance, and a new terror surged through me. I hadn't considered the nocturnal animals that stalked the woods at night. I wished I could stay in the canoe until daybreak. At least nothing could reach me out here. But the water continued to seep inside the boat, the rising liquid having the same effect as a ticking bomb. I had to survive. There was no other option. Jenna's statement from the other night—that coyotes ate rodents—allowed me to catch my breath. I refocused on paddling. I could make it to shore before the canoe sank.

It seemed like I'd been battling the current for hours by the time I reached the opposite shore, but it had only been twenty minutes. The boat missed the beach by about a hundred feet. It was close enough. Lake water rose around my ankles as I exited the canoe, but it only took a few steps to reach dry ground. I slid the knife into a side pocket of my pack and hoisted it onto my shoulders, setting down the flashlight while I pulled the canoe toward me. Dense vegetation grew across the shoreline next to the beach and provided a decent hiding place. I shoved the canoe under the overgrown bush to cover my tracks. With the light angled down,

I turned on the beam again. My feet edged around protruding branches and along the water until I reached the camp's beach. An uneven stairway constructed from logs led me to the grassy area that housed the camp's buildings. I kept my head down and trotted toward the far cabins, remembering their unlocked doors and rows of bunk beds.

I had the sensation of floating above my body and watching myself, a hawk circling a terrorized mouse. *How had I gotten here?* We could have avoided the whole thing. That was the worst part. Only a minor change here or there would have done the trick—a few minutes more spent researching before booking the trip or a different decision made last week or twenty years ago. Instead, every choice led to this terrifying place. My breath heaved from my lungs. My soaking shoes tumbled over each other as I scurried across the uneven ground, searching for a hiding place. The night was silent and black around me, the air so filled with terror that even the stars hid behind the clouds. *Never ignore your instincts.* That's what I always told my clients, but I hadn't followed my own advice. I'd been pushing away the tightness in my chest and pangs in my gut for days. Now my body's animalistic instincts consumed me, muscles contracting, and fear exploding through every cell. I could barely see where my next footstep would land, but my legs stretched forward, again and again. Sturdy tree trunks materialized from the shadows like strangers waiting to capture me. I kept running.

A twig snapped through the darkness, and my feet stopped, my throat constricting. The faces of the dead flashed in my mind. Even the release of breath might give me away.

My thoughts spun toward alternate realities as I darted into the cover of the trees. Why hadn't I made up an excuse to stay home with my family? It would have been easy enough to lie. Or I could have insisted on hosting the get-together at my house in the safety of suburbia. Or twenty-two years earlier, the people at campus housing could have placed the incoming freshmen in different dorms and hallways than the ones they'd chosen for us. Then I would have made another group of friends, friends who would have insisted on meeting at a less remote location and who steered clear of reckless decisions. They might have been friends who, when we hugged, could have detected the sour odor of festering secrets.

I paused beside a tree, gathering my wits. I couldn't dwell on what could have been because my life was in danger *right now*. I listened for approaching footsteps or any sign of a struggle, but only the hum of cicadas rose above the lapping waves. After two minutes of relative silence, I turned on my light and continued skittering toward the cabins.

Six utilitarian huts stood in a row. I chose the third one in, reasoning that if Charlotte looked for me here, she'd start at one end of the row or the other. I might have a chance to hear her approach. I stepped from the rain-soaked ground and up the two wooden steps. My hand pressed against the door and it creaked open, revealing a shadowy bunkroom. My light scanned the room. No one else was there. I crept to the furthest bed in the corner and sat on the lower bunk. I released the breath I'd been holding and closed my eyes. I envisioned the staff cabins located through the path in the woods and realized there must have been a road for the counselors to access their living quarters. There must be a parking area somewhere behind those cabins. Where else would they have left their cars? Maybe there was a road that led out to the main road from there. That was the direction I'd head in at daybreak.

My feet were soaked and cold inside my shoes. I untied them and set them on the floor to air out, replacing my socks with dry ones. I tried to be thankful for the small luxury but couldn't feel anything beyond my hyper-aware state. My stomach growled. The slice of pizza I'd eaten several hours earlier wasn't enough to get me through. I set the flashlight on the mattress and took off my backpack, removing a power bar and unwrapping it. I choked it down in four large bites, followed by some water. I'd save the other bars for the morning. It was impossible to know how many miles I'd have to travel before my phone would work, or I found someone to help me. The shiny edge of my phone caught my eye, and I pulled it out, checking for any hint of reception. There were zero bars. Cursing under my breath, I zipped the phone back into my bag and removed the knife, placing it on the bed next to me. Creating a makeshift pillow, I propped the bag behind my head. My legs stretched across the bare mattress. I kept my wet shoes untied next to me in case I needed to run.

I moved the ring of light around the walls of the cabin, careful not to shine it near the windows. The inspirational messages painted across the walls seemed to mock me. Someone had painted the words: *Keep smiling!* in hot pink around a yellow-and-white daisy. The next one read: *We can do hard things!* Beyond that, purple words encircling a yellow star read: *Positive thoughts plus positive actions equal a positive life!* A bitter laugh escaped my lips. I wondered if Frida had chosen those slogans. Had Frida helped paint the bright words across the walls before Charlotte bashed in her head?

My chest swelled at my tainted memories of Frida. I'd gotten her all wrong. I'd been too quick to judge. Frida King had been a strong and determined woman who had overcome the odds, getting an education, and separating herself from her strange and abusive parents. She'd made it her mission to help others, maybe kids like herself, who'd had unhappy childhoods. In my memory, her eerie and unflinching eyes had always been watching, staring, leering. But now, the filter shifted on my dark perception of Frida's mannerisms. I realized she had only been observing—learning how people who lived normal, happy lives looked and acted. I'd been too immature back in college to notice the difference. And that night in the Mexican restaurant when Frida had seen me kissing Pete, she'd never told anyone—at least, as far as I knew. I'd run into her several times after that, and she'd never mentioned it. She'd only smiled and asked benign questions, like "Are you enjoying the weather?" or "How are your classes going?" Charlotte had never even hinted at my indiscretion with Pete. Neither had Jenna. I was sure Frida hadn't told them. I wouldn't have been capable of keeping the same secret on her behalf. Frida had been a better person than me. She hadn't owed me anything, but she'd been loyal to me anyway. And now she was dead.

My thumb slid the switch of the flashlight backward and I sunk into the darkness again. "I'm sorry, Frida," I said under my breath as tears leaked from eyes. I pulled my knees into my chest and rubbed my toes through my cotton socks. Despite my current situation, I silently repeated the advice written on the walls. They were messages from Frida. I had the strange feeling she was helping me again, reaching out from the grave to give me hope, even though I didn't deserve it. I had to focus on a positive outcome if I wanted to get out of here alive. I didn't know for sure what had happened to Jenna. Maybe she woke up and saw that I was gone and went looking for me. There was still a chance I could save her.

I envisioned myself running down a camp road in only a few hours, stumbling upon a clear and easy path to the main road. A police car would drive past and stop for me. We'd find Jenna—tired and hungry—but otherwise fine. Twenty-four hours from now, I'd be home with Marnie, Wyatt, and Andrew. That's how it would go—only positive thoughts. I was safe here. Soon, this would all be over. I lowered my eyelids.

CHAPTER TWENTY-SEVEN

A floorboard creaked near my ear. Even before I opened my eyes, I heard ragged breathing and smelled the earthy scent of another person. My body bolted upright in the bunk bed, my hand fumbling for the knife but coming up empty. Muted light slipped through the window. It was morning. I couldn't believe I'd let myself fall asleep. Charlotte loomed over me, pointing a rifle at my face.

"I took your knife." Deranged satisfaction gleamed in her dark eyes as the corner of her mouth twitched.

I held my hands up, feeling like I might throw up. Charlotte looked sickly. Her skin was waxen, her lips dry and cracked. Despite the fullness of her cheeks, her eyes sank into purplish hollows. Any speck of doubt that remained as to whether she was responsible for Sam and Kaitlyn's deaths dissolved at the sight of her.

My muscles coiled like a cornered dog. I fought the urge to attack her, to call her a psychopath. I could tell she was in a fragile emotional state. I forced myself to forget about what she'd done, and pretended she was a distressed client who needed my help. Yelling at her would only cause her to become defensive and lash out.

I locked eyes with her. "Charlotte, please. You don't need to point a gun at me. I'm your friend."

"Ha. Right. Just like Sam and Kaitlyn and Frida were my friends?"

"Yes. They were your friends, too." I noticed she hadn't mentioned Jenna and wondered if that meant Jenna was still alive.

Charlotte scowled and held the gun steady.

"I don't understand." I fluttered my eyelashes. "Have we wronged you in some way?"

"That's the understatement of the century. The five of you destroyed my life."

I maintained eye contact with her. "But you have a great life, a beautiful life. Think of Oliver and Reed. Think about how hard you've worked to become a physical therapist." I bit my tongue, regretting the words almost as soon as they'd left my mouth.

"I lost my job six months ago. They said I was rude to one of the patients, that I hit her. That bitch filed a complaint against me."

My mouth opened, but I hid my shock. I remembered Charlotte's confessions about her emotionally abusive and sometimes violent upbringing, and I wasn't entirely surprised she'd lashed out at a patient. "I didn't know you lost your job." I kept my voice steady to cover the lie. "I'm sorry. That must have been difficult. I wish you'd told me."

Charlotte glared at me.

"Why did you bring us all here?" I braced myself against the bed, afraid to hear the answer.

"To expose your lies."

"What lies?"

"Our friendship is a lie." Charlotte's upper lip snarled. "You're not the great friends you've always pretended to be. At least, not to me."

I swallowed but didn't respond.

She stomped her foot against the wooden floor. "Your actions have consequences."

My heart slammed against my ribcage. I wasn't entirely sure what Charlotte was getting at, but I needed to keep her talking. I couldn't let her escalate the situation. As long as she was talking, she wasn't killing me.

"What happened before we got here, Charlotte? Why did we meet at this place?"

"I found the cabin because of Frida. She bought Camp Eventide five years ago and turned it into a retreat for troubled teens. I knew about her camp from Facebook."

"What happened to Frida?" I forced the squeaky words from my throat.

Charlotte's opaque eyes stared past me. "It took me weeks to find a lead on a new job, but neither of my previous employers would give me a referral. I emailed Frida for a recommendation, but she never responded. Then I called her, but she still wouldn't stand up for me. She said she didn't feel comfortable."

"Why did you ask Frida for a recommendation?"

Charlotte lowered her chin. "No one else would step out on a limb for me. Frida used to be my supervisor when we volunteered together at the hospital. I thought she would vouch for me, considering I was her only real friend in college."

I nodded as the blood drained from my face. Charlotte and Frida hadn't worked together since before Oliver was born, at least fifteen years ago. Of course, Frida wouldn't feel comfortable writing a professional recommendation. They didn't even work in the same field.

"I knew I wouldn't get the job without a recommendation, so I drove up here a few months ago and surprised Frida with a visit. Travis's cabin was pretty much the only place to stay."

My chest seized. The story Charlotte was telling me matched what I'd discovered in Travis's box of papers.

Charlotte continued talking as if I wasn't there. "I sneaked into the camp and followed Frida to her cabin while the others were eating dinner in the mess hall. She was so shocked to see me. I thought she wouldn't be able to turn down an in-person request for a recommendation, especially after I'd driven all the way up here. But she did. Even after everything I'd done for her." Charlotte pinched her colorless lips together. "I couldn't believe how she could betray me so easily. I saw my entire future falling away. When Frida tried to give me a hug, I shoved her away from me as hard as I could. She fell backward and hit her head on the metal corner of the table. There was a lot of blood. I didn't mean to kill her, but I didn't help her either. With a camp full of troubled teens, I figured no one would suspect me."

I lowered my eyelids. *Poor Frida.*

"The funny thing was, I felt so powerful, leaving her there to die. It was like I'd finally stood up for myself. I'd finally made someone pay for wronging me."

My feet wobbled beneath me. I stretched taller, setting my jaw. Stories Charlotte had shared with me long ago surfaced in my consciousness—her father had beaten her for her younger brothers' wrongdoings, and her mother had been an emotionally distant alcoholic. Parenting like that could cause irreparable damage to a child's psyche.

Charlotte frowned and blinked several times. "I didn't get the job, even though I was overqualified. It was Frida's fault. After everything I'd done for her." Charlotte shook her head. "Seeing Frida again reminded me how I don't have any real friends. Her accident got me thinking about how easy it would be to do the same thing to the rest of you."

I pressed my heels into the floor, struggling to keep my face still. "You do have friends, Charlotte."

Charlotte rolled her eyes. "When Jenna sent the email about the weekend away, I knew the cabin was the perfect spot to get back at the rest of you for ruining my life. I didn't want to kill anyone else." Her eyes blinked rapidly. "Really. I didn't. But I did want to scare you enough to teach you a lesson. I wanted to watch you turn on each other, to show you our so-called friendship was a sham, and to make sure we never planned one of these ridiculous weekends again. But Sam couldn't stop provoking me, and one thing led to another."

Tears burned my eyes at the mention of Sam's name. "It sounds like Frida really hurt you. But what did Sam do?"

"Sam stole MedTech from me."

"What?"

Charlotte jutted out her chin. "MedTech was my idea. It was *my* company. I described the entire concept to Sam back in college one night at Campus Café. She stole it from me. She never gave me any credit or offered to compensate me. Instead, I've struggled my entire professional life. I've had to stay in unhappy marriages just to make ends meet."

I swallowed, noting Charlotte's faulty logic. Sam had worked for years to build MedTech into the successful business it was. She'd completed medical school and worked in a research hospital while Charlotte chose to take a break and stay home and raise her son. But Charlotte was balancing on the edge of something dangerous, and I didn't dare to argue.

"Sam should have given you a seat on the board," I said, hoping to appease her. "I never realized the company was your idea."

"Sam never told anyone that part. It felt so good to sneak up behind her in the woods and loop that cord around her neck. It felt like I was taking back everything that should have been mine."

I gasped, raising my hand to my mouth. Poor Sam would never have suspected Charlotte of being violent. She wouldn't have thought to run or fight back.

"With Travis living next door, I knew the rest of you would assume he was the one who killed Sam. Especially after I saw that tattoo. Man, you're all so predictable." Amusement danced in Charlotte's eyes. "And when you shot Travis, that was beyond perfect. I thought I had it made. Travis wouldn't even be around to defend himself."

I thought back to the way I'd snatched Travis's gun from the floor and pointed the barrel at him, deciding not to shoot. But Jenna and Charlotte had lunged toward me when Travis jerked forward. I'd never been sure who had squeezed my hand, but now I knew Charlotte had done it.

"I couldn't have foreseen what happened with Kaitlyn afterward. I had no choice."

"Why Kaitlyn?" I asked, struggling to keep my voice from cracking. "How could you hurt her?"

Charlotte scowled. "She had such a perfect life, didn't she?"

My throat was so dry I couldn't make a sound.

Charlotte shifted the rifle to her other arm and shook out her free hand. "Kaitlyn brought her fate on herself."

"How do you mean?"

"She was on the couch, still awake, and waiting for the non-existent tow truck when I came downstairs for a midnight snack. She told me again how she saw me in the woods near the spot where Sam died. She'd seen my orange shirt and heard a struggle. Kaitlyn kept asking questions about what I was doing out there. She practically accused me of killing Sam. I told her she was wrong. I said I could explain everything, but I needed to get a glass of water from the kitchen first. Instead of getting a glass, I took the rifle from the cellar and forced her down to the lake. I used the same cord to strangle her, holding her head under the water. Then I hid the gun in the woods so you and Jenna wouldn't get your hands on it. You have to understand. I couldn't risk having Kaitlyn expose me."

I gasped. Kaitlyn had been on to Charlotte before any of us. She had known Charlotte killed Sam. Even if she'd only had a lingering suspicion, I wished she would have come to Jenna or me instead of confronting Charlotte directly. But that was just like Kaitlyn. She always wanted to see the best in people. She never wanted to talk behind anyone's back.

"But even if Kaitlyn hadn't seen me, I had reason enough to hate her."

"Why?" I held my breath, unable to imagine how anyone could hate Kaitlyn. She was kind to everyone. Not in the fake, over-the-top, stab-you-in-the-back way of so many suburban moms; she had been genuinely compassionate and down-to-earth.

"Kaitlyn stole the man I was always meant to be with."

My heart raced. "Reed?"

"No. Not Reed," Charlotte huffed. "Derek!"

"Derek." My mind reeled, struggling to make sense of Charlotte's explanation. "Kaitlyn's husband?"

"Yeah. Derek was supposed to have been mine. I was the one who invited him to our party the night he and Kaitlyn met. He was in my chemistry study group and we'd been hanging out for weeks. We were only friends, at first, but there was so much more there. We talked and laughed so easily together. Sometimes he even walked me home after class. I was the one who ran into him standing in line for coffee at the student union the day before. I invited him to the party because we had such a strong connection. And he liked me too because he showed up to see *me*. But then Kaitlyn butted into our conversation with her tall, skinny body and perfect teeth. Her big boobs were practically hanging out of her tight sweater. Derek never looked at me again."

I swallowed. Charlotte's delusions were even more severe than I realized, but I played along. "That must have been hard for you. Especially at their wedding."

"I didn't go to their wedding, remember?"

I nodded, although I'd forgotten that Charlotte hadn't been there. "At least you have Reed," I said, immediately wishing I'd veered toward a different subject. I felt like a wild animal caught in traffic, narrowly avoiding the crushing wheels of a car only to find a semi-truck barreling toward me from the other direction.

"Reed and I were happy for a while. But it's not the same life I would have had with Derek. Kaitlyn was so smug with her charity benefits, garden clubs, and all-inclusive vacations. Derek was too good to her. Derek wouldn't have lost interest in me the way Reed has."

I shifted my leg, at a loss for words. Charlotte's version of events skewed so far from reality that I couldn't speak. I worried about what Charlotte would accuse Jenna and me of doing, and I pressed my heels into the floor, dialing into therapy mode.

"It's going to be okay, Charlotte. You didn't mean to kill anyone. Frida was an accident. Sam was in the heat of the moment, and Kaitlyn was an unfortunate witness. I'll keep your secret. You know I will. So will Jenna. This nightmare can end right here. We can blame the deaths on Travis. No one will question our story, just like you said."

Charlotte chuckled and readjusted the barrel of the gun toward my forehead. "Do you really think I'm that stupid? You and Jenna. You two are unbelievable. So high and mighty. I should thank Jenna for helping me, though. She made things so much easier for me when she twisted her ankle. Once I'd punctured my tires, there was no way anyone was leaving. Her injury trapped you here."

I gulped for air. "You're going through so much, Charlotte. Do you want to talk about your relationship with Reed some more? Or your unexpected job loss? It helps to talk about things."

"I don't need your fake tears. Or your useless marital advice."

"I'm sure Reed can support you until you find other work. I can lend you some money."

Charlotte's lip peeled back. "Reed doesn't know I got fired again. He thinks I already found a new part-time job. We keep separate accounts. But he'll leave me when he finds out I was lying. He was already on his way out the door. A stupid vacation isn't going to fix that."

"People can be more forgiving than you realize sometimes," I said, hoping it was true.

Charlotte only stared at me.

"Charlotte, where is Jenna?"

"I tied her to a tree and gagged her. Her hands and legs are bound. She won't escape."

Jenna was alive. I hid my relief out of fear that Charlotte would fire the gun if I made any sudden noises. *I could still save Jenna.*

"Charlotte, you need to let me and Jenna live. We'll promise to backup your story. You're going to need corroborating witnesses."

Charlotte glared at me. "I can't. I've already headed too far down this road. There's no turning back now. Besides, I don't trust either of you. Not after what you did."

"What did we do?"

"Like you don't know."

"I don't."

"You and Jenna are equally responsible for what happened to me. You two are the worst friends of all. You think you can toss me aside like a piece of garbage on the side of the road."

A cold sweat prickled across my skin. I forced myself to breathe. "Charlotte, can you tell me what we did so I can apologize? I know I've made mistakes, but I promise I never did anything intentionally to hurt you. I'm sure Jenna didn't either."

"You should have apologized twenty years ago."

Twenty years ago? I looked at my hands, equal parts confused and terrified. "For what?"

"For leaving me at that party!"

My mind tumbled backward through the years, struggling to recall a specific party. "Which party? I don't know what you're talking about."

"It was spring of junior year. You and Jenna invited me to go to a fraternity party at Sigma Delta Epsilon because Jenna knew someone there. It was a Hawaiian luau-themed party. Do you remember now?"

A photo from Kaitlyn's album flashed in my mind. Charlotte and Jenna wore flowered shirts and shell necklaces. I *did* remember the party. It was the night Jenna bolted after seeing Pete. But I didn't understand what Charlotte was getting at. "I'm sorry. I don't remember it. Can you tell me what happened?"

Charlotte shifted the rifle to her other shoulder, keeping it aimed at my face. "You abandoned me at the fraternity. I didn't

251 THE LAKE HOUSE

know anyone. I went to use the bathroom, and you and Jenna left without bothering to tell me. I didn't have a cell phone back then. I couldn't find you." Worry lines creased Charlotte's forehead. The painful memory still affected her. "I wandered all around that enormous old house, checking the upstairs bedrooms for you. A guy was sitting alone in one of the rooms. I told him my friends ditched me, and he felt sorry for me and invited me inside. He seemed nice. I drank a couple of beers with him, but then he told me he wasn't a student. He was a few years older and happened to know someone who lived there." Charlotte paused, lowering her gaze. "The guy put his hand on my leg. I wanted to leave, but he blocked me and locked the door. He wouldn't let me out. He squeezed my throat and pinned me down. You can guess what happened next." Tears slid down Charlotte's face, and I could see how raw the memory still was for her. I didn't like where the story was going.

"Charlotte, I'm so sorry. I believe you when you say that guy attacked you. But I don't remember leaving you at a party. I had no idea anything like that ever happened."

Charlotte rolled her eyes. "Yeah, right. Some therapist."

I shifted my legs, thinking again of the photo album in the cabin, thinking of a way to make Charlotte question her memory. "You said it was the Hawaiian luau party at Sigma Delta Epsilon?"

"Yeah."

"I didn't go to that party."

"Yes, you did. You were there, and then you left."

"No. I didn't. I have proof. It's in the photo album back at the cabin. Jenna and Kaitlyn took you to that party. There's a photo of you and Jenna before you left."

"I know. You're in it too."

"No. Kaitlyn and Jenna went with you. I had a babysitting job that night. Remember the Maloneys? I was so bummed I had to miss the party to watch over a spoiled six-year-old."

Charlotte didn't respond.

"Jenna was in the photo with you. You were wearing Hawaiian shirts, and Jenna had a big blue flower in her hair. I'm probably the one who took the picture. Maybe that's why you remember me being there."

"I know it was you who walked through the door to that fraternity with me. That's why I don't feel too bad that I have to kill you."

"It's been twenty years, Charlotte. Memories fade, even for people with sharp minds. They've done studies on it. Can you at least let me show you the photo before you kill me? I have two kids. Remember Marnie and Wyatt? Don't you want to make sure you're killing the right person before you take their mom from them?" A sob rose in my throat at the thought of my sweet children, but I swallowed the emotion. Keeping my composure was essential if I wanted to see them again.

Charlotte's eyes flickered toward the window, and she lowered the gun. Something I'd said had gotten through to her. At a minimum, she was willing to hear me out. "You can show me the photo, but it won't make a difference."

I nodded, slowly standing from the bed. "Okay. I guess we'll see who is right."

She motioned with the gun. "Put your shoes on."

I forced my feet into the wet shoes and tied them.

"You go first. Keep your hands raised."

"Can we get Jenna?" I asked, attempting to keep my voice light and airy.

"No. I'll be pointing this gun at your back. I'll shoot you if you try to do anything stupid. We'll cross the lake in the canoe you brought over here."

I shivered, imagining how Charlotte must have been lurking in the trees and watching me the night before. I thought I'd been so clever. My legs lumbered forward, marching across the campground in the light of dawn like a prisoner of war. At least I'd bought myself some time. I could tell from the desperation in Charlotte's eyes that she needed a friend. She wanted to believe my version of events—that I hadn't been to the Hawaiian luau party. But when she saw the photos in a few minutes, there was an equal chance the images would bolster her memory because Charlotte's recollection was correct. Jenna and I had been with Charlotte that night at the fraternity house. And we'd left her there.

CHAPTER TWENTY-EIGHT

"Smile!" I held up the camera and clicked. Charlotte and Jenna leaned close to each other and flashed exaggerated smiles. We wore Hawaiian-printed tops and shell necklaces, and we'd tucked cheap plastic flowers behind our ears.

"Do you want to be in it, Megan?" Kaitlyn asked, pulling her work apron over her clothes. "I can take another one."

"Nah. I'm good." I waved her off and adjusted the grass skirt I'd secured over my jean skirt. "Wish you could come with us too."

Kaitlyn hoisted her backpack onto her shoulder. "I have to serve pizza to drunk college students who leave crappy tips. I swear, I'd rather be studying all night like Sam."

Jenna chuckled.

"We'll catch you next time." I turned toward Jenna and Charlotte. "You guys ready to go?"

"Are you sure it's a luau theme?" Charlotte asked. "Because it would be embarrassing if we showed up dressed like this if it wasn't."

"Yeah. It's definitely a luau. Let's par-ty." Jenna balanced on her crutches as she clapped her hands together and laughed. It had been nearly three months since the car accident, and I was relieved to see how well she was getting around on her own.

Charlotte applied a fresh coat of lipstick, and the three of us tumbled out the door. We trekked across the dark sidewalks toward fraternity row, the fifteen-minute hike taking longer because of Jenna's leg. None of us had the money for a cab.

"*Too bad Sam and Kaitlyn are missing out,*" *Jenna said as she limped along.*

The bass thumped inside my chest as we approached the party. Tiki torches lined the walkway to the front door. Despite the chilly April night, women in bikini tops and grass skirts stood in clusters on the small front lawn, talking to men wearing Hawaiian shirts.

"*Let's go inside,*" *Jenna said.*

Charlotte went first, approaching the front door where two frat boys stood guard.

"*Evening ladies.*" *One of them waved us forward.* "*Welcome to the tropics.*"

"*Nice flowers,*" *the other said.*

Jenna glanced back at me and made a face, and I stifled my laugh. Charlotte held the door for Jenna. I followed behind her.

People swarmed the two front rooms, where a line of partygoers snaked from a keg. Steps led to a dance floor in another room. Reggae blared from the speakers. Lights flashed along with the beat of the music, and a DJ bobbed his head behind a turntable. The air swirled with the odor of stale beer and occasional whiffs of weed.

We joined the line, waiting for our drinks. Charlotte recognized a woman from her Organic Biology class and introduced us. A few minutes later, Charlotte's classmate returned to her crew, and the three of us got our beers. We wandered into the next room where a couple of guys approached us and asked Jenna how she injured her leg.

"*A car accident,*" *Jenna said. She didn't mention that I was the driver, and I thought again about how she was the best kind of friend. After the two men discovered Jenna had played on the soccer team, they offered to get us refills and wandered toward the keg.*

Charlotte made a face and held out her empty cup. "*I have to pee.*"

"*I think the bathroom is on the other side,*" *I said, pointing past the hordes of people in the front room.* "*We'll wait for you.*"

I took Charlotte's cup and she wove her way between groups of people.

"*Oh my God.*" *Jenna's hand tightened around my arm.* "*Pete's here.*"

I followed her stunned gaze to the opposite corner of the room. Pete's broad shoulders dwarfed the people around him. He touched his fingers to his square jaw and laughed. I'd barely talked to Pete since he'd kissed me at the Mexican restaurant a month earlier. I'd only spotted him in passing in the auditorium where our Abnormal Psychology professor held her lecture. The Monday following the kiss, Pete had approached me with a smile on his face, but I could only see Frida's damning eyes staring back at me. In the most detached tone I could muster, I told him I didn't want to see him anymore. Then I hurried toward a seat in the back corner of the auditorium, making a point never to look in his direction. Amazingly, he hadn't bothered me after that.

The sight of Pete here at the party made my heart race. At the same time, Jenna's presence clogged my veins with dread. It felt as if a giant spotlight was shining on me, highlighting my betrayal to the entire crowd. Jenna had never mentioned my dinner with Pete or the kiss. I'd spent nearly two weeks of sleepless nights worrying about the fallout before I realized Frida wasn't going to rat me out.

"He's here with Grant, his roommate." Jenna bit her lip. "Should I go talk to him?"

A warning bristled through me. "No," I said, shaking my head. I knew Jenna hadn't gotten over Pete. I hadn't gotten over him either and we'd never really even been a couple. I wanted to stay as far away as possible to ensure no one exposed my secret. "Let's ignore him. Those other guys will be back in a second with our refills. The taller one was really into you. When Pete sees you talking to him, it'll make him jealous. He'll realize what a dumb piece of shit he was."

Jenna's lip curved into a smile. Her eyes flickered around the room but landed back on Pete. Just as quickly as it had formed, my friend's smile faded, and her hand dropped to her side. I followed her line of sight. A slender woman with a shiny braid, mirrored sunglasses, and a bikini top sidled up to Pete. He draped his sturdy arm around her bronzed skin and kissed her on the lips. They pulled apart and smiled, then kissed again. The woman looked vaguely familiar, and I realized where I'd seen her before. She was one of Jenna's former soccer teammates.

I sucked in my breath and turned toward Jenna. Her face crumpled as she swiped the back of her hand under her nose. "I have to leave." She forced her way through the crowd, using her crutches to clear a path.

I searched the crowd for Charlotte as I chased after Jenna. "Jenna, wait!" I yelled, but Jenna couldn't hear me over the music. I couldn't let her walk home alone on her crutches, especially when she was this upset. I noticed a stairway just ahead and climbed up to the third step to survey the room. Charlotte's brunette hair and purple flower caught my eye. She wove her way through boisterous groups of people, then stopped. She'd run into her biology classmate again.

"Charlotte!" I yelled, but she didn't look toward me. It was impossible to hear anything over the music. I thought of Jenna hobbling down the dark city street alone and couldn't bear it. There'd been a string of muggings on campus, and Jenna would make an easy target. I pushed through the crowd and went after her, reassuring myself that Charlotte knew a couple of familiar faces at the party. We didn't all need to leave. Charlotte could stay and still have a good time.

I stumbled down the steps and through the front door. Jenna needed me. I'd explain everything to Charlotte later.

CHAPTER TWENTY-NINE

Charlotte's feet crushed the tall grass behind me as I marched a few steps ahead. Memories from the night of the Hawaiian party swarmed my head, the music and colors becoming more vivid after Charlotte's disturbing revelation. I had no idea someone had assaulted her that night. I shook my head, acknowledging "assaulted" wasn't a strong enough word. She had been raped.

More photos from Kaitlyn's album scrolled through my mind. The ones of Charlotte with her black clothes, black makeup, and piercings at the end of our junior year suddenly made sense. Her drastic change in appearance started right after that fraternity party, but I'd never made the connection. She'd been sullen and withdrawn. She'd traded her preppy clothes for drab colors and heavy makeup. She'd gained weight, binge eating in her bedroom, and sneaking food when she thought no one was watching. These were potential signs of trauma. I'd missed them all. I'd mistakenly believed Charlotte's change in behavior stemmed from guilt over Jenna's car accident.

Why hadn't Charlotte told us? I tightened my fists as I walked, trying not to be annoyed with her. She'd been the victim. As with many victims of sexual assault, she probably felt shame. Maybe she even felt responsible. Or maybe she didn't want us to feel bad for abandoning her at the party. But if I'd known what had happened to her—if I'd had any clue—I would have insisted that she report the crime to campus police and undergo counseling. Charlotte was right about one thing—I hadn't been a good friend at all.

"Even if you're not in the photo, I can't let you live." Charlotte's tightly strung voice yanked me from my thoughts. "I can't risk having witnesses walking around."

"I'm your friend. I promise I won't tell anyone."

Charlotte didn't respond.

I spoke louder. "Not many people have true friends. You've always been that person for me. It's rare to find a friendship like ours. I'm sorry I never told you that sooner."

Charlotte huffed out a breath. "If you're such a true friend, why don't you ever call me? Why haven't you made any effort to get together in the last five years? We live half an hour from each other."

I dug my fingernails into my leg as I trekked toward the canoe. "You're right. I don't know. Things have been busy, especially with the kids. My weekends aren't free anymore. And, like I told you, Andrew and I have been struggling."

Charlotte's breath heaved from behind me. "I'm going to blame all the deaths on Travis. I'll say I shot him in self-defense and then escaped."

I nodded. "Yeah. That's a good plan. I'll backup your story. Travis was such a hateful person. No one will question it." I kept my voice steady, hoping she'd believe me.

Charlotte didn't argue with my response, and I took that as a good sign. We descended the steps to the water and arrived at the canoe's hiding place. The aluminum end of the boat stuck out beyond the brush. I turned to face her. I'd done an amateurish job covering my tracks.

Charlotte motioned with the barrel of the gun. "Flip it over. Let's go."

I closed my fingers around the edges and heaved the canoe onto its side, letting it fall face-up at our feet. A hazy mist rose off the still lake. I scanned the shoreline for any sign of Jenna but couldn't find her.

"Pull it into the water and get in." Charlotte directed me with the gun, never lowering it from my direction.

"There's a leak."

"You made it across last night."

I pushed the boat into the shallows, ignoring the way the cold liquid seeped through my dampened shoes and into my socks. Gripping the oar, I stepped into the canoe and sat on the seat closest to the front. The boat tilted to the side as Charlotte climbed in behind me and shoved us further into the water.

"You should row since you're in the back." I kept my eyes trained ahead of me so that Charlotte couldn't detect my scheme. She would have to set down the gun if she took the paddle, giving me a chance to grab the firearm and defend myself until I could escape.

"Nice try," she said. "Start paddling. You know the way."

My body was hollow and aching, but I paddled, aware of the gun pointed at my back and the puddle forming at my feet. I pulled the oar through the water twice on one side before switching over to the other. The boat was heavier now, and each stroke produced only a weak boost forward. Using this inefficient method, I zigzagged us across the glassy lake as more water seeped into the boat.

The only way to make it out alive—to see Marnie and Wyatt again—was to establish a convincing bond of friendship and trust with Charlotte. I had to make her believe I was useful and that she needed me for her plan to work. She would soon see the snapshot of herself and Jenna wearing their Hawaiian outfits just before we left for the party. Kaitlyn wasn't in the photo. Would Charlotte remember I was the one who had taken the picture and that I'd been wearing a flower-print shirt too? I had to convince her she was misremembering things. I was running out of time.

"Want to grab dinner once we get back to the suburbs, and things settle down?" I stopped paddling and let the canoe glide through the water.

Charlotte grunted.

"We need to keep our stories straight. You know, after all this. Plus, we're going to need our friendship more than ever now that we both have rocky marriages. We can plan a weekly ladies' night out. Won't that be fun?"

"I doubt that will happen."

"Why wouldn't it?"

"Keep paddling, Megan. I don't have time for your bullshit."

"It's not bullshit. I'm your friend, Charlotte. I may not be perfect, but I've always been your friend." Water splashed against the side of the canoe. A rugged shoreline appeared in the distance just as the water inside the boat rose past my shoe. "Your trip to Europe sounds fun. Tell me more about it. What city are you flying into?"

Charlotte waited several seconds before responding. "Paris. I'm not going now that I don't have a job. Reed was supposed to go with me."

"I can go with you. I'll pay for our tickets. I've always wanted to go to Paris."

"I think I'll wait to see the proof from the photo album first. Keep paddling."

"Okay." My blood turned colder than the water surrounding my feet. Would the photo without me in it be enough to convince Charlotte I hadn't left her at the party?

I guided the canoe toward the stretch of rocky beach I'd escaped from only a few hours earlier. Returning to the desolate spot without outside help felt devastating. My body was weak. I was out of options. There was no choice except to play the part of Charlotte's loyal friend and hope that she'd spare me and that I could somehow save Jenna, too.

The canoe scraped against rocks near the shore, and we bobbed in place. It had only been two days since we discovered Kaitlyn's lifeless body in almost this exact spot. Three days since we'd found Sam lying in the woods. If only I'd realized that Charlotte had been responsible. She'd seemed so upset at the time, but maybe she'd merely been reacting to the aftermath of her own heinous actions. I pulled my eyes from the water's smooth surface and stared at my dirty fingernails. Nausea ate away at my insides.

"Get out," Charlotte said. "Pull me onto the sand. No sudden movements."

I stood slowly and plunged my foot into the lake. I turned to face her, finding the gun still raised in my direction. My fingers closed around the front of the canoe, and I tugged it up to dry land. Charlotte stepped onto the rocks, lifting her chin toward the wooded incline. "You go first."

I climbed up the hill toward the cabin, my feet sliding beneath me on the uneven path. I searched over my right shoulder through the trees, looking for any sign of Jenna.

"Eyes straight ahead," Charlotte said.

I refocused on the narrow path, wondering what Charlotte didn't want me to see. Maybe Jenna was tied up somewhere nearby. A few steps later, a putrid scent hit me in the face. I stopped walking, covering my mouth with my hand. I'd smelled the same odor last year when I'd found a dead mouse under the hood of my car. It was the smell of death. Only this was ten thousand times more intense. The bodies were decomposing. It was unbearable.

Charlotte coughed from behind me. A breeze drifted through the trees and offered temporary relief. I pulled in a breath of the fresh air and continued trudging up the hill and onto the deck.

"Go inside and get the album. I'm following you."

I opened the door to the kitchen; the foul odor suffocated us as we stepped inside. I shielded my mouth and nose with my arm. Charlotte made a gagging sound. The photo album lay on the living room table. I grabbed it and held it up for Charlotte to see.

She nodded and motioned toward the door. "Take it out to the deck."

I gasped for air as we exited the kitchen. It was easier to breathe outside. Still, the stench of Travis's decomposing body clung to me, permeating my hair and clothing. I paced toward the table, feeling like I was walking the plank. My fingers felt thick and awkward as I flipped through the pages.

Charlotte's eyes sunk into her face like black pebbles. "Where's the proof that you're not an awful person?"

"It's in here." My frantic hands flipped through the album. Two pages stuck together. I opened near the back of the book and found a photo of "morbid Charlotte" staring back at me. She wore heavy black eyeshadow and lipstick, a chunk of neon pink hair fell into her face, and she had multiple nose piercings. In retrospect, Charlotte's altered appearance was so obviously her response to the attack. She'd tried to turn herself into someone else to escape the pain. *How had I not seen it?*

Charlotte saw me staring at the photo. "Are you going to take another dig at my lipstick?"

"What? No. I wouldn't. Especially after what you told me."

The middle pages separated, and I located the photo. Jenna stood a half-foot taller than Charlotte, looping her arm around Charlotte's shoulder. Although it was the middle of winter, they wore summery, floral tops. Necklaces made of shells encircled their necks. A purple flower was propped behind Charlotte's ear. Jenna wore a blue one. Mine had been pink, but I wasn't in the photo.

I pointed to the photo. "See. I wasn't with you."

Charlotte's lip curled back. "This is your proof? This doesn't prove anything other than you weren't in the photo."

"I took this photo," I said. "I'm sure that's why you remember me being at the party. But I didn't go with you. I was babysitting for the Maloneys like I usually did on Saturday nights. After seeing this picture again, I remember it clearly. It was Kaitlyn who'd been with you and Jenna. She was wearing a flower behind her ear just like these." I jabbed my finger at the picture. "Except Kaitlyn's flower was pink. And she was wearing a straw skirt over her denim skirt," I said, describing what I'd been wearing that night.

A question flickered behind Charlotte's eyes. She was deciding whether to believe me. Maybe the details were causing her to doubt her memory.

Something thumped against the side of the house, like a bird flying into a window or a branch hitting the roof.

Charlotte's eyes stretched wide. "What was that?"

"Oh no," I said in a loud whisper. "It's probably Marlene. She must have smelled the bodies."

Charlotte stood, heaving the gun in front of her. It was the first time she had lost her focus on me. I had no reason to think Marlene had caused the noise, but my theory urged Charlotte to investigate. With her back to me, Charlotte crept toward the side of the house. Several empty wine bottles sat near the wall of the cabin, and I recognized the opportunity. I drifted over to the line of empties. My fingers tightened around the neck of the closest one, a bottle of Chardonnay with a ripped black label. I held my breath as I lifted the makeshift weapon above me, slowly and silently. Gathering energy from every cell in my body, I swung the bottle down on the back of Charlotte's head. The glass landed with a crack. Charlotte collapsed.

I lunged toward Charlotte's limp body, noticing the rise and fall of her chest. She was unconscious but alive. I removed the rifle from her hands and inched around the side of the house, gasping with relief when I found no one there. Only a broken branch leaned against the cabin's wood siding. Tears dripped down my cheeks, and I didn't try to stop them. Looping the gun strap around my shoulder, I turned and sprinted into the woods, praying Jenna was still alive.

CHAPTER THIRTY

I raced through the trees, heading in the direction I'd been looking when Charlotte told me to keep my eyes pointed forward. Jenna was likely somewhere in the area, and Charlotte hadn't wanted me to spot her. I refused to let my soggy shoes slow me down. I plodded faster, ducking under branches as my eyes scanned across dozens of tree trunks. I clutched the rifle in my hand.

"Jenna!" I yelled. I paused, wanting to believe I'd heard something.

"Mmff!"

There it was again. My head swung toward the faint noise, and I clamored to the top of a ridge. A flash of blue caught my eye through the trees—the same color as Jenna's shirt. I saw her then, sitting against a thick trunk. A bandana gagged her mouth, but her eyes pulled me to her.

"Don't worry," I said. "We're safe. We're getting out of here." Tears streamed down my face, rolling onto my neck and under my collar as I ran. *Jenna was alive!* I crouched down when I reached her, setting down the gun and untying the knot at the back of the bandana.

She spat it from her mouth and sputtered for breath. "It was Charlotte."

"I know. I'm sorry I left you."

Jenna's eyes flitted over me, crazed. "Where is she?"

I tipped my head toward the cabin. "I knocked her out. She's unconscious." My fingers tugged at a knot in the rope that bound

Jenna's wrists. Finally, the rope was loose enough for her to break free. She reached down as we untied her ankles together.

Jenna panted, deep wrinkles forming around her eyes. "She wants to kill both of us. She said we ruined her life, but she wouldn't tell me what we did."

I nodded, pulling her to her feet. "I'll explain everything, but first, we need to get out of here. Can you walk?"

"I'll do whatever it takes."

I leaned close to Jenna as she draped her arm around me. Her hand touched mine, her skin cold. She was shivering, and I realized how freezing she must have been exposed to the rain for most of the night with no coat. I unzipped my windbreaker and gave it to her. It was a size too small for her, but she thanked me and put it on.

With the rifle strap on my opposite shoulder, we hobbled away from the cabin at a decent pace, aware that Charlotte could regain consciousness at any minute and surprise us. At least this time, I had the gun.

"Can you make it back to the camp? I think there might be a road leading out behind the staff cabins."

"Okay. Yeah."

Jenna winced with every other step she took but never complained. I told her everything I'd learned about Charlotte and why she'd snapped. My words spilled out jumbled and in no particular order. Jenna gasped at each new revelation—Charlotte's beliefs that Sam had stolen her business and Kaitlyn had swept away the man she was supposed to marry; Kaitlyn spotting Charlotte in the woods. Breathlessly, I explained that Frida King had been the owner of Camp Eventide, Charlotte had accidentally killed Frida back in June because she wouldn't provide Charlotte with a job recommendation, and Frida's death had set off the current string of events. Then I told Jenna what happened to Charlotte at the party twenty years earlier.

Jenna stopped walking and buried her face in her hands. "Oh no. I had no idea."

"Me neither."

"We left her there."

"Yeah."

We stood next to each other, the weight of our mistake cementing my feet to the ground. Jenna began to cry.

I touched her arm. "We didn't know. She never said anything. And we couldn't have known it would lead to this." I motioned in the direction of the cabin. "She's had some bad stuff happen recently. She didn't tell anyone she'd been fired from her job, even her family. Now Reed is cheating on her. She convinced herself that everything was our fault."

Jenna blinked at me. "Everyone has a breaking point."

I nodded, again remembering tidbits of stories Charlotte had relayed to me over the years. Charlotte had been so relieved when she'd escaped to college, safely away from her abusive parents. But I knew from my studies that childhood trauma was one of the main predictors of future violence. Ingrained patterns were difficult to break. I'd missed the warning signs.

I swallowed against my parched throat and nodded toward the path. "We should keep moving." Jenna slung her arm over me again, and we continued the trek.

It took us over an hour to reach the camp. We found a bench in the clearing near the zip line and sat on it. My shoulder ached from supporting Jenna's weight. We hadn't even reached the private camp road yet, and it seemed less and less likely we'd make it out. I remembered my backpack. Charlotte had taken my knife, but my pack was still sitting in the cabin where I'd slept the night before, filled with power bars, a water bottle, and dry socks.

I turned to Jenna. "I have an idea. My backpack is in one of the cabins. How about we get it so you can eat and drink something?

Then you can hide in one of the staff cabins. You keep the gun and I'll run to the highway for help."

Jenna pressed her lips tight like she was trying not to cry. "I wish I could come with you. I'm sorry. It's such a long way, and my ankle hurts so much."

"It's okay. I'll move faster on my own. You'll be safe with the gun."

"Yeah. It's the best plan we have."

I stood up, and Jenna tugged my arm.

"Megan, thank you."

I turned toward her. "For what?"

"For not leaving me tied to that tree. You could have run out on your own by now, but you didn't." Jenna nudged me with her elbow. "You're a good friend, no matter what Charlotte said."

I nodded, my eyelashes blocking my tears. I debated whether to confess to kissing Pete at the Mexican restaurant all those years ago but I bit my tongue. Revealing another painful betrayal now wouldn't serve a purpose.

"Thanks," I said instead. "You're a good friend too."

We made our way past the mess hall and the office and toward the row of tiny cabins, entering the middle one where my backpack lay atop the bare mattress. I collected it, giving Jenna three power bars and my water. I took off my shoes, affixed a new Band-Aid, and replaced my wet socks with the dry ones from the bag. Jenna devoured the bar and gulped half the water, handing the bottle back to me.

"You should take this."

I nodded, stashing the water in the side pocket of my pack. I handed Jenna the rifle, and she positioned the strap over her shoulder. It took another ten minutes to trek over to the staff cabins. Jenna pointed toward the one closest to the woods. It stood next to the cabin encircled by yellow police tape.

I followed Jenna inside the dim and dusty room, making sure she had a comfortable place to sit. "Don't leave. If Charlotte shows up, shoot her in the leg if you have to."

Jenna nodded.

"I'll be back soon. With help."

"Good luck."

We hugged. I clutched the straps of my pack against my chest as I headed out the door and jogged down a narrow path through the woods. Just as I suspected, it led to a gravel parking lot. I followed the road, my legs stretching farther now. I remembered my breathing tricks from my marathon training days, pulling air into my lungs in measured breaths.

The road curved through the trees, stretching on and on. Ten minutes passed. Then twenty. Then thirty. My legs were weak and shaky, but I never slowed my pace even as I pulled my phone from my pocket and checked for bars. Still there was no reception.

At last, I reached a wooden sign suspended between two trees: *Welcome to Camp Eventide* it read. I coughed out a laugh at the marker. I'd reached a public road. I continued running down the barren dirt road, listening for the sound of a distant motor, but only the plodding of my running shoes against the muddy gravel echoed back at me. I stayed near the edge of the road so that I could dart behind the trees if I needed to. It would be devastating to have Marlene and Ed spot me after I'd made it this far. I kept going, Marnie and Wyatt's faces dangling in front of me like carrots. A cramp stabbed my side, but I ran through it. I estimated my pace at ten-minute miles. If I kept up the pace, I'd be close to the two-lane highway in a little over two hours. There'd been cell-phone reception there.

The miles passed, slowly but steadily. There were no cars on the craggy road leading to the abandoned camp. Only trees surrounded me. They were pine trees, mostly, but occasionally maple or oak trees grew between the evergreens, their leaves changing to shades of brown, orange, and yellow. Once in a while, the faded, peeling bark of a birch tree would pop from the others. After an hour of running past the endless forest, my breath heaved. I squeezed the cramp in my side and walked until I could jog again. Every mile was a step closer to kissing my kids' pink cheeks, to repairing my marriage with the good man I'd married, to getting Jenna and myself to safety. *One, two, one, two.* I only focused on the sound of each step, and on the distance covered. The road unspooled in front of me, never-ending. But I pressed forward. More trees appeared around every bend, a repeating landscape I'd thought I'd passed already. I searched for hidden driveways and remote cottages but did not find any. I remembered Kaitlyn telling us about the land trust. No one lived in this enormous expanse of wilderness because it was a nature reserve.

After I'd been running for nearly three hours, my feet were blistered, and my insides were twisted and breathless. At last, the dirt road met up with a paved road. My feet stopped. I yelped and blinked my eyes, confirming I'd reached the two-lane highway and feeling like I'd discovered a drinking fountain in the middle of the desert. This road was my lifeline. I craned my neck, searching for a car. I ran south, in the direction of the laughably small town we'd passed a few days earlier. That's when I heard it—the rumble of a motor. I hopped up and down and waved my arms.

"Stop!" I yelled.

It was an SUV, silver and battered. It whizzed past me. My knees buckled and I slumped over, despair flooding my body. I'd been so close to finding help. The vehicle disappeared around the bend.

Something vibrated against my hip. My hand pressed against my pocket, feeling the phone beneath. Afraid of getting my hopes up, I removed the cold object and stared at the screen. Three bars appeared where there had previously been none. I threw my head back as a stream of text messages and missed call notifications filled the screen. I resisted the urge to respond to them, especially the ones from Andrew. That would have to wait. My trembling fingers swiped past the main screen, and I finally pressed the numbers I'd been yearning to dial for four days: *911.*

CHAPTER THIRTY-ONE

Several minutes later, I huddled under a Mylar blanket in the back seat of a police car. It was the first time I'd felt safe in days. My 911 call had been a vague and urgent cry for help. Now I filled in the details for the officer who had rescued me, a heavyset, forty-something man with graying sideburns named Officer Hopke. My thoughts were frantic and scattered, my story told in a random order.

The officer wanted to call an ambulance, but I refused. We had to go back for Jenna first. I told him about Jenna's ankle injury and how she'd been tied to a tree all night. I urged him to send another police car and an ambulance to the rental cabin where Charlotte was injured and possibly dangerous. I told him about Marlene and how she might have a gun—or several.

The officer studied me with a furrowed brow as I described how Charlotte had murdered Sam and Kaitlyn, and how we were quick to blame the deaths on Travis—because of his tattoo and creepy demeanor—and on his friends because of their association with him. I told the officer that I knew who killed Frida King, the director of Camp Eventide. It hadn't been one of the campers. Charlotte had been responsible for Frida's death, too. His eyebrows raised at the information.

More of the story flooded from my mouth. The officer tilted his head and widened his eyes when I told him Travis's body was in the root cellar. I didn't care what he thought of us. We'd feared for our lives. We'd done what we had to do to survive. Besides, I wasn't the one who'd pulled the trigger.

"Can you direct me to Jenna's location?" he asked.

"Yes. She's hiding at Camp Eventide. In the cabin next to the one where Frida King died. Please hurry." The siren beeped above my head, lights flashing across the pavement as the car did a U-turn on the highway. I fumbled through the texts, gathering my energy to call Andrew and talk to the kids without falling apart. I needed to make sure Jenna was safe first.

Carried by the speeding police car, it only took a few minutes to lose my phone reception again and reach the parking lot behind the staff cabins. The policeman drove through the opening in the trees and pulled next to Jenna's hideout.

I doubled over with relief when the cabin door flung open, and Jenna stumbled outside. She squinted, stunned, into the flashing lights, offering an uneasy smile in my direction. Officer Hopke exited the car, carrying another Mylar blanket, which he wrapped around her as he escorted her into the car next to me.

He leaned through the window into the back seat. "I've got two more officers heading to the rental cabin. I'm taking you both to the hospital now."

Jenna squeezed my hand. "Did you tell him what happened?"

"Yeah."

She rested her head against the seat cushion and released a breath, followed by a hiccup and tears. I let my eyelids close as the car rumbled over potholes and loose gravel. Several minutes later, we were back on the highway, the movement over the smooth pavement nearly lulling me to sleep.

My phone dinged with a new text. I rubbed my eyes and sat up, hoping to see Andrew's name, but it wasn't him on my screen. The message was from the other man, the one with whom I'd been having an affair. The thought of him sickened me. I never wanted to see him again.

"Is that Andrew?" Jenna asked.

"Yeah." I averted my eyes as I lied. I angled the screen away from Jenna and read the text:

I've been so lonely without you. When can I see you again?

My jaw clenched, anger surging through me. I didn't recognize my former self, the version of me that would have been excited by this illicit invitation. This man's words disgusted me. I disgusted myself. I'd betrayed my husband and my kids. Charlotte's haunting pronouncement echoed in my ears: "*Your actions have consequences.*" Charlotte should have killed me when she had the chance because she was right. I wasn't a good friend. I hadn't only betrayed Andrew. I'd betrayed her, too.

I squeezed the phone, my fingers shaking as I typed my reply: *I'm sorry, Reed. It's over.*

A LETTER FROM LAURA

Dear reader,

I want to say a huge thank you for choosing to read *The Lake House*. If you enjoyed it and want to keep up to date with all my latest releases, just sign up at the following link. Your email address will never be shared and you can unsubscribe at any time.

www.bookouture.com/laura-wolfe

My novel takes place in pre-pandemic 2019, but I started writing the first draft in the spring of 2020 when we were a few weeks into quarantine/lockdown. At the same time, I received notification that my kids' summer sleepaway camp had been canceled. I thought about the sprawling camps sitting empty in the woods. How strange to have cabins, dining halls, climbing walls, and beaches with no one to enjoy them. It was an eerie vision and I thought it would be perfect to somehow work it into my story. Suddenly, the idea for Camp Eventide was born.

False friendship is an especially sinister concept to me, and I wanted to explore this idea by writing about a reunion weekend gone wrong as plenty of long-buried secrets rose to the surface. While all the characters and circumstances in my novel are purely fictional, the happy sentiments in the story (and the spreadsheet) were inspired by my own annual reunion weekends with a group of college friends from the University of Michigan. Thankfully, nothing nearly as traumatizing as the events in my novel have ever happened during any of our reunion weekends. I hope after reading this novel my friends will continue to include me on future invitations (and spreadsheets!).

I hope you loved *The Lake House,* and if you did, I would be very grateful if you could write a review. Reviews make such a difference in helping new readers discover one of my books for the first time.

I love hearing from my readers—you can get in touch on my Facebook page, Goodreads, Instagram, or my website.

Thanks,
Laura Wolfe

LauraWolfeBooks

@lwolfe.writes

1908042.Laura_Wolfe

www.LauraWolfeBooks.com

ACKNOWLEDGMENTS

So many people supported and assisted me in various ways along the journey of writing and publishing this book. First, I'd like to thank the entire team at Bookouture, especially my editors—Hannah Bond, for guiding me through the early stages of planning and structural edits—and Therese Keating, for smoothing out my novel's rough edges and holding my hand through the finish line. Their insights into my story's structure, pacing, and characters made the final version so much better. Additional gratitude goes to copyeditor, Lucy Cowie, and proofreader, Shirley Khan, for their keen eyes, and to Bookouture's top-notch publicity team led by Noelle Holten and Kim Nash. They have gone above and beyond in promoting my books. Thank you to those who continuously support my writing and provide inspiration and encouragement, especially Lisa Richey and Karina Board. Thank you to my parents, siblings, mother-in-law, and other extended family for supporting my books, and to Lindsay Nalbert for assisting me with my Milwaukee-area research. I appreciate everyone who has taken the time to ask me, "How's your writing going?" or has left a positive review. Most of all, I'd like to thank my kids, Brian and Kate, for always cheering for me and for finding creative ways to occupy themselves, so that I could have time to write, and for my husband, JP, for supporting my writing. He read every version of this novel over the many months I spent writing and revising it, and I wouldn't have made it to the end without his encouragement.